Derek's In Trouble

As funny as ever and as unlucky as always, Derek is going through another unexpected crisis in his life. A local reporter with the partner of his dreams, his life is all set to be perfect. So, how will he explain his foray out in his wife's dress? Then, there's the leggy lady intent on making a lasting impression …on top of that, there are everyone else's problems to sort. Is his Gran, the secret Radio agony aunt, capable of helping anyone?

Mac Black

Current occupation: a writer of humorous fiction.

Previous working background: shipbuilding on the River Clyde, tyre manufacturing in Dundee and working in the food industry in Fife (in jobs that didn't make his hands too dirty).

He was born in Glasgow and lived there for about half a life before moving to Carnoustie and then to Cupar, his present home.

He has been married for a long time.

Current titles by Mac Black

Please... Call Me Derek
Derek's in Trouble
Derek's Revenge (Autumn 2012)

Why not check the publisher's website www.uppublications.ltd.uk or follow Mac on www.macblack.info

First published in Great Britain in 2012 by U P Publications Ltd
Head Office: 25 Bedford Street, Peterborough, UK. PE1 4DN

Cover design copyright © Mike Peers 2012

A CIP Catalogue record of this book is available from the British Library

ISBN 978-1908135117

9 3 5 7 0 8 6 4 2 1

Also published for Kindle by U P Publications under ISBN 978-1908135230

FIRST PAPERBACK EDITION

Published by U P Publications - Printed in England by The Lightning Source Group

www.uppublications.ltd.uk
www.macblack.info

DEREK'S IN TROUBLE

Mac Black

U P Publications
2012

1

It was late afternoon on Saturday, barely five-thirty, as she came tottering towards his cab. He accepted this to be just another fare – another female who had been out celebrating, if maybe a little earlier than normal today. He was well used to the behaviour of the younger generation. He liked a few drinks himself, but he was a family man and well past all the showing off and silly stuff. A beer or two, in front of the telly with his wife sitting beside him, was good enough for him nowadays.

This caring father thought about each young female who chose to use his cab in the same way he thought about his own youngster – *with apprehension*. He worried about them all and for what passes nowadays as modern behaviour.

His daughter wasn't as old as this one and *his* daughter would be behaving herself. She would be studying at this time on a Saturday – *not*. She was now at university, living away from home, coming home every fortnight – with washing. What mischief was she getting up to, he often wondered?

If he'd been asked at that precise moment, he might have claimed that he cared so much for this passenger that he even opened the cab door for her (but really it was because he had been standing outside having a fag). 'Get it yourself,' was usually his motto, caring dad or not.

The young lady climbed unsteadily into the cab. She did not look comfortable in those heels, and there was a certain lack of allure as far as he was concerned. The state she was in she obviously needed his protection to see her safely home and as a conscientious taxi-driver he would do his duty and take her right to her front door. He would treat it as both a requirement of the job and a pleasure – as long as she paid her fare.

Some young lady ...he would recount to his wife when they next came face to face...

So ...Derek got in and lay back in the taxi seat feeling full. No, not just full – stuffed, well and truly stuffed. The silly smile on his face was a good indication to the taxi-driver that this was someone who had enjoyed several glasses more wine than his capacity. He had drunk more than he should have, eaten more than he should have, talked more than he should have, and he was wearing clothes that perhaps he really should not have...

He kicked off the shoes. How Sally could wear these high heels all day and not complain, he would never understand, and as for her bra ...it felt tight, but then again so did her skirt and blouse. The simple fact was, she was slim and he was not. Another simple fact was that if ever she were to see him dressed like this, there would be ructions...

Sally would not be returning home until after seven she'd said. She was visiting Muriel, his dear mother-in-law, while he was out for lunch, an extended lunch with his father-in-law – Alexander's idea and his treat – a special father-in-law / son-in-law bonding lunch, but with neither of their wives being aware that it was a meeting of two males in female clothing. If they had known, they might not have been quite so pleased to encourage the idea of the get-together.

Derek went along with it to humour Alexander and, although it was exciting and amusing actually to be in public wearing a blonde wig and some of Sally's clothes, for him it was definitely a one-off experience. However, he wasn't so sure about Alexander.

Previously, his father-in-law's excuse for dressing-up was associated with the Slatterfoot Amateur Players, but now he seemed to be enjoying it too much. Derek feared that, after his recent excellent performance as the female lead in the play, Alexander was letting the adulation go to his head.

"Take me to Toozlethwaite Manor, please, my good man," said

Derek to the taxi-driver in a slightly slurred, but recognisably male voice. If he could have seen the taxi-driver's face, he might have noticed a change in the expression – the raised eyebrows, followed by the contemptuous rearward glance at the lolling shape in the back of his cab.

"And where might that be, *sir*?" the driver enquired, in as diplomatic a manner as he could muster. His wife had been saying he'd been needing specs for a while – and he had laughed at the suggestion. Maybe she was right...

"Everybody knows *(hic)* it's the cottage, halfway between Newingsworth Road East and the Macintosh Farm," Derek slurred back, "...I call it a *(hic)* the manor. Look for the sign to 'Tipsicorus International'. You'll have to be careful, and not drive over the edge of the lane, or you could get stuck *(hic)* with me. Hee-hee! Hee-hee-hee!"

I'll make ruddy sure I'm careful, mate, don't you worry, the driver said to himself and cared a little less about seeing this one safely to the front door. You just never know with these blokes. Just get him, *or her*, out of the cab – after she's paid.

He was careful in the lane, and although it was a bit dicey doing the tight turn, he managed. He had to. His working period still had many hours to go and Saturday was his busiest night – he couldn't afford any hold-ups. However, when it came to the paying, his passenger had more of a problem than he'd had turning the taxi. Manipulating male fingers into the small purse to pay the fare was almost impossible. Of course, this 'lady' being slightly inebriated was a good thing for the driver – the tip handed over was more than generous.

In the end, it was a happy chappie who drove off abandoning Derek. The caring taxi driver went quickly back down the lane, glad to be rid of the pervert. Would this be the sort of strange bloke his own daughter could pal up with some day – maybe to bring back home for him to meet? He shuddered at the thought, which made him worry even more about her...

Derek tottered along the cottage path in stockinged feet, with a pair of high heels dangling from his hand.

A light had obviously been left on when Derek left this morning, which was not very clever. Here was the person who trumpeted on about so many pet hates – street lamps being alight during daylight hours, rubbish casually thrown from vehicle windows, and natural resources continually overused.

He also hated men or women who ate and drank to excess, and people who didn't make use of public transport.

This was someone who, when sober, believed that no one, other than himself, cared about the environment and all that gubbins. To have to recognise *his* electrical power wastage, in this case, was most disappointing.

As he stood, feeling bloated and steaming drunk, watching his privately hired cab drive off down the lane, he should have appreciated the irony in at least two of his pet hates, but to be truthful, he was incapable of appreciating anything at that moment.

On top of that, he was failing in the simple task of inserting the key into the keyhole.

It was not easy and took time, but he proved it was not impossible. Then, having eventually succeeded in opening the door, removing the key from the Yale lock in his condition also proved difficult – but he was in.

He pushed the living room door open and staggered inside. His head was spinning. He needed to sit down but stopped suddenly as his eyes tried to focus. He was not alone.

"Shally..."

The name came out as a fearful, gurgling, choking sound as his world collapsed around him.

The plan was spinning way out of control. "I have ...uhmmm... *(hic)...*"

Derek may have been shocked coming face to face with his wife, but not half as shocked as Sally.

Standing in front of her was this dishevelled, slightly overweight and blonde, cheap version of herself, still upright but frozen in terror and looking at her with eyes almost popping out.

Sally displayed very little sympathy as a moment later his body started swaying.

He then proceeded into a dead faint, and dramatically toppled over onto the sofa. It was obvious that Derek was in serious trouble.

Yes, he'd blown it. There they were – in his hand – he had ruined her best shoes...

2

It was a very sad day for Hamish, as he prepared to close the kitchen door for the last time. The farm was no longer his, the old place was going, it was all change! *Good luck 'Tipsicorus'*, he thought, *whoever you are.* As the new owners of the farm, perhaps they would have more success than he'd had.

Wandering around the inside of the farmhouse, collecting the few things he would take, he'd been stopping in each room encountering many poignant reminders – the smells, the colours, the old bits of furniture, curtains, the slightest things today sparking off moments long forgotten. Some he could have done without, but most thoughts were of tender and passionate times.

"Och, michty me..." he murmured sadly, over and over, as he moved around the old building, old even back when he and his folks moved in. *"...It's bricks an' mortar, ya silly ould gowg! Ye should ken ...it's jist a hoose!"* ...but it still hurt to leave.

His younger brother never made it here, but the memory of him lingered. As boys in their early teens, they were extremely active, almost always out of doors in daylight hours, especially in school holidays, and living on the farm with freedom to roam had been great. With only two years between them and having done most things together, they were close. Many months before his death, illness had restricted Tom's movements and becoming housebound, made it so much worse.

Tom died a year before the move.

As he looked around the rooms, Hamish recalled with surprising ease the good times he and his brother enjoyed up north at the old place – thoughts put aside for a long time. It was always presumed that the two boys, Hamish and Thomas, would take over the running of the farm when they were old enough, permitting their father to retire, or just do less. Tommy's death changed the plans.

So, as it was, the remaining Macintosh members would leave Scotland, sad to be one less, but determined to take only happy memories with them. That move, though a long time ago, was still clear in Hamish's mind. There was a wry smile as he realised he was nearly thirty years older than his father had been at that flitting.

Goodness ... surely ah've no' been here furr fifty-five years!

Departing their Scottish home had been discussed several months before Hammy was due to leave school. To his father and mother, it seemed the right time to up-sticks, a time for change. They would be going from a smallholding they had owned and run in the Scottish hills since well before Hamish's birth, to join Grandad and Granny Macintosh down south. Back then, Hamish was delighted to be leaving school. Not being a particularly outstanding pupil, he was looking forward to real work, especially as it would be alongside his father.

Hammy remembered all those years ago being destined to grow up 'elsewhere', another young Scot to live and work away from his homeland. The 'elsewhere' would be Newingsworth, this farm, the farm being left behind, the farm where three generations of the Macintosh family had worked and lived happily, but, it was all over now – small wonder he felt bad about it.

Dinna look a' me like tha'... Ah couldnae help it!

Strange ...him feeling he had to explain to the faces in the photos as he lifted them from the sideboard to be placed carefully in the cardboard box. His thoughts went unheeded. They continued to look at him critically: his wife Sybil, his mother, his father, gran and grandad. It was probably a trick of the light and a dripping tap that caused him to think his grandad was 'tutting' and shaking his head disapprovingly...

The Newingsworth farm was originally purchased by Hamish's grandad whose move out of Scotland occurred at a low point in his life. Fortunately, Hamish's dad was old enough to take over from him and, as a consequence, Grandad moved from the Scottish farm on his own terms.

Nearly fifteen years later, Hammy and his folks were to join him and his wife, because Newingsworth was being kept in the family and passed on – exactly the way things still ought to be...

The future had looked bright for the younger Macintosh family fifty-five years ago – this chance to go south – an exciting opportunity with the elderly Grandfather Macintosh taking a fancy to retiring to a comfortable chair. His choice was to relax, after a long hard physical life and do something he'd missed out on – to just sit and read some good books. He'd had enough and decided the youngsters could take over at Newingsworth. This was a much bigger farm than the one being worked in Scotland, and for them it would be a challenge.

Arriving at Newingsworth, sixteen years old, the young Hamish was at an age for trying his hand at everything and anything, and that's what he did. His days were full and tiring; he thrived on the hard physical work – it was so much better than school. Great times, Hammy recalled, and to have been able to live happily in the place where two previous generations of Macintosh's survived and worked successfully – that just couldn't be improved... Unfortunately, the third generation mucked it up!

Nearly fifty-five years had passed since coming south, and his Scottish accent still prevailed. He was proud of it, even though it was very different from the way they spoke around this area. Getting used to the local accent had been hard but he coped and, to be honest, although difficult for him it was worse for the poor locals. They were forced to decipher what the heck *Hammy* was talking about...

All the furniture was being left behind. Being no housewife, and with few of the rooms in use, everything was covered by a thick layer of dust. Anyway, the furniture was brought from Scotland when they moved initially and was old. It had served adequately over the years and owed him nothing.

Somehow, dust seemed appropriate.

When he and Sybil married, his father, Macintosh Senior, had been Hamish's one and only employer, and that was the way it would remain. The newly-weds lived conveniently near his folks, not quite on the farm but close, in the family cottage. After lying empty for a year after Grandad died, it became theirs for a time.

Aye, rare an' handy furr work, i' wiss, Hammy mused...

Now, Sybil was no longer with him; he was alone. They'd met in Newingsworth. She had been his right hand, the one with the business brain, the one who gave the advice and guidance to keep the farm successful when Hamish took it over from his father. It was a marriage that lasted forty-seven years, and it was only four years since she passed away. When she died, it became a tougher challenge for him and, from that day on, gradually proved too much.

He had let Sybil down and felt guilty, but he just hadn't expected her to go so soon. He had not prepared himself. She'd been good at what she did. The physical part had been his and he did it well, happy to leave the rest to Sybil – the accounts, the tax bills, the ordering, all the things he didn't want to be bothered with. She took care of them so competently. Things weren't meant to change like that. She'd been a younger woman – he had expected to go first.

At the time of the handover of the farm to Hammy, he and Sybil agreed to swop houses with his mum and dad. His parents went into the smaller cottage, blending graciously and generously into the background, permitting Hammy and Sybil to have freedom to run the farm in their own way.

However, not long after relinquishing authority, there was a surprise for Mr and Mrs Macintosh Senior – no, more of a shock. Their son and his wife would be ending the milk producing business – established so carefully during their tenure. It would remain a dairy farm, but with no milk production – their fame and fortune was to come from *eggs*...

It was the early nineties when they changed direction: Sybil's idea. It could have been a disastrous decision because they were to supply a market which was only *starting* to recover from a massive salmonella crisis (Edwina Currie take a bow?) – a major factor which they chose to ignore...

The cows were sold off at a good price, into a reasonably stable market, and the milking equipment sold on as second-hand, also for good money. Had they continued, they decided, the equipment would have required a costly upgrade to keep pace with regulations. The money obtained was quickly put to use with poultry being purchased and egg production began.

Sybil came from farming stock and for all her life her family had been involved in the poultry industry. Though her parents suffered seriously when the egg market collapsed in the late eighties, this ambitious young couple did not let a small matter like that deter them.

Oh aye ...ambition... Hammy reminded himself... *We hudd plenty o' tha', aw richt – an' no' a care in the world...*

Mr Macintosh Senior found it strange but, having given his word not to interfere, he didn't. Anyway, he was getting old but Hammy's parents lived long enough to witness and appreciate the smart and successful transition that took place. Of course, it could have just been luck...

Hammy was a quick learner and, with Sybil as an excellent tutor, they converted their barns and moved into the selective market of Free Range Eggs. It wasn't an instant success. They both had to work hard with a small team, a team which proved loyal over the years, and they did alright to produce a reliable product, which was purchased happily and regularly in the area. They secured good business with the majority of the smaller local outlets and then, with hard bargaining by Sybil, they moved up a level to become one of the suppliers to the big supermarket, Bisko's.

The negotiating and sales were all done by Sybil. She had a cheery but confident approach to customers, usually sympathetic and eager to please, but with a steely core when it came to the finances. Hammy could never have done what she managed. He had neither the confidence nor the patience, and probably there would have been a language difficulty as well.

Today, it was a lonely man who was wandering aimlessly around. If anyone had been there to observe, the impression he would have given was stooped, sad and old looking. Normally, he was a bustling, full of energy sort of bloke who didn't look his age and certainly didn't make a habit of acting it.

Of course there were regrets, like not having his own family. It would have been nice to have someone benefitting from the farm being handed down, like his father did with him. That thought triggered tears – not a normal reaction for him, and the tough exterior crumbled a little. He stopped at the top of the stairway, and sat and wept. It was not lack of family that caused the waterworks – it was the stupidity of thinking any descendant could have benefitted – *there was nothing left to hand on.*

Y'urr a stupid auld so-an'-so, he remonstrated with himself. *Ye've furgoatten ye've hudd tae sell the bluddy place. Y'urr no' broke, but thurr wid be nuthin tae gie the poor wee souls – if we'd hudd oany.*

So, logically, as he stood outside the kitchen door holding the handle, he concluded that it made sense to have been childless – part of life's big plan. He pulled the door closed, concluding a long period of his life with a simple turn of the key.

A last look in the barns, though there was little to see other than the mess remaining after the collecting of the poultry – off for humane slaughter; the feathers still blew about...

He slid the large barn door closed one last time and it moved beautifully. The rollers worked perfectly. That was one thing he'd always insisted on, back in the days when he worked with machinery – maintenance.

It was always done when due.

Nothing was left to break down.

Hoses and expendable parts were replaced routinely, grease nipples and rollers greased, all movable parts kept moving, and moving smoothly. Squeaks had not been permitted, and that included the lock for the kitchen door.

All to no avail...

The result of the final bank visit caught him by surprise, but he couldn't fault Mr Donaldson. The man had supported him on so many previous occasions, getting him out of panicky scrapes and helping him find the way to carry on – until the next crisis. Full of hope and optimism, sitting in Mr Donaldson's office, he was expecting to listen to the wise words, as usual, but instead his hopes were dashed – there would be no more cash!

"I'm extremely sorry, Mr Macintosh, I've considered very carefully and it would not now be in the bank's interest to give what you require. It pains me, after all the business we've done over the years but, from what I can see of your situation, selling might be the best option. And anyway, isn't it about time you sat back and took it easy?"

So, that decided it. His ambition to retire on a high wasn't to be, and, if he looked at it philosophically, he wouldn't be the first in the country to go with a whimper.

The straw that broke the camel's back, in Hammy's case, was the Range Rover, his very own birthday gift. Being alone and feeling a bit low, he stupidly indulged himself by buying a new expensive vehicle, maybe not one of his best decisions. Once all the debts were settled, this could possibly be an asset – with luck.

Selling to Mr Donaldson the separate cottage down the road also helped. It had been to Mr Donaldson's benefit, of course, and a bargain for him anyway at the time – the cottage had been lying unoccupied for several years. Hammy derived some pleasure from seeing the building modernised for a young couple and serving its proper purpose once more. It was to be a home for Mr Donaldson's newly married daughter. What a coincidence too – old Hector's grandson turning out to be the husband.

Young Sweaty! 'Call me Derek, please...' He's aye sayin' tha'.

He met them the other week when they were over at the place, working on it – a nice young couple. He should really be saying cheerio to them but maybe he'd come back another time and do that. Today, he wasn't in the mood. At least he had a home, rented from a kind friend. He put the important items he was taking with him into the vehicle, a few cardboard boxes with the pictures and photographs, and his clothes, and some other odds and ends. His new place was furnished, and he was fairly certain it would be more comfortable, and cleaner, than what he was leaving behind.

He started the engine and drove over to the gate, feeling there was something important he should be taking, but he was darned if he could think what it was. He swung the gate closed, feeling odd to be closing a barrier that had always been open, and that's when he noticed the key he'd put in his pocket, out of habit, for the farmhouse kitchen door.

"Och, they'll no' miss this," he said, and drove off without looking back.

3

Waking bright and early in the morning, with the sun streaming into the room, and hearing the birds outside chattering and chirping away, was one of life's little pleasures that for several months, ever since moving into this cottage in the country, Derek had experienced. It was idyllic – on a normal morning – but this was not a normal morning. In fact, the question in his mind was, at this precise moment, was it morning?

Derek tried lifting his head. The blasted sun was shining in his eyes, so he couldn't see, and the birds sounded too ruddy cheery, both damn things highly irritating, especially when his neck refused to move his head without pain. There was pain in his head, and in his eyes, and his shoulders. Could he even move his legs?

What was he doing on the sofa? He was in the living room!

Why?

"Sally... *Sally...* I don't feel well..." and he didn't sound it...

There was no reply.

He could hardly breathe. There was a sort of – tightness – it was like a band around his chest, the sort of thing they warn you about on television adverts. Oh-oh... He was having a heart attack... He clutched at his chest. What were the lumps? What was happening to him? He looked down. He had a bust. These clothes – they weren't his. They looked like Sally's...

"*Sally's...?* Oh my God..."

Suddenly, there was clarity. It didn't make his head any less painful. In fact it made it considerably worse. The agony of a memory flashed into his tortured brain, the memory of finding that Sally had arrived home before him, what had she thought? Did she comment? Had he given her a satisfactory explanation? Where is she now? What day is it? Very pertinent questions under the circumstances, but he dreaded some of the answers awaiting him.

Turning awkwardly, he landed on the floor for his trouble. These clothes of Sally's were too tight. He should have realised that when he was putting them on yesterday morning. What if they were damaged? Would she mind?

Ah, it's *Sunday...* Well, at least one question answered... He clambered off the floor and looked out into the garden – no sign of Sally ...so he went into the kitchen and put on the kettle. A cup of thick black coffee with two sugars should help, he hoped. He reached up for a mug and something pinged! Better change into bloke's clothes, he decided.

The bedroom was a mess but at least he couldn't be blamed. That was Sally's trademark, like her bedroom when she was with her mum and dad at Cloverton. Her clothes were everywhere. Those he was wearing, if he just threw them into a corner, would she notice he'd used them? It could be too late for that unfortunately – she was on to him. He could perhaps have talked his way around a rumour if it had fed back to her, but she was here wasn't she? Saw it with her own eyes – in real time.

Look ...at least she left a note, taped to the front of the wardrobe. He would give her a ring in a moment and apologise. Maybe if he contacted her on her mobile while she was in a public place she wouldn't start shouting at him too loudly. It may be well-deserved, but his head wouldn't cope.

So, what had she written? '*Dear Derek ...*' Oh, oh, that's a bad sign – she usually lovingly called him 'Sweaty'.

'*...How disappointing to see that you and my dear father are tarred with the same brush. There is a time and a place for everything, and though it may seem prudish I consider a certain amount of respect should be given to normal conventions for the clothes being worn, and the size of body being squeezed into them. I'll never be able to look my friends in the face again if any of them* *recognised that it was my clothes on your podgy body.*

As for my shoes – squeezing your size nine feet into my size six high-heeled sling-backs was not funny. Choosing to wear and ruin my very best pair is totally unforgivable.

When you eventually waken from your drunken and embarrassing stupor, remove my clothes immediately and take them to the dry cleaners for fumigation. Do not mess up the bedroom by just leaving them lying around.

Your strange childish behaviour has greatly disappointed me and I had difficulty last night believing that this was the person I married little more than three months ago, the one who'd said he'd love and cherish me – the same person who goes out and makes a fool of himself in my clothes – and ruins my best shoes.

I am going back to my parents and whether or not I return will be very dependent on your future behaviour. I will be having words with my father as well, for agreeing to go along with your silly ideas. At least he is a grown-up and he knows right from wrong.

Working alongside you on Monday at the office is something I am not looking forward to, so do not tempt me to do something there which I could regret. You have been warned...

Your loving wife,

Sally xxx.'

4

Alexander walked in his own front door at six-twenty-five precisely on Saturday evening. He had been a bit wilier than Derek. He still hadn't given up the flat in the middle of town and he'd been back there, changed out of the female attire, removing the make-up and all other female traces, before returning home to Cloverton. Last night, his wife, Muriel, and his twin sister, Thelma, suspected absolutely nothing untoward.

"Did you have a nice meal, darling?" Muriel enquired as he joined them for a quiet drink, yet another after his session with Derek, but he liked to think it was without showing any effect of his earlier consumption. He could hold his liquor.

How disappointing it had been for him to see Derek unable to consume the wine without losing control. Derek only had two bottles spread over several hours. He was saddened by his son-in-law's lack of drinking capabilities, and he didn't like being saddened; unfortunately, it was too late to turn the clock back. Sally and Sweaty were married and it was all official now, so Sweaty would remain his son-in-law, whether he could hold his drink or not...

"And did Sweaty behave himself?" Thelma added.

"But of course..." he answered, although he'd thought the blouse Derek wore had been the wrong colour for the rest of the outfit, and he'd applied the make-up a little carelessly perhaps – but maybe, as an expert, he was being over critical. He certainly didn't mention this to his wife and sister.

"Where's Sally?" Alexander asked. "I thought she was going to be here until I returned. It would have been nice having a chat with her. I haven't seen my dear daughter for weeks."

"Not feeling too well. She left early with a headache. She would probably be back at the cottage before Derek," his wife informed him.

Oh-oh, thought Alexander at the time, poor Sweaty. You are in trouble young man...

The thoughts he'd had last night about Derek came back to him as he sat down to breakfast this morning, but he didn't let it spoil his anticipation of the food. He was relaxed. Breakfast for Alexander on Sunday mornings should always be a leisurely, quiet, peaceful affair. This morning, the newspapers had been delivered, Muriel had created a high cholesterol selection of just the sort of food he loved to have for the early Sunday meal and the three of them had taken the utensils in their hands to begin eating, when the doorbell rang – insistently.

Ding-dong, ding-dong, ding-dong, ding...

Sally, of course, had decided to return here, her previous home, this morning – early – in a foul temper, ranting and raving to her mother about the state Derek was in when he'd arrived home at the cottage last night, "...in *my* clothes".

Now, it wouldn't be just Derek who could be in trouble, Alexander suspected. Supplementary questions were about to be asked regarding yesterday's outing, and he guessed he was in danger of being put in the spotlight. He was well experienced in what his daughter could be like. That's why he'd been delighted to see her married and out of the house months ago. They'd had many heated discussions over the years, most often criticisms of him. He probably deserved them, but didn't like being told, especially when he was being told by Sally.

The peaceful intentions of Muriel, Thelma, and Alexander to sit having a civilized, not bothering each other – engrossed in their own newspaper sort of breakfast, all went flying through the window when Sally appeared, hot and perspiring from the cycle ride, and apparently spoiling for a fight – with everyone.

It all poured out fast. She'd left Derek and was coming back to stay with them – back home. This news immediately disturbed Alexander, but he was disturbed even more when she turned on him...

"Derek came back steaming drunk and dressed in my clothes last night," she began. "I hope he didn't disgrace himself when the pair of you had lunch yesterday. Did he, Daddy? He was dressed that way when you saw him, I presume – in my clothes. How he squeezed into them, I do not know. It must have been terrible for you, Daddy. Did you not feel uncomfortable sitting opposite, with him dressed so ridiculously?"

"No," replied Alexander with honesty, hoping that the probing would not go any deeper, but Sally's words started the cogs of Muriel's brain clanking a little more than they had last night, and her husband's developing habit came to mind...

"You didn't say anything was odd about Derek last night, Alexander. Why not? You weren't by any chance wearing something odd too, were you?" and she stared straight into his eyes. "What were you wearing, Alexander?"

Alexander's stomach rumbled ominously. He had been looking forward to breakfast this morning, but he'd consumed very little of it and it was beginning to look as if he'd be having very little more.

"The, ehm ...check suit..." an honest answer, he told himself.

"With the long skirt?"

"Well..."

"And the silk stockings?"

"Umm..."

"Oh Alex-an-der..." came as a condemnation from both Muriel and Thelma.

"Not you too, Daddy..." came from Sally. "Was it your idea, or Derek's?"

"Well, Sweaty didn't argue against it too much, and we were just doing it for a giggle..." He felt the calm breakfast was over as he rose from his chair. An escape was called for. It could only get worse. "You'll have to excuse me a moment. I'll have to make a phone call, urgent business..."

"Daddy, the bank is closed. It's Sunday, remember."

"When you are the manager, it never really stops. You should know that Sally," he blustered, as he abandoned the breakfast table and went upstairs to the bedroom. He grabbed his mobile and selected

Sweaty's number. It rang, and rang.

"Hello," answered a pitiful voice.

"Sweaty, they're on to me as well. I'll have to get out. Three women in the house and I've a feeling my life could become a living hell if I remain. I could go to the flat, but I sense, at a time like this, you could do with some strong support. If I packed a few things, I could use your spare bed. I'll bring a couple of bottles of malt whisky with me and we could drown our sorrows together, and support each other in this hour of need. OK?"

The reply was not immediate, and Alexander considered for a moment he was talking to himself, or else it was a wrong number he'd dialled.

"Sweaty, is that you? Are you still there?"

"Yes," said the sad voice. "Sally's left me... She said she was going back home... Is Sally there?"

"She is – and she's one of the three reasons I want out – fast..."

"Is she really mad at me?"

"Yes, my dear boy – couldn't be madder. You are in big trouble." He said it, he thought, in a jocular manner to lighten the conversation a little, so the wail now coming from the phone was a shock to his hearing. "Relax, Sunshine, help and comfort are on the way," he added and hung up, but he guessed that if any more drinking and drowning of sorrows was to be done, he would be doing it on his own. This young lad couldn't handle it now the going was rough.

Of course, Sweaty hadn't been married as long as he had. He would toughen up through time...

5

'Little Radio fm' was the local independent radio station serving Newingsworth and Slatterfoot and surrounding districts. The jingle, and slogan, from the very first broadcast, was synonymous with the posturing of the smaller man. *'We may be LITT-LE – but we pack a lot of punch'* could be heard singing out many times – many, many times – on air throughout the day.

It seemed right to support the local station, so their programmes were playing regularly in the Smith house. Most recently it was at a high volume when it was on. Neither Granny Smith nor Grandad would normally be in the room beside the radio.

When Derek lived there, as he did for all his life until he met up with Sally, the volume was regularly reduced, but the combination of the hearing of the two pensioners having diminished over time, and with Derek no longer there to control, higher volume reigned...

Daisy Smith was always out the house when one of Hector's new favourite programmes was on: The Granny Wisdom Show, once a week on Monday mornings, for two hours. He didn't mind his wife being out because he could listen to the radio without regularly being requested by her to do minor tasks. That could be really annoying.

The presenter was a real duffer and hadn't a clue about what she was doing – reminded him of his own wife at times. Daisy was never at home at the right time to hear this programme and make any comment, or to appreciate that he was likening her, his dear wife, to this silly old woman on the radio... Daisy had always been out at Bisko's when this was on. For her, recently, Monday had become an essential-to-be-shopping day.

'Little Radio fm' was a relatively new radio station for the region. It had been on the airwaves for only about two years, specialising for its revenue in having local attractions and businesses to advertise on air. So far it was successful enough as a low-budget operation, and managing to survive. Today, being Monday, all the radios tuned to 'Little Radio fm' were broadcasting to the audience for The Granny Wisdom Show, for two hours only. This programme was a mixture of music and chat, not unlike most of the broadcasts by the larger organisations, but what this programme had, that the others hadn't, was Granny Wisdom herself.

It had started harmlessly enough five weeks ago, a live phone-in programme with a presenter who didn't seem to know how the business was supposed to be run. She would press the wrong buttons, throw the wrong switch, or play music different from what she'd said, and be talking when her microphone should have been off. However, to those who phoned in, she'd give homely and friendly advice, provided she could hear what they were saying. Mis-hearing a comment on a bad phone line was common and could lead to some very strange and unrelated replies.

Sometimes it was the lovelorn and lonely, genuine broken romances and broken hearts, but it could be mischievous callers forcing her to dodge answering overtly sexual questions in her overly amateurish manner. The haphazard effect had added to the listening figures for the station, and was particularly liked by those who enjoyed the non-visual version of people slipping on the proverbial banana skin. Granny Wisdom was an expert at slipping...

Her following of listeners had built up remarkably quickly, considering she was so incredibly bad at what a professional would consider the job should be.

One of broadcasting's most professional humble bumblers sent her an email asking if she would be starting her own mob of old groupies like TOGs. He'd suggested she could call her followers – the MOGGIES. This he explained could stand for '*My Old Godawful Granny Is Extra Special*'. She was delighted to have received his comment, although her producer, Carol, wasn't too sure if it was meant as a compliment... Granny Wisdom didn't care – it was recognition....

Very few people knew Granny Wisdom's identity. Derek knew. It was his idea – due to bumping into Curly, his buddy from their younger days. Curly was known to his staff by his correct name of Mr Graham Stockman or alternatively – the Boss.

Derek had gone to meet a producer, Carol Stevens, at the studio of 'Little Radio fm' to propose an idea of his own. His suggestion was to be a programme to boost the charity efforts of his two gardening pals, Arthur and Charlie, and promote the marathon in which they'd be competing later in the year. He hoped a radio programme could be aired in conjunction with the current features he was doing in the Newingsworth Weekly Gazette, and take the project a leap forward by generating more cash for charity.

When he was introduced to Carol, his first thought was 'My God, she's only a child'. He was thirty, going on thirty-one, but sadly feeling like an old married man wanting to remain young, finding life rattling past at a much increased rate – too fast in fact.

Walking along the corridor of the small studio, he stepped aside to let someone pass and it was quite unexpectedly a face that he knew – *Curly*. Graham was back to town.

They were both now adults, but Derek still thought of his pal from their boyhood gang by his anointed nickname.

Graham had immediately responded with, "No... It can't be, yes it is... It's Sweaty. How are you, old mate? It's been ages since I last saw you."

He, surprisingly at thirty-one, still had a head of ginger hair to match his old nickname. Derek's first thoughts were that chemicals and a bottle had been involved, but he could have been wrong.

Curly was the same age as Sweaty. It had been the same gang when little, the same class at school, and the same desires for making it big in the world.

Derek had been given the opportunity of joining the Newingsworth Daily News and decided journalism would be his thing. He'd remained at home.

At about the same time, Curly left to live in London to work at his first job in broadcasting and things progressed well for him.

Commercial radio was where he'd developed. Although he'd always been ready for the BBC calling and could have been tempted, they didn't call.

He didn't let that dampen his enthusiasm and reached a turning point a few years back – he wanted to be the boss and run his own station, even though it would have to be small and in local radio.

He researched and identified that his old stamping ground had no commercial coverage so he invested his savings, obtained approval to broadcast, and here he was.

It was comfortable being back on old territory. When he met Sweaty he felt guilty at not having re-established relationships sooner – but he had been busy, very busy. It was a warm feeling bumping into Sweaty again...

"You... You are married? ...You?"

Derek wondered why Curly should be so surprised. He wore glasses, yes, and was not the smartest dresser in the town, but he didn't think of himself as a geek, or particularly unattractive.

"If I'd known you were back, you'd have been invited to the wedding," said Derek. "It's strange – this being married – four weeks and three days, and never a cross word. You will have to come over to meet Sally. She's wonderful, the perfect wife. She says I'm ok – but only on my good days..." Graham's expression disturbed Derek a little – he seemed to accept that as the truth, rather than a joke.

When they had met, Curly was enthusiastic about going along with Sweaty's idea of having more publicity for the marathon. It wouldn't do the station any harm being involved in a charity drive, but he also asked him, as an old pal, and one with an artistic flair, if he would like to be involved in devising a new programme for the station. Derek was flattered.

"Something different is what I want, something no other station has, if possible. Think about it ...but, enough about work – how are the old folk, your gran, and your grandad – still well? I'll have to pop round and see them sometime. Are they glad to be rid of you? Did you ever stop the good-bye kisses on the doorstep? Oh yes, I remember – even when you were just going messages..."

Graham could visualise himself as the teenager standing waiting for Derek to come out of the house, and how Granny Smith always insisted on the peck on her cheek on every occasion. She only demanded it from Derek and not from him, thank goodness, but Graham was the one who would feel embarrassed. That was not a practice encouraged in his family, but then again, it had been Derek's gran, and not his mother.

Yes, he remembered Granny Smith as being a nice, but a dominant force. She'd brought Derek up well and always thought the world of him.

Derek left Graham, not feeling particularly hopeful of being able to help. Had Curly just been flattering him by suggesting he possessed an artistic streak? For goodness sake, he was still trying to establish the correct direction for his own career, and his ambition to be a published author still seemed distant.

Proving his ability to write was even still in question, partly because the current choice of subject was now looking decidedly dodgy and proving to be a struggle. After all the fuss last year about his father-in-law acting and doing female-impersonation, Alexander turned out to be surprisingly good at it. This had given Derek the inspiration to write about the strange practice of men dressing in women's clothes; well, he had thought it strange ...*not something anyone would catch me doing, no sir*, he told himself.

At least, he'd made a start to the story, but only just. A first chapter had been typed out. It was sitting on the PC looking lonely – the only chapter in the file that, many weeks ago, he optimistically entitled 'Incognito'. As usual, he had a distinct lack of confidence in his own ability to come up with all the goods and to a great extent the chosen theme was blowing hot and cold. He gave the subject a fair bit of thought though – this dressing-up lark by men. Surely, dressing-up was a game that little girls played, stealing their mummy's lipstick and suchlike, and messing up the wallpaper in the process. Why would grown men choose to do it? Could they not prevent themselves? Was it a gender-bender problem? Anyway, where do they get the clothes? Going into a woman's clothes shop was certainly beyond Derek's imaginative capabilities.

Should his book become a factual psychological assessment, or remain fictional? He also wondered, should he try the experience himself? Was he brave enough to try it? He could see little likelihood of that but, as usual, so many questions were generated it caused his whole creative process to come to a grinding halt.

The Newspaper Office was not too far from 'Little Radio fm' and walking was part of his daily routine. Walking not only gave him the chance to think, it was essential exercise because recently his waist had been developing too rapidly.

Could it be due to Sally cooking rich and tasty meals, and him being pampered? Yes, it could be, partly ...but no, not just that. They hadn't been married long enough to affect his waistline, surely. It was more likely caused by being spoiled all his life, by his gran. He'd never had to cook or do any housework, thanks to her. It also could be, of course, that since joining the Gazette, he was not jogging each day as he used to, and there was probably little doubt that he needed more exercise.

Perhaps he should join Arthur and Charlie for the marathon!

As he turned the corner into Dobson Street, his mind, as it was prone to do, wandered in another direction. His thoughts went back to dressing up – but not him dressing up. The picture being constructed in his head was of Sally – in an extremely skimpy nurse's outfit – he was tied to the bed and she was coming towards him! She was going to...

Wait a minute! Who was he trying to kid? Dream on man... Nothing like that is likely to happen. Sally is not that sort of girl! Think of other things, Derek!

The brisk walking did help and, as he crossed the road at the zebra crossing, surprising the driver of a delivery van, he had a sudden inspiration, a divine intervention almost. Why not a radio programme which used someone's lack of talent: someone who was totally ignorant of the whole broadcasting process: have them trying to present a programme. He or she could maybe bumble through a radio show, talking to phone-callers and just chatting, with musical interludes. It could even be a problem-solving phone-in sort of thing, with wise but meaningless words being dispensed to people who shouldn't have phoned-in in the first place...

Who could fit the bill for something like that? Anyone he knew? Sally? No, too down to earth and wouldn't think it a funny idea – too honest at times.

How about Alexander? No, he was a bank manager and working full-time already, earning a fortune.

Muriel? Maybe, but she used computers at Bisko's and was capable of dealing with technical stuff. She was well aware of the ways of the world, too practical and capable, so, no, not Muriel. Anyway, at times he was unsure if she had a sense of humour...

Thelma? She was looking for work, or if she wasn't, she should be, but she'd been a manager and knew something about electronics – not ignorant enough.

What about Grandad? Derek imagined a radio programme with his grandad introducing it, stuttering along and getting absolutely nowhere. *It hadn't been done before, had it? No, but he couldn't envisage inflicting that on the public.*

There was his gran, Granny Smith? Now, there could be a possibility. She was old and wise, could work a vacuum cleaner, and a washing machine, but not a mobile phone, or a computer... Would she become flustered if things went wrong? Possibly, but that would fit the bill. Had she a sense of humour? Hmmm, sometimes it was questionable but fun for others can come from the pompous person walking into a lamp-post, can't it? Does she get annoyed? At Grandad, yes, definitely, but she was not too bad with others. Would she like some extra money? Who wouldn't?

Clearly Granny Smith knew nothing about broadcasting, but she did have opinions that she was willing to state, and she had lived a long time. Would she enjoy the experience? Why not give her the chance? It might be amusing... No... It was too stupid ...but original? No-one had ever been daft enough to try it on a radio station, had they?

Derek was well aware that Graham knew, and liked, Granny Smith, although he'd always thought her somewhat eccentric ...then he suddenly realised he was going way beyond his remit, *Can you think of an idea? It wouldn't be his decision as to who would be the presenter, that is, if the idea was accepted in the first place – it was all up to Curly.*

Anyway, he might think of a better person, and whoever it is, he's paying ...but Granny would be good.

6

To Derek's amazement, Graham went for it. Reluctantly at first, and yes, he agreed it was stupid; however, it was so stupid it might work, though only with the correct person. It couldn't be someone completely incompetent though. They'd have to get to know how the equipment functioned even if they couldn't use it like an expert, or they might destroy the studio. A sense of humour was a necessity, and they mustn't be self-conscious, or be easily embarrassed. Non-stop talking, when necessary, could also be a benefit, but most importantly, whoever it was would have to be able to get on well with the show's producer – and a vital essential – they must always be available, without fail, early morning every Monday.

Graham added, he would want an air of mystery created about her – he'd now fixated on a female. She could maybe be a sort of failing agony aunt, billed as 'the wise one' ...but be the exact opposite?

There they sat facing each other in the office slurping coffee, Graham and Derek, each trying to give the impression to the other of being an important executive, but both feeling twenty-five years younger, and back in 'The Gang'. They were comfortable being together again. It was a warm feeling, and they were finding it impossible to talk without using the old nicknames.

So, Sweaty, and Curly yapped on....

Curly was enthusiastic and saw this as a programme that could be introduced at very short notice. The producer would be Carol – Sweaty knew her – so she was invited to join the meeting in the Boss's office, which, in the heads of Sweaty and Curly, was now the gang hut. Creative juices were being helped by more coffee, and next on the gang's agenda would be deciding a programme name.

On joining this creative discussion, Carol felt slightly uncomfortable calling these two males by their nicknames, but soon got the hang of it. In no time at all, she began to feel peeved at just being called 'Carol' and wanted so much to be part of their gang. Then she found that she was taking on the role of chairperson as the two little boys, sitting beside her, started recounting stories of what they'd done together back in younger days, and her task became one of dragging their chattering back to the business in hand – as usual the males were having all the fun.

A title for the show please ...she demanded.

'*The Newingsworth Oracle*' – sounded like a newspaper – no.

How about, '*Wisdom from an Oracle*'? Hmm... No, much too heavy.

'*The Pearls of Wisdom Show*'? No...

If she were an older woman, it could be, '*Your Favourite Granny Show*'. No...

How about '*The Granny Wisdom Show*'? Now ...that had more of a ring to it. Yes ...that's what it could be, **'THE GRANNY WISDOM SHOW'.**

Right, the title is decided, now, the big question, who could do it? Whoever it is will have to be able to keep the secret – discussing it with no-one other than the ones who would be involved in the programme production. A first timer, trying to control a computerised talk and music show – live on air – there was no chance of making it work like clockwork – it could be perfect...

When Derek suggested his own granny, Graham just grinned. Yes. He remembered her as appearing scatty – but really being a smart cookie underneath. Would she still be the same? He hadn't seen her in a long time.

"Would she?" he asked excitedly, "And could she keep it a secret if she was the chosen one? A bit of mystery... That I think is important."

Derek thought how, over the years, he had never managed to wheedle out of his gran why he wasn't being brought up by his rightful mother. At the drop of a hat, she always was able to produce a variety of untruths, which just came tumbling out, mischievously hiding the real truth from him. He never succeeded in catching her out, so he was able to say categorically, "Definitely..." and it was agreed.

Daisy Smith, Derek's gran, would be given the first option...

"How soon can you speak to her?" asked Curly.

"Now," replied her grandson.

Speaking to her on her own was easy enough. Derek just had to lift the phone and ring, and it could be done from Curly's phone, with the other two listening in.

"H-h-h-hello..."

"Hi, Grandad, how are you today?"

"Is that you D-D-D-D-Derek?"

"It sure is, Grandad. Did you get wet today?" He was still managing to do his daily paper round, on his squeaky bike, seven days a week...

"B-b-b-b-bloody soaked, D-D-D-Derek, thinking of g-g-g-g-giving it up." How many years had he been repeating that intention – every time it rained? "C-c-c-c-could c-c-c-catch my d-d-death of c-c-c-c... d-d-d-death of c-c-c – pneumonia..."

"Could I have a word with Gran, please? Is she in?"

"She is. She's d-d-d-doing one of her c-c-c-c-c-c-crosswords. I'll g-g-g-go and g-g-get her f-f-f-for you. Hang on..."

It was a slow business talking to his grandad, and he had to be very careful if he chose to tease him about his stutter. It would always be face to face, and Grandad would have to be in a receptive mood. If Derek did chance it and tease, it had to be done in a kindly way, or it could mean a sulk for many days...

"Hello, Derek. It seems ages since you phoned and it's so nice to speak to you. How is Sally? Are you having problems? I haven't seen her in ages either. Why have you phoned? I hope you haven't... Is Sally all right? Oh, it's not you ...are you in trouble again? Hector, turn the radio down... How can I help?"

Curly nodded to Carol – she'd passed the non-stop talking test...

"No, Gran, nothing like that. How'd you like to earn some

money?"

"Oh, yes, of course, who wouldn't? Supplement the pension, it would, but what would I have to do? Do you want me to come round and clean for you and Sally? Don't ask me to do the gardening though. I don't think my back could cope."

"Oh no, Gran, it would be much more exciting, and much better money – but you couldn't tell Grandad about it. In fact you couldn't tell anyone about it."

"Ah ...so you want me to be a spy?" It was said quietly, and guardedly, with her hand over the telephone. One couldn't be too careful...

"Well, maybe not that, but would you like to meet me tomorrow in town. I can't tell anyone about this either, other than you. I can't even tell Sally. If we meet in W. H. Smith's it won't matter if one of us is late, just in case it's raining again – I'll see you at two o'clock?"

"Derek..." and she said it guardedly once more, "Should I wear a disguise?"

They'd found the lady who was about to become Granny Wisdom... The three of them sat there smiling, but Carol's smile was bigger. It looked as if this little exclusive male gang would have to be submitting to some girl power in the near future...

7

The other two could feel the tension. Having one member of the staff who was unwilling to speak to another member of the staff, and one who was totally broken-hearted, was putting a great deal of strain on the two remaining members.

In the office, Sally was reluctant to communicate at all with Derek. The one who had been 'behaving stupidly' was him, and Sally had no doubts about that. Therefore, he was the one who had to suffer. Sally had done absolutely nothing wrong, but neither had Spider or Rob, yet they were suffering too. Curt emails, and occasional text messages, were the nearest the squabbling pair came to having direct contact.

Spider hadn't volunteered, but when Sally and Derek were in the room together and verbal communication had become essential, he somehow became the one who was landed with the unenviable task of acting as go-between. Sally wouldn't listen to anything that Derek tried to say directly to her, though, on the first Monday, there was very little being said, by either.

Rob, being the boss, felt he could justify shutting his office door and hiding inside, away from the ill-feeling and unpleasant atmosphere. Spider would cope, and anyway, if he couldn't – tough... The boss shouldn't have to be involved unless there is a failure to meet deadlines for the printer. So Rob played on his computer, checking the current odds for the three-thirty at Newmarket, and took difficult decisions about the best bet for the day. He still had an account at Saddanbroke's and although it was rarely in the black, it was not excessively in the red either. His winning bet was waiting – it just had to be selected...

Having worked for over a year at the Gazette had been good for Spider, and he had become an essential member of the team, due to Sally in the first place – even though his employment had been by mistake. In consequence Spider felt a deep loyalty to the organisation, and in particular, to Sally. Today, he was almost as broken-hearted as the two non-communicators.

The highlight of Spider's year, so far, had been Sally and Derek's wedding. He was invited, together with Rob and Elizabeth Sheldon and their two little boys and, ever since, the office team of Sally, Derek, Rob, and himself, had seemed more like a happy family than just colleagues: they were bound together: a tightly-knitted team – until now...

What had gone wrong between Sally and Derek? He would have liked to know, only to be able to help more. He was not just being nosy, the two ex-lovebirds were being annoyingly tight-lipped about the cause. He'd a vague idea of what had gone wrong, something to do with clothes and shoes in particular, but clothes and shoes were not subjects he'd studied and therefore he was not qualified to help. Clothes kept him warm, shoes were at the end of his legs, and until now this knowledge had been sufficient, standing him in good stead – what more should he know, he wondered?

"Spider, would you please tell him that I can't read what he's written here." Spider went over and collected the piece of paper from Sally, and then crossed to the far corner desk.

"Derek, Sally says she can't read what you've written here..."

"Please tell her, Spider, it's perfectly obvious to me," Derek informed him. So back Spider went, trying to make out what it was himself, but without success. He knew where this was going and he didn't fancy walking from one end of the room to the other, all day.

"Sally, Derek says it's perfectly obvious to him."

"Right, thank you Spider," and she typed in 'perfectly obvious to him'. Spider wasn't sure if that was what had been meant, but kept his mouth shut, and sat down at his own desk.

The suspicion of something not being right started first thing today, when Spider arrived just behind Sally. She didn't appear from the usual direction. Derek and Sally cycled in together from the cottage normally but Derek appeared later than usual, and looked a bit dishevelled. No doubt the knowledge would come out as the day progressed. Someone was bound to say something ...*but Spider did not find out.*

Derek went out, on a news hunt, he said.

The office radio was switched on at low volume by Spider, as had become a recent habit. It was almost eleven o'clock: time for The Granny Wisdom Show. This was only the sixth week and it was still sounding chaotically crazy. He didn't know why, but for Spider it had become compulsive listening.

Yes, he was just in time, the music started, and then it stopped, and started again at the beginning. Whoops – the sound was like a needle being scratched across a record on an old-fashioned turntable. Surely that wasn't what had happened. Don't they use CDs nowadays? Maybe it was intentional – to surprise listeners. You just didn't know with Granny Wisdom. Surely no-one could mess it up quite so much, unless it was deliberate, but then again...

"Is this the right button, Carol? No... Which one is it then?" Granny Wisdom's voice came through the ether, and as she was talking the middle of an Abba song came blasting out. "Take a chance, take a chance, take a..." and stopped.

"Hello everybody and good morning to MOGGIES everywhere," sang out the voice. "Welcome again to 'Little Radio fm' and to..."

'We may be LITT-LE – but we pack a lot of punch', sang out the jingle.

"Oh ...was that me Carol? Yes? Oh dear, but welcome anyway to 'The Granny Wisdom Show', on another rip-roaring Monday morning. Here I am again, ready to take your calls and try to help you with your little problems of life and, if I can press the right buttons and move the correct switches, there might even be some music. Are you as excited as me? I won't be able to tell you what the music is going to be, but we might be able to guess after it has been played – if it gets played... So who's the first caller today, Carol?"

"It's Susie from Slatterfoot – go ahead Susie," Carol prompted Daisy.

"Hello Granny Wisdom. Can you help me please?"

"Tell me your problem and I'll try, Susie," said the calm soothing voice.

"It started with my budgie. It escaped and flew into a tree. I've got a tiger-striped cat that lost its tail in a fight with the milkman's dog, and it's gone up the tree after the budgie – and got stuck – the cat, not the dog. Now I've asked my boyfriend if he could get the cat down for me, but he's said no. So, I asked the man next door, and he said no as well, but my problem is, if I'm having fish for tea do I have to have white wine with it, or would it be alright to have red?"

"Well, I'm not very good with wines, Susie. After a wee glass of sherry I'm anybody's, if you know what I mean. So, I'd say you should drink whatever you fancy with it, or better still have steak pie, and then you could drink your red wine happily without the neighbours suggesting you don't know the proper etiquette. Whatever you drink though should be in moderation. There's too much bungee-drinking going on these day – or is it binge-jumping? How's the cat doing?"

"It's still up the tree – oh, but my boy-friend must have changed his mind. He's half-way up the tree to get it. Oh ...he's fallen off... I'll have to go..."

"Bye Susie, it's been nice talking to you, and I'm sure we are all hoping your budgie flies back to you. Which button, Carol? I know you told me before, but I can't remember... Now don't make that face – it doesn't suit you... No need to lose your temper... That one? See – and you thought I couldn't do this..." The talking stopped...

There was an awkward silence ...and nothing filled the gap!

...And then the beautiful strains of the 'Titanic' love theme swept in... *"My heart will go on,"* sang Celine Dion as sweetly, and as cloyingly as only she can. For those listening, it was impossible to avoid the pathetic image ...an enormous sinking ship ...giant floating icebergs ...and Granny Wisdom donning her yellow lifejacket!

On the music flowed, full of heartfelt emotion, until a sudden break in Celine's vocals caused by Daisy bumping a button as she spilled her coffee... "Have you a cloth please, Carol?"

" ...Once...more...you ooooopen the door..." Celine continued, and the music moved towards its climax, with listeners expecting at least a loud splash at the end, but no, the sound faded out in a controlled professional manner, so unlike normal. The novelty of the professionalism was thanks to Carol having taken temporary control to avoid the crackling from Granny's controls and the dripping coffee...

"And who do we have now, Carol?" Granny asked her very able producer.

"It's a young man, who won't give his name, Granny, but calls himself 'Broken-Hearted'. I'll pass him to you now..." There was a pause and then Carol's voice came through again. "...the blue button, you silly old..."

"Thank you, Carol. Hello caller, and how can I help you?"

"Hello Granny Wisdom. Thanks for taking my call but I am at my wits end, because my wife has left me..." and the voice gave a sob, and a tear sat waiting in the eye of all the MOGGIES listening. This was going to be a sad one. "I did something stupid."

"Another woman was it, Broken-Hearted?"

"Oh no, Granny Wisdom – it was even worse. I ruined her best shoes..."

"Oh now ...that doesn't sound too big a problem. Surely if you buy her another pair, she'll come back home?"

"Nothing so simple. There was a problem with her clothes too."

"Oh my, in what way, Broken-Hearted?"

The radio at Spiders desk was still on. Spider had gone to the loo – obviously it was all much too exciting. The sound was down low. Sally hadn't been listening but suddenly she thought the voice of the caller was familiar. She moved over to Spider's desk and turned up the volume. Rob Sheldon had almost fallen asleep in the office, but because these were only wafer-thin walls, the sound of the radio startled him and he listened in too.

"I wore her clothes. She might have forgiven me if I'd been slimmer, I think, but I shouldn't have done that, and I'm sorry, and I want her to come back – please ...and I'll buy her new shoes – and anything else she might want..."

Spider came back into the office and stood beside Sally. He

couldn't understand why there was a little tear running down her face. Rob heard the part Spider missed, and as he wiped away the little bit of dust in his eye, he was making an educated guess.

"Are you going to tell us your wife's name, Broken-Hearted?"

"Oh no, I couldn't do that. I've humiliated her enough."

"Does she listen to this programme do you think, Broken-Hearted?"

"I hope so (sob), I really do hope so, because I so desperately want her back. I love her, and Granny Wisdom – thank you (sob). Someone ...somewhere (sob) is so lucky to have you as their real granny... Thank you, thank you, thank you... (...sob...sob)."

Sally was in tears, Spider was in tears, and back at the radio station Carol was in tears, all of Newingsworth and Slatterfoot, and surrounding districts, and all the MOGGIES were in tears.

Derek Toozlethwaite was probably the only one in the area who was smiling. With any luck, that call would win his wife back, if she was listening, but even better, it would have boosted the future ratings for the Granny Wisdom Show through the roof...

He hadn't spoken in advance to anyone at the studio about his intention to make the phone call, especially not to his gran, and he was feeling rather smug about the success of his little ruse, until a thought struck him – *what if his granny actually recognised his voice? What the hell would she say to her grandson, her dear Derek, for dressing up in women's clothing?*

She'd never forgive him either...

8

Derek was 'feeling the burn'. Attempting to keep pace with Arthur and Charlie was progressively taking its toll. He just wanted to stop and die, quietly, at the side of the road – if possible in a clean and dry part of the verge. At any moment, he was sure he would fall over, but he was being choosy where. His two running companions were fit, and it showed. Similarly, very obviously even though he tried hard to hide it, it showed that he was not.

He was also on a psychological downer.

Obviously, he was not forgiven for dressing-up in her clothes. Sally hadn't returned to the cottage, even after his call to Granny Wisdom, and here it was, Saturday again.

Maybe she hadn't been listening to the radio on Monday morning, or simply hadn't been won over by his plea. He hadn't said either her name or his when he phoned, had he, so why should she have known it was him? She certainly hadn't come back.

His hope, so high at the start of the week, had diminished by the end, and the office contact, or lack of it, certainly gave him no hint of early forgiveness. So for Derek it was a long week and, sadly, it looked like his punishment could be lasting a lot longer...

On top of that, his father-in-law was now in residence with him at the cottage. Neither male had any talent for cooking and they were living on an assortment of takeaways and ready-made meals which had lasted now for ...oh, goodness knows how long? He'd lost track of time. Had it only been a week? That sort of food was not doing anything for his stamina, or his waistline.

So, running off the excess fat was his target. It was a beautiful morning and the spring countryside was beginning to display seasonal colours. This beauty unfortunately was accompanied by the occasional unpleasant smell caused by the energetic work being done by local farmers. Taking deep, gasping gulps of breath, so necessary for him to stay alive, meant Derek had lungs filled by these less than pleasant aromas.

This didn't help his feelings of discomfort. He couldn't go on...

He would have liked to have shouted to his two companions in front that he was stopping for a momentary rest. Yes, 'would have liked to' – if he had been capable of actually shouting out a joined-up sentence.

"Arth..." was all that came forth. Presumably it was an attempt to shout 'Arthur', although it could have been "Arghhh..." as he fell to his knees, who knows? Maybe, when the two in front reached the hut again, twenty miles on, they would notice he was missing...

Looking and finding his training routine on the internet was smart. The one chosen as his personal programme said: 'By week 6 a newcomer to marathon running should have the capability of achieving a twelve-mile, walk-and-jog combination – but don't push too hard,' it warned.

Arthur and Charlie, having done three marathons previously, had obviously maintained their fitness, using their own personal training regime. Plus, the big bonus, as far as physical activity was concerned, they did a manual job daily, but Derek was determined to show them that he could keep up. He ran from the start, and kept running but, after maintaining pace for about six miles continuously, he was now lying flat out, face down on the grassy verge, and reluctant to start up again. Not walking these last four miles was being deeply regretted.

His running companions, would they even remember he started out with them? There seemed to be very little effort involved for Arthur and Charlie to run and carry on a continuous conversation, all about how successful they'd been with the bulbs they planted last year, especially after the winter being so long and hard. As gardeners, he supposed talking shop for them was bulbs, flowers, turf, trees, shrubs, compost, and the inadequacies of Newingsworth Parks Department, of which they considered themselves to be essential pieces. Then they'd chatted on about their other activities – without missing a step, or a breath.

These two guys were now well known, thanks to their friend 'Sweaty'. Since Derek had the inspiration and published the original newspaper article about Arthur and Charlie, they had become minor celebrities, and not just in Newingsworth. Not only were they now doing a regular gardening section in the Newingsworth Weekly Gazette but, every so often, they were invited as guests on the regional TV channel show 'Around the Towns', and had become well known as the experts on gardening in the area. They even chanced their arms and covered for the music critic on the Slatterfoot Evening News, when the dear old lady who'd done the column for years, was ill and off work for three weeks with 'ladies problems'... Credit for the career extensions of Arthur and Charlie was almost entirely due to Derek but, as time passed and their personal success grew, nearly all that seemed to have been forgotten.

To be fair, a while ago, they were kind enough to say how Derek had been their 'little helper' in the early days. They didn't actually use the name 'Derek', of course – who did? They habitually called him by his nickname, Sweaty... During those first months involved together, he'd continually pleaded with them in the same way he did with everyone he met, "Please... Call me Derek", but without success. Being repeated over and over made no difference and he eventually realised he was wasting his breath. So, he gave in and now answered automatically to Sweaty. At least, he told himself, it was meant affectionately – most of the time.

With difficulty, Derek raised his head and looked around.

Arthur and Charlie were nowhere to be seen. Why was he pushing himself like this? Running a marathon – it really wasn't his scene. It had seemed like a good idea at the time ...and how many people have said that over the years? He had been fit enough to cope with the fifteen-minute jogs he'd been doing for a long time but twenty-six miles was a long distance. Taking a bus is the way he should be travelling for journeys of that sort, surely....

Sally had repeatedly attempted to stop him behaving like an idiot, but somehow behaving like an idiot was in his blood, and the training continued.

He was a newspaper man, first and foremost, generating publicity for the forthcoming attempt by Arthur and Charlie, but done from the comfort of an office chair was surely not right, was it? The guilt at not being involved himself got to him, so it seemed correct to get up off his backside and join them. This week Sally wasn't there to try stopping him and, being on his own, it was something to do.

The newspaper competition running currently was asking suggestions for suitable costumes for the celebrity pair to wear on their next big run. The locals were showing interest and enthusiasm. Some superbly outlandish ideas were being submitted, but the right one hadn't yet come out of the bag.

Because they were gardeners, pushing a wheelbarrow loaded with smelly manure was popular, but probably antisocial. Another was for them to be dressed in arrowed convict outfits with a real ball and chain attached to their ankles: obviously a contribution from a true sadist – or a fellow competitor.

Flat out, with his nose in the grass, Derek was surprised at the amount of miniature wildlife he was able to observe, and all seen through steamed up spectacles. It was like a diminutive forest filled by its own tiny population. No need for any microscope here. He could see tiny jumping things, tiny creeping things, tiny crawling things and tiny other things, looking very busy, masses of them – giving the impression of a little army, which was moving rapidly in his direction – ANTS.

He sat upright abruptly, but the dizziness was still there. He flopped backwards and just lay there again, gazing at the beautiful sky and the fluffy white clouds, not having the strength to care if the ants had come to carry him off or not. He would have been happier if it had started to rain, to freshen him a bit.

Lying there in a sort of stupor, he didn't notice the large executive car drawing up alongside. The driver seemed concerned for him, but was having difficulty finding the correct button to press. Eventually, the window slid down.

"Are you all right?" was shouted to him.

"No," he replied then added, "Ohhhhh..." for effect.

He had intended telling whoever it was, to bugger off and not bother a dying man, but when he turned his eyes to look at the speaker his mood changed.

She climbed from the driving seat, came over, and looked down at him. This was a beautiful short-haired blonde and she was standing staring at him with a concerned expression on her face. In his dazed condition he gazed upwards – at long legs vanishing into a mini-skirt that he could see barely covered a g-string, which in turn, barely covered other interesting parts, which of course, as a gentlemen, he didn't look at.

"You seem to be having some difficulty. Can I give you a lift?" she asked.

Having difficulty – me, a trainee marathon runner, just because I've fallen over and am lying here gasping? Of course there is nothing wrong with me... That was the convoluted reply he considered he should be giving – but what he actually said was, "Oh, yes please," in a pathetic voice.

"Jump in," she told him, as she stepped carefully over the grass in her high heels, and climbed back into the driving seat. Jump in? He would willingly have obliged her if he had been able, but he could barely rise and hobble to the car door. He opened it and flopped into the front passenger seat – gratefully – and then her perfume struck... God – what an effect!

Gone was the weakness from his head and his body. It was over-powering... He ...he ....*wow* ...*he felt randy*... It must have cost her a fortune to buy a perfume with such a kick.

You are a married man, he reminded himself. You have a lovely wife, and your lovely wife loves you. Think of Sally, even though she is currently despising you and still living with her mother. Do not be tempted by this beautiful girl who's lured you into her car, and who obviously fancies you, even though you are a sweaty lump of lard at the moment... *Jeez – what a perfume... Sally who? Oh yes...*

He didn't feel they had met in the best of circumstances. He was perhaps not adequately dressed for the situation – in fact, he was almost undressed... T-shirt and running shorts – he felt naked. He was afraid to look at her. He sat upright, fastened his safety belt, folded his arms trying to breathe very little of the intoxicating perfume, braced his legs firmly, feet apart and pushed himself back in the seat, desperately trying to think only pure thoughts to make him feel exhausted again.

Then her hand was suddenly on his bony knee...

"OUCH...!"

9

"Another cup of coffee, Mum?" asked Sally.

"Yes please darling," said Muriel, as she reached for a little piece of the cherry cake. No work today: Muriel was delighted to be just relaxing with Sally and Thelma, and considering what husband Alexander might be getting up to at this very moment. He wasn't at the cottage when they'd arrived, but neither was Derek.

At least they knew that Derek went running on Saturday mornings – Alexander would certainly not be with him, doing that. Being Saturday, Alexander wouldn't be at work either, of course. Banks don't open to suit the public, a well known fact, and his certainly didn't. At least when he was at work, Muriel knew that he would be behaving himself in a professional manner. Otherwise, she felt she ought to be nearby to keep an eye on him.

It will be a nice surprise for Derek to return to the cottage in a short while and find them here, Sally was thinking, particularly when he is told that he is forgiven.

Her dad almost certainly had been the instigator of the little clothes escapade. She was convinced now and willing to forgive Derek, but it had been a slow process. Luckily, and to Derek's benefit, Muriel understood Alexander better than Sally. Derek wouldn't even have thought of getting dressed up in her clothes without encouragement, she told her daughter. The boy was probably taunted into doing it by his father-in-law. Alexander likes little jokes.

I over-reacted, Sally told herself. Sweaty wouldn't do anything intentionally to hurt me, she just knew. Now ...if it had been another woman, then she would have had good reason, not only to be upset, but to be totally justified in clobbering him as well...

Derek would be doing road training for the marathon. Out early on Saturday mornings had been the pattern for many weeks now, building up his stamina. In actual fact, Sally doubted his ability to complete a marathon, but she didn't want to disillusion him yet, by telling him.

If only he'd gone on his usual Saturday routine last week, he wouldn't have been pushed into the dressing-up nonsense. While away from Derek, the more she thought about it, the more she was convinced – her father had been the root cause.

For moral support, was the commendable reason given by Muriel and Thelma for being at the cottage this morning, and their own idea. It made sense, them being with Sally on the promise of attending to the retrieval and removal of Alexander from the premises. Getting him out and leaving this recently married pair in peace, to make up on their own after their very first fall-out, must be the correct thing to do.

Meanwhile, as they waited for the return of the two males, it was very pleasant just lazing about. Saturday couldn't be used in a better way when you've been working ...not necessarily working hard in Muriel's case but working nonetheless for five days. Saturdays and Sundays were Muriel's times to sit down and relax.

Still at Bisko's Superstore, still the cash supervisor, and still cycling to the store every day – the cycling for Muriel was now addictive. After each outing on her bike she felt the benefit. She knew she was having more than enough exercise and therefore at the weekend she could be bone lazy and not feel guilty, especially now Thelma lived with them. The pressure of minding the Cloverton house had been removed from her shoulders by Thelma. Absorbing the responsibility for cleaning and shopping, as she was doing, was also giving Thelma some purpose in life, however, that arrangement wouldn't last forever. At the moment, although Thelma didn't have a job, she was about to start looking. Actually earning money again would be nice because she'd thought of a way to spend it!

Muriel's sister-in-law was quite different from Muriel and Alexander in that she had never been a bike person. She couldn't even balance alone on a two wheeler before she came to live with them. Thelma couldn't be left out said Muriel so, thanks to her arm-twisting, Alexander generously provided Thelma with her own two wheels, and the skill quickly followed. With Muriel running behind holding on to the saddle for ten minutes, Thelma discovered she had excellent balance.

With her Raleigh racer and encouragement from her sister-in-law, Thelma's leg muscles developed quite nicely over the months. She even stopped complaining of the pain when they returned from a long ride – now there was progress, but the push-bike was turning out to be only a stepping stone; she was becoming more ambitious. A faster two-wheel transporter was wanted, one she didn't have to pedal. Muriel hoped that Thelma's notion would just turn out to be all talk because her sights were set on a motorbike!

Sally had cycled to the cottage on her own this morning, which made Muriel and Thelma feel naughty and slightly guilty – they'd used a taxi.

"We are glad you managed so well. You are obviously skilled," they said, complimenting their driver, because it was a tricky task doing a three-point-turn in the narrow lane, the only access to the cottage. They told him of the difficulties most visitors had when tackling it for the first time.

He accepted their congratulations modestly. He didn't bother pointing out that he'd had practice, having been before, and not very long ago, delivering a strange she-man to this very address.

So, as the cups of coffee were downed and topped up, the plan was agreed. Muriel and Thelma were fairly confident that if Sally remained at the cottage, it was unlikely that Alexander would want to stay. Although they hadn't spoken to him yet it was pretty certain he'd want out. He would be leaving with his wife and sister.

"More coffee for you too, Aunt Thelma?" said Sally, being the perfect hostess.

"You don't have something stronger do you, dear – a little brandy perhaps?"

"Thelma... It's barely eleven o'clock in the morning. You promised that you would give up any thoughts of alcohol during the day," her sister-in-law reminded her.

"Just joking," Thelma added, though she thought if she'd been here herself Sally might have sympathised, and a little brandy could have been available. Another coffee was poured for her by Sally whether she wanted it or not.

Almost a year now since she'd seriously consumed alcohol, and although Thelma felt sort of smug at the thought, she also knew it would take very little encouragement to return to the old habits. An odd glass of white wine was the limit, and though having her sister-in-law to hold her in check sometimes felt a damn nuisance, it was helping her to stay in control. Coffee was fine this morning, sitting together like this in the spring sunshine.

Sally's garden was at the rear of the house and caught the sunshine almost all day until the large sycamore, just beyond the fence, created shade late in the afternoon.

In reality, there was no chance of Sally offering her aunt any strong drink. At this moment, the atmosphere was perfect, and could remain so, but only if all participants stayed sober. At Cloverton, she'd seen how alcohol would encourage earnest discussion to develop into serious argument very quickly between Thelma and Alexander particularly, and occasionally with her mother too.

This fact became apparent to Sally after Thelma took up residence. With Alexander and Thelma being twins, and both strong willed, alcohol would cause any tolerance for the other's viewpoint to vanish rapidly. It was very understandable to Sally why Aunt Thelma left home all those years ago – Dad could be a pain, but no matter, it was nice for her aunt to have moved back to live with them in Cloverton. They could all be one 'happy' family again – provided alcohol wasn't involved...

The cottage was not far from Newingsworth but, with access being along a farm track, and with banks of trees and hedgerows and the stream flowing along at its side, civilisation seemed far away. With distant traffic hardly audible, there was a feeling of tranquillity in the garden. At times when she sat on her own, Sally found that she could feel at one with nature.

Some large trees bounded the cottage, old and majestic looking, not yet into leaf at this time of year but still very nice, which made the view delightful, but there was one tree, the sycamore, which both she and Derek suspected could be dangerous in a high wind. The cottage would be flattened if it decided to 'drop in' and something would be required to be done to make it safe – certainly before the winter, but Derek could be so slow.

To be fair though, there was uncertainty about whose responsibility it should be to maintain the safety of that tree. It wasn't really part of their garden and neither she nor Derek had met the new owners of the farm yet to discuss it.

'Tipsicorus International' sounded a large organisation. She'd heard they were foreign. Local gossip questioned even if the people who were there could speak English ...so she hoped it wouldn't be too difficult to communicate with the local representatives, that they would be friendly and, once informed, would do whatever was required to render the tree safe.

Toozlethwaite Manor, as Derek liked to call their home, once belonged to the previous owner of the farm – her father bought it from him. Receiving this cottage, as a wedding gift from her father and mother, had been a surprise to the young couple.

Sally scoffed at Derek's theory as to why it was now theirs. He claimed it was to keep them quiet – a thank-you for not rocking the boat after Muriel's hostage ordeal, and that this was her father being excessively generous for a very good reason – their silence – to which Sally responded by telling him not to be so ridiculous, and to stop sounding priggish. Unfortunately, she knew he was correct, but there was such a thing as family loyalty and her husband would do well to remember that. He was now part of the family, and should just be grateful...

As for Derek and his behaviour, from Sally's viewpoint, although an intelligent person he could be so stupid at times. A blind man walking a tightrope could tell he couldn't hold his drink; it would have been obvious to anyone he was with that he was not in the habit of having a lot. It's almost certain, when they were out together last Saturday, that her father would have realised, judging by the condition Derek was in when he returned. Anyway, it would have been her dear father's idea of a joke, to push Derek too far. He'd caused this separation.

Drinking a lot had never seemed to affect her father much and he should have been capable of preventing Derek getting into a state. Sad though it was, Sally told herself, he would have found it enjoyable to watch, and probably encouraged his son-in-law to get sozzled.

However, her father's fault or not, Derek was a grown man and would have to take control of his own life if he wanted to stay married to her; and, of course, there was the messing up of her good clothing...

It would have been bad enough if he'd been dressed in casual clothes – and she didn't mean her casual clothes – the least he could have done would have been to appear home in a drunken condition in male attire...

Admittedly, he would still have suffered, but she wouldn't have abandoned him. She would have waited until he sobered up and then he would have had to contend with a serious lecture. With him sober, she would have inflicted maximum suffering on his ego and yes, she would certainly have made him feel bad, but although he wouldn't have forgotten it, it would have been over and done with by now.

As it was, she couldn't turn back the clock. He'd misbehaved and she had reacted the way any sensible girl would, by letting him stew for a while, but enough was enough. He'd served his time. The important thing was to separate her father and her husband, and regain normal married life.

So ...*his penance is over*, she decided. *When Derek returns, my being here will be a nice surprise for him, won't it...?*

10

Muscular pain, collywobbles and various other unfamiliar animal passions: a curious mixture of emotions was being experienced and, without making it too obvious, he eyed the door pocket hoping to see a sick bag. Because her driving was sure to cause another emergency he wanted to be prepared. His attempt at blanking-out the screeching tyres on corners, the swinging of his pained body from side to side, and trees and hedges flashing past, was not being successful. This one was no slowcoach!

What Derek didn't know was that the lady driver taking him home usually drove her own Mini-Cooper. She drove it at speed, and she drove it hard, considering herself driving always in competition with the best males. As an ardent fan of Top Gear, she enjoyed speed immensely but today she wasn't driving her own car.

Only moments before, she automatically reached for the gear lever to zoom off in her usual fashion, hoping to change gears rapidly and impress this temporary, male passenger with how a woman could really drive.

What she reached for, and failed to twist and slam into first gear, was his kneecap! She immediately apologised for appearing overly familiar, and though still in partial shock, this disappointed Derek. For an exciting moment he thought she did it deliberately and was about to take advantage of him in his weakened condition.

"Sor-ree!" she sang out as she zoomed along. "Creature of habit, I'm afraid. Unfamiliar with the controls and disappointed in the general driving performance of this hired car – big and ponderous," he was told. "But I am a bit of a show-off, too," she admitted.

As she appeared to be embarrassed and apologetic for the misplaced hand, he smiled a no-problem-it-doesn't-matter sort of smile back, and noticed how ineffective her perfume had suddenly become. Probably the pain, of what seemed like a dislocated kneecap, was creating an overpowering antidote.

"I'll take you home, if you'd like?" was her earlier offer, an offer which was graciously and gratefully accepted, and as she drove along the introductions followed. Sophie Clerkenwell-Brown was the name of this perky young blonde driver, with the difficult to control hands.

"How do you do, Sophie Clerkenwell-Brown," he said stiffly, trying to avoid turning his head unnecessarily. "I'm Derek, Derek Toozlethwaite, but my friends always call me Swea..." and he stopped himself just in time. "...My friends call me ...Derek."

"What do you do then, Derek, and do I see a wedding ring on your finger?" she said teasingly, knowing full well it was. She had attacked the knee of a married man in a hired car, yet again, and he thought it accidental. He wasn't really a challenge, this one was surely too innocent.

"Yes, I'm married, quite recently, and exceedingly happy with my new wife," he said, to bolster his own confidence more than anything else, but it didn't. "...And I'm a journalist – with the Newingsworth Weekly Gazette – oh, and I'm writing a book at the moment," he explained, with gravitas, but then hesitated...

Should he explain that it wasn't progressing very quickly and it might even be the wrong subject he'd chosen to write about – but would that be telling her he was an intelligent man, writhing in the depths of his emotions – or just that he was a wimp?

"Well, what a coincidence. I'm an editor with a publishing company," she told him, changing gear a little more successfully this time, he noticed, and without looking.

Derek was pleased he'd held back on explaining his lack of creative talent. It would be wise not to expose weaknesses to someone who could help him in the future. In fact it could be quite enjoyable to get to know this young lady a lot better. Having her as a contact could be beneficial. She seemed the frisky type who would want to know her authors intimately, but probably only if they were successful.

His mind was drifting... *And he was in the hotel room discussing the new deal for his fourth novel with his new editor, the blonde Sophie... Just him ...and her... She reached out ...and touched his knee...*

Oh, she was talking again!

"I've driven up from London to meet a new client who lives in this area – in Cloverton. That's an estate in Newingsworth isn't it? A lady, her first attempt at writing ...about a hostage situation. Sorry, shouldn't be telling you this – client confidentiality."

Female: lives in Cloverton: first attempt: a hostage? No... It couldn't be ...but yes, it could!

Good grief! He knew which lady – but she wouldn't...

"Muriel Davidson!" he blurted out.

"What made you say that?" asked a surprised Ms Sophie Clerkenwell-Brown, screeching round a corner to the consternation of a pheasant, which only narrowly avoided becoming road–kill.

"My mother-in-law..." and although he said it nonchalantly, inside he was perturbed, to add to his other discomforts.

"Well, no, it's not her, but I couldn't tell you anyway, could I, even if it was...?" she smiled.

Of course it was her – client confidentiality indeed – how could Muriel do this to him? She hadn't even said she had been writing, never mind having secured a publisher... What a super subject too, and after what he did for her, and she's beaten him. She's written a hostage book...

A thought suddenly brightened him up – she was bound to have given him a starring role. He would probably be her principle character. It was a large and active part he played at the time, and he had been a hero, certainly in his version of events. That's how he and Sally came together.

Had Sally known her mother had written this book?

Of course, if his wife had still been living with him, or they'd even been talking together like other newly married couples, she might have told him, he supposed.

Imagine that ...Muriel succeeding in writing a book, the task he'd set himself, a task at which he should be excelling – considering writing was his livelihood – and his efforts were a dismal failure. His mother-in-law had beaten him to it. That was rubbing salt in the wound. Damn!

One good thing to come from this knowledge – it had taken his mind off her driving...

"Are we anywhere near where I should be taking you?" asked Sophie, bringing Derek back to reality. Unfortunately, currently proceeding in the easterly direction was incorrect. It should have been the opposite. Derek had been somewhat disorientated since the first whiff of the perfume.

"Take a right turn at the next junction," he hurriedly contributed, and they continued for a quarter of a mile then, "Right again," he said.

She gave him a questioning look. "We've just turned totally about...?"

"Short cut," he smiled foolishly...

11

In Derek's humble opinion, the car they were in was too big for a person like Sophie Clerkenwell-Brown to be driving. It wasn't just her diminutive size that generated this thought. It was the car itself. It was simply too big, bigger than required for the purpose and, furthermore, on his list of hated gas-guzzlers; ruining the environment, they were.

He was also unsure of her driving skills, and the pain from his right knee would probably stand witness to that. If she would just drive calmly in this tank of a vehicle, rather than practising for the Grand Prix he would, maybe, feel more comfortable.

The environment was something Derek liked to think he cared for. It was a strong feeling, sometimes displayed overtly to others, like an annoying halo. Driving a motor vehicle was not one of his accomplishments, but he never wanted to. For him, getting about by foot, or using public transport was adequate, well ...that was until they moved into the cottage. Having to access the cottage via the farm road for half a mile, and then another half-mile of rough narrow track that had never received any decent surfacing, forced him to resort to buying a mountain bike – and the occasional use of a taxi. The track ran alongside a stream, which rose and fell depending on the weather and, luckily, hadn't flooded while they'd been in the cottage – so far...

So, after an embarrassing detour, the large vehicle Derek was currently travelling in was at long last getting close to his home.

"Turn left at the sign to *Tipsicorus International*," he told Sophie. "It used to be *Macintosh's Chooky Hens* but the owner changed recently. We haven't met the new people yet, but we think they are foreign."

At least she slowed down to take the corner successfully as they left the main road but, to Derek's concern, her natural, instinctive need to regain a brisk speed, created clouds of dust along the minor narrow road. They were now travelling along towards the farm. Derek hoped that they wouldn't meet any other vehicles coming towards them and, in his anxious state, failed to point out that they were quickly approaching the right turn into the cottage lane – until she flashed past it.

"Ooops..." He apologised for failing to warn her, and she slowed a little.

"I'll turn at the end of the road," she decided.

Carrying on for another mile, they reached the farm's entrance. Derek hadn't ventured along this road recently, not since before old Hammy Macintosh sold up. Things were very different. The old wooden three-spar gate, there to bar the entrance but which, previously, would have lain open at all times, was no longer even there. Both the gate and the low wooden fence had been removed, and in their place stood a galvanised steel ten foot high version, with a matching chain-link fence going all round the edge of the farmyard and the buildings.

It must have cost a packet, Derek thought. This new gate was closed and padlocked. The new company sign at the start of the road showed this organisation to be a vegetable supplier. Derek was puzzled, it didn't make sense. The new owners must think the people in this area really dishonest. Did they imagine the locals would break in and steal bags of potatoes, or whatever? Potatoes and other stuff grew in fields. Didn't they realise that everybody here would just dig them up and pinch them straight from there, like they usually did?

Returning, Sophie drove with a bit more caution to make sure the corner to the cottage was not missed. Over the fragile-looking railway-sleeper bridge they went, and along the disturbingly narrow track – a track that was rutted and considerably narrower than any she'd previously driven on with this big car.

"You can do a three point turn at the cottage, but you'll have to be careful. The edge of the road is a bit crumbly," warned Derek. "The alternative is to reverse for the half mile again?"

"Reverse – in this? No thank you..." The three point turn was obviously the wisest option.

It seemed so obviously the wisest option, but only if achieved without mishap, in a smaller car and driven by someone who was a little more in sync with the controls.

Unfortunately, the front wheel on the driver's side found the crumbling edge Derek was warning about. Sophie revved but only managed to dislodge some more of the banking – and the car tipped. She revved again, and the car tipped farther. Cutting the engine, she turned to him in dismay.

The car was angled down on her side and the passenger side was sitting about two feet higher than it should. At this point, Derek regretted not having continued with the marathon training – *if only he'd said, No thank you, when she offered the lift. It would have been less trouble to run home.*

Suddenly, exiting the car on the passenger side had become more like a commando training course and he did not feel up to it but, looking at the shocked face next to him, he could feel only compassion. This was a new situation for this terrified young lady. It was all up to him. What could he do in a situation like this, he asked himself, other than be the hero?

"I'll climb out first," he said, "...and help you out in a minute."

He tried to open the door. Of course he had to push against the weight of the door, outwards and upwards. He managed, but not without feeling pain in his already aching joints.

Having an active imagination can be a benefit to an aspiring writer – sometimes. He looked out of the door and it seemed a long way down. To him, it was like leaping from an aeroplane without a parachute... A film came to his mind ...similar dangerous circumstances – 'The Italian Job' and, at the end, the balancing of the bus and the gold. No one ever knew what happened because the film ended just then. This could be his 'Italian Job'. When he jumped, would the car and Sophie, go over the edge?

He slithered out, eyes shut and fingers crossed, and hit the road.

It was only three feet ...and as he landed in a heap, he whipped his hand clear, just in time, as his door swung, 'clunk!' closed again. Relief... He'd made it, and the car hadn't moved. Sophie was safe.

She might have been less than impressed with the heroic action, if she'd been able to see him at that moment – lying on the road in a crumpled heap, but he'd made it, and safely, and in his head he was still the hero. Looking at the driver's side, there was little difference in his mind between a sheer drop over a high cliff edge and this sloping ditch, but a damsel was still in distress, and it was his duty to save her. Thank goodness Sally wasn't at home to see all this fuss, he thought – she would just panic. How should he tackle it?

The rear corner of the car was almost touching the muddy stream water. Tackling it from the front, seemed best, clambering along the ditch face and once beyond the door it could be opened, and he would help Sophie out. So, he held onto the wing mirror and reached towards the door handle.

Gently now, don't open it yet, get passed the door first ...but he should have told Sophie that he'd open it, and then he wouldn't have been pushed into the stream, with her assistance... It didn't really matter, he was dressed in his running gear, and luckily the stream was more muddy than deep. Sophie was still safe in the car. Back up the banking he went. Her door was now lying open.

"Right Sophie, carefully turn and put one foot on the banking and I'll hold you," he instructed, but her seat belt was still fastened. She loosened it – and then fell out. Derek went backwards again, but at least he was still being the hero, by performing the job of a cushion – a wet cushion.

"Ouch! I've twisted my ankle!" Sophie cried out, as she tried to climb back up the banking, still wearing stiletto heels, of course, and with a married man supporting her buttocks. Again Derek thanked his lucky stars that Sally wasn't here to see this, but some parts of this catastrophe were more enjoyable than others because she was a nice handful and the use of both hands was essential to make sure she wouldn't slip again.

Sophie was wet and covered in mud, and was wearing a blouse which was now clinging, and a mini-skirt which Derek could have sworn had shrunk to be even shorter. And now, with a painful ankle, she couldn't walk.

Derek would have to carry her.

For someone who had collapsed in agony just a short time ago, he rose to the occasion, just grateful that she was only a dress-size ten. He struggled to hold the damp body while he fumbled for the house door key, kicked the door open eventually and they tumbled in. "You'd better get those wet clothes off and have a hot shower," he said gallantly. "That stream can't be very clean and I'll get you my wife's dressing gown."

So, Sophie immediately did as instructed and removed the blouse and mini-skirt. As they dropped to the floor, Derek swallowed his tongue, and stood gazing, feeling his temperature rising quickly. He gulped out, "The shower room is just behind you..."

Sophie turned around, but seemed in no rush. Derek gazed at the perfectly formed bare buttocks, and as he stood there, the back door was opened quietly, and in tip-toed three people he'd thought were many miles away – Sally, Muriel, and Thelma.

"Surprise!!!" they all shouted...

12

One hastily called taxi, driven by the same caring gentleman who delivered them earlier, returned and found his two previous passengers now in a different frame of mind. As they climbed into his cab, he sensed the tension. There was also a third person joining them for this journey – a young one, and she was very upset: extremely agitated!

"Cloverton!" was given curtly as the destination. "Just get me away from here – and quickly!" the youngest tersely instructed.

The asperity, he thought initially, was because they'd been forced to walk the length of the rough lane to meet him. He could see that the far end was now blocked by a car. It looked, to the taxi-driver, like someone had been on a kamikaze-car mission to have finished up in that position, but that wasn't the reason for their anger... It did not surprise the driver in the least that something untoward had been going on at that cottage; something bad was bound to occur there – he'd sensed it earlier. Unfortunately, his natural curiosity, and his endeavouring to listen and hear the cause, spoiled the concentration he should have been giving to his driving – leading to a collision being only narrowly avoided with another taxi. The other vehicle, travelling slightly more sedately, had been about to turn into the single-track, farm road, at the sign for 'Tipsicorus International'.

At least, the driver of the other taxi was a man enjoying the peace and tranquillity being diffused by his passenger and therefore concentrating more fully on the task. He stopped quickly and safely, without his passenger even realising the near miss.

It goes without saying that the pressured driver in the faster taxi, the one going in the direction of town and carrying three irate females, would very quickly pick up the gist of the problem. He could not have avoided hearing about it the way they were going on: *a den of iniquity: another woman: her naked body: marriage had been a big mistake: (and the cherry on top) if he thinks he's getting off with it this time, he is greatly mistaken, oh ...yes...!*

Having transported them a little more than an hour before, this taxi driver remembered the intentions being discussed by the two older women on the way there. 'Forgiveness', would be the young one's watchword, he'd heard them say, of a husband, and of a father. The two in the cab would be doing the supporting act mainly, he'd understood, although one of them appeared to be there just in case she missed out on anything...

The results were all there to hear (not that he was listening, of course) ...a total reversal in the space of a few hours, the forgiving approach nullified. Not one of them could actually believe the bare cheek of it. She just stood there, almost naked, and as for Derek...!

Sally was absolutely furious, and Muriel sympathised with her daughter. To the taxi driver, Thelma was the one who commented least and seemed to be struggling to suppress a grin. She hadn't missed out on anything – it had been a fun morning for her.

The other taxi contained a gentleman, a banker, who'd spent a very enjoyable morning relaxing in Newingsworth Public Park, reading the Financial Times. This gentleman was full of good spirit, because he took the precaution of having a quick drink before returning to the cottage, with the intention of a sparse late lunch at his temporary abode with his son-in-law, Derek.

The taxi, having stopped for a moment to avoid the other exiting rather hurriedly, for the first time gave Alexander the chance to read the large freshly-painted new sign now displayed at the lane entrance. For years it had been a simple, peeling, painted board directing the lost traveller to Macintosh's Chooky Hens, a farm which had been at the far end of the lane for as long as Alexander could remember. Regretfully, he was well aware of the change in ownership, having advised the previous owner, Hamish Macintosh, to sell up.

This colourful sign was now proclaiming it to be the route to 'TIPSICORUS International'. The script under the name read 'Specialist Vegetable Growers'. So at least it was still a producing farm, Alexander was pleased to observe. There was even a slogan, 'We have the stuff you REALLY need – you'll soon be hooked', and a web site.

So, *www.tipsicorusinternational.com/specialvegetation* was duly noted. He would be needing that later.

Who deals with their finances he wondered because, unusually, the organisation's name wasn't familiar to him; he made a point of knowing these things. As a banker he hoped cautiously to obtain some of their business, though he feared for their survival in these difficult times. Starting up a business just now needed a lot of confidence, and courage, and sound financial backing.

He would ask Derek if he'd looked at their website yet. *Unlikely though – Derek's mind seemed to be more on other things just now. The poor lad was still in mourning for Sally having gone home, and it had all been because of a pair of shoes, hadn't it? Sally had always been a self-righteous little prig...*

Her father knew her well. *Once Derek has been married a few more years, he'll look forward to breaks like this*, Alexander thought sympathetically.

"Something's wrong up there, guv," stated the driver, turning round to speak to Alexander through the glass panel, and pointing along the lane. "It looks as if a big car's gone over the edge of the ditch. I'd never get turned again if I went up this lane, and I don't fancy reversing all the way back along. I've been here before."

"Oh..." said Alexander, unenthusiastically because he was one step ahead, anticipating what was about to be asked of him...

"Would you mind if I dropped you here and you walked the rest?"

He did mind but any irritation was reduced by the effect of his earlier imbibing, so he paid and smiled at the driver. He turned and saw the large car in the distance, sitting at the funny angle, and wondered what nonsense Derek had been up to this time. *Hadn't he said he was going out running...?* He strode along singing quietly to himself, wondering when Sally would return here to her own place. Although the spare bed in the cottage was comfortable enough, it would be nice to return to Cloverton and normality, but it would have to be without Sally there, bugging him for every goddam reason.

The cottage door wasn't properly closed. He pushed and it swung open, and he entered the little vestibule. As he sat on the stool to remove his slightly muddied shoes, and give no excuse for criticism by his daughter, he heard voices. One was Derek's, but the other? No, never heard it before – maybe one of the new occupants of the farm, down to do the introduction bit.

"Alright, so I had no clothes on, but, Derek... they sneaked in at the wrong moment. That was all," said the female voice.

"That's not what Sally thought," moaned Derek.

"They had no right to jump to that conclusion had they? They didn't even ask why I'd no clothes on."

"She'll never forgive me now, and she was coming back to me," he sobbed.

"Well, she picked the wrong time didn't she."

Alexander could tell, these two had passed the introductory stage. This female was becoming irritated by Derek's failure to even try to put up any defence – and then she seemed to have a change of heart.

"Come here," he heard, "A wee cuddle..."

Sophie was feeling bad about the way she was treating Derek. Why was she being so hard on this poor bloke she'd just met, a guy she had no strong feelings for, but who obviously desperately needed someone to sympathise with him?

Alexander, opening the door with his cheery comment of "Not interrupting, am I?" frightened the life out of the pair of them.

Not again...! That was Derek's disturbed thought, the situation being almost déjà vu, but with clothes on this time. Both jumped up. Sophie forgot for a moment that her ankle was now swollen and painful as she put her weight on it. "Ouch!"

"I didn't do anything," Derek immediately shouted out, expecting the same criticism as earlier. Sally's dressing gown, which was just a little too big for the diminutive Sophie, fell open to reveal to

Alexander the tiniest of bras and pants, but it was a short lived pleasure as the gown was quickly wrapped back around her.

"Been having fun?" Alexander smiled. "When the cat's away... Good for you Derek. I didn't think you had it in you."

"It's not like you think it is," exclaimed a panicking Derek. This was Sally's father, remember. "We've had an unfortunate incident..." Derek started to explain.

"You didn't get caught again, you idiot, did you?" Alexander sounded disgusted.

"Hell's bells..." Derek was getting a little annoyed. "Now you are thinking the wrong thing. Sophie gave me a lift. She couldn't drive the big car properly, and went over the edge of the ditch. We fell in the mud, and I carried her in, and Sophie took off her clothes, and..."

"Derek, I'd rather not know all the sordid details," said Alexander, with a wicked glint in his eye.

"Excuse me," interrupted an increasingly irate Sophie. "I will have you know that I am a respectable professional."

Alexander's eyebrows rose in surprise...

"Not that kind of professional! I was a witness and I know exactly what happened, and it was next to nothing. Derek appears to be an innocent for whom the worst is being presumed. He's done nothing wrong, and I have done nothing wrong, and poor Derek intended to do nothing wrong, did you Derek?"

Sophie gave him no time to answer because she feared he might be stupid enough to say something incriminating. She had sensed some exciting vibes between them earlier, so there may have been some intention – if his family hadn't disturbed them.

"...And I consider there is no justification for the treatment both of us have received from Derek's hard-hearted family. He has my deepest sympathies for the situation he is in – because this man is innocent!"

Alexander applauded.

"A beautiful speech for the defence, young lady and now, can I introduce myself? I am Alexander Davidson, Derek's father-in-law, and probably the one who got him into the original mess, but I'd deny that vehemently if I were in a court of law. And you are?"

"I'm Sophie, Sophie Clerkenwell-Brown, how do you do?" and as she reached to shake Alexander's out-stretched hand, the dressing gown fell open once again. Alexander didn't complain, but Sophie was quicker this time to spoil his enjoyment.

"So..." said Alexander, "...the car is stuck, and unless we arrange to have it moved into a better position, you could also be stuck, overnight, and with a lecherous old man, and an almost as lecherous young man."

"Wait a minute. I'm not..." Derek began to protest, but thought better of it as Alexander gave him an all-knowing look...

"Therefore, it would be wise to move the car, don't you think?" and as he said that, Alexander brought out his phone, and took control.

Having good contacts always proved useful to Alexander and he used them freely. Today, the favour was being requested of a garage owning friend, but Alexander was niggled. Yes, he would come out specially, right away, and tow the offending vehicle back onto the level, but...

Alexander wasn't pleased. *Even though it was a friend, and a favour being called up, it was still to be a double-time charge for a Saturday afternoon. Some friend*, he thought, *and some favour.*

He put a special little tick against that name...

Two hours later, Sophie was wearing clothes, had applied some make-up, and the hire car was back on level ground. There was one little snag, Sophie couldn't drive – her ankle was still badly swollen. Probably a torn ligament was the guess of Derek and Alexander, the penalty of high heeled shoes and a dodgy landing. It was certainly not practical for her to drive back home.

The plans made for her visit to the secret client in Cloverton were abandoned. It wasn't desperate that it happened today anyway and the person she was to meet hadn't been warned. It was to have been a pleasant surprise but the visit could be done another day.

Annoyingly for Derek, the secret client remained a secret, and no matter how cleverly they probed, neither Alexander nor Derek could find out the identity of the individual in Cloverton she'd planned to meet. Derek remained convinced it was Muriel, but didn't say this to Alexander. They were left with the rescued car to be returned to the car-hire company, but the small branch in Slatterfoot agreed to accept it only if delivered to them immediately. Anyway, it couldn't be left where it was in the lane outside, nothing could turn, and driving backwards could be awkward, if another vehicle came to the cottage.

Sensibly, Sophie decided to reject the offer to remain overnight. Were they joking about being a couple of self-confessed lechers? Was this really a den of iniquity – with threesomes? Well, not for me, thank you. She wasn't into kinky, despite the rumours spread back at the office... How to get home then? The railway could be an alternative, so train timetables were hurriedly consulted. There weren't many trains for London stopping at Slatterfoot Station on a Saturday, but one could be caught if they were quick. Alexander would take her, in her hired car. Farewells would have to be swift.

Alexander hurried out to start the car, leaving Sophie to follow.

It may have been only a painfully short and eventful time Derek and Sophie had spent together, but when it came to saying goodbye – a twisted ankle for her, and a dodgy kneecap for him – Derek found Sophie ever-so sexy again: she had reapplied the perfume, and boy, was that farewell kiss enjoyable...? *Phew...!*

Moments later, as he waved farewell and they sped off down the lane, Derek was left standing alone and forlorn on the doorstep, but with a fond memory.

What if she had stayed, he wondered...? The aroma of her perfume was there again – the smell still lingered on his arm. Suddenly, he did feel lecherous...

13

Not many people can play a baby-grand, and not many houses are large enough to house a baby-grand piano but, then again, not many people these days would want a baby-grand...

At Cloverton, the house was big enough for a baby-grand piano to sit in the back room – the room that looked out onto the large well-tended garden and in this house there was someone, living here at least temporarily, who could actually play a baby-grand piano. The 'someone' was Sally and, if the piano was ever to be removed from the music room of her family's home, she would be the one who would miss it.

Each day of this week, after being at the office seeing Derek coming and going but having no communication with him, meant each evening she was returning to Cloverton, exceedingly glum and grumpy.

With her refusing to speak directly to Derek, Spider had been taking all the flak, being go-between. She was well aware that Spider didn't deserve the way she was treating him, but Derek did! Every little bit of it. Sally was in no doubt – he deserved to suffer. This was their second marital tiff – the second in the space of a week. Their married life could be reaching its limit already – it was barely even four months.

Of course, if it had been just the one misdemeanour on the previous weekend – the getting drunk with her father, and the wearing of her clothes – then it would have been all over by now, and they could have been sitting cuddling together on the sofa, as usual. Admittedly, she would still have been casting it up though, about him ruining her best shoes – he wouldn't have been let off lightly with that one, but it hadn't even reached that stage...

Now this second shocking discovery: his affair: his secret woman. He'd denied it, of course. They both had – the blonde and him – the reaction one would expect – said they'd just met and she had kindly given him a lift: all totally innocent. Pull the other one... and her, standing there in the bare buff! They'd obviously been at it!

The music being played by sad-Sally this week, after all those years of tuition by dear Miss Flanders, was only of a sombre and wistful nature, minor keys being to the fore. If depressing music was what was wanted, this was the place. The selections Sally succeeded in dredging up were from the saddest part of her musical memories.

The other two occupants of the house looked to the evenings with trepidation, dreading what would be inflicted on them as the 'dirge of the day' (as Muriel entitled the little tunes). By Wednesday, Muriel and Thelma were suffering melancholy too, but didn't like to hurt Sally even more by complaining.

In an attempt to lighten the mood that evening, when Sally left the room and her tear-stained piano for a loo break, Muriel and Thelma crept in to demonstrate they had skills too. Muriel played her speciality, 'Chopsticks', with two fingers very capably. Thelma took the opportunity to do hers then, 'Old MacDonald had a Farm', and although using only her forefinger, performed it exquisitely, she thought. They were on their third repeat when Sally returned to find them both smiling and proud of their performances, waiting for applause and a shy little smile of pleasure from Sally.

And did their brilliant efforts cheer her up?

Sally went to bed in a huff...

Friday was here. Last night was a repeat of the doldrums, but tonight, Muriel and Thelma were sitting in the front room, out of Sally's earshot, because the doors into both the front and the back rooms had been closed. In the back room Sally was still playing her dirges, and thoroughly enjoying being miserable. The other two savoured the relative tranquillity of the rustling of pages of their reading material, being turned to the accompaniment of the now muffled background music.

Alexander was still at Derek's. The phone-call from Muriel inviting him to return to Cloverton had been politely refused, on the basis that Derek couldn't cope on his own.

Afterwards, Muriel wished she hadn't mentioned Sally's piano playing at the start of the call. She should have known Alexander always found Sally's repertoire to be almost as irritating as her continual criticism of his behaviour.

The reading material for the two women was very different.

Reading most evenings was now normal and pleasurable for Muriel. Finding joy from a good book began during her 'short exciting adventure away from home', as she termed the time she was held hostage, and though all types of writing was appreciated now, she had become particularly attracted to tales of vampires. Tonight her eyes were closed as she visualised herself sinking her teeth into Alexander's neck and drinking his blood, as they do...

Would it be worth consulting one of Freud's manuals to discover what this meant? There could be a sexually frustrated vampire sitting inside her, waiting to escape... Should it be set free? Would it be acceptable for her bank manager husband to go to work with teeth marks showing? Could he wear a scarf?

Oh, must remember the dentist appointment – where's the calendar?

Thelma was sitting daydreaming. Her reading material was lying open on her lap, The Most Modern Motorbike Magazine, published every month for fourteen years and bought by Thelma for the first time this afternoon.

Her eyes were sparkling because she had taken a fancy to a motorbike and today, by buying the magazine, was moving one step closer. What a selection she was finding in these pages, the power of the engines, the braking capabilities, the tyres, the road holding ...and what a lot of shiny bits. Each page was gazed at rapturously. She'd even chosen which bike she wanted, and tomorrow she would go out and buy it, but there was just one small obstacle, something to prevent the new dream from immediately becoming a reality – money – Thelma had very little of it.

Her sister-in-law had been horrified to hear the motorbike idea stated out loud. "Thelma, act your age," had been the staid retort from Muriel, almost bursting Thelma's bubble of enthusiasm. Almost, because what it actually did was spur her on to start thinking realistically in more detail of what to do about the money.

Her moderately well-paid job down south had been left behind when the reunion occurred, when all was forgiven and she had been invited to return to the family home at Cloverton. It was nice to be back as a part of the family again.

When occasionally she thought back to the arguments she had with her mother and her father, and with twin brother Alexander, before she left to go it alone, she still felt the cold chill of regret wash over her.

When her mother died, she didn't attend the funeral and probably contributed to her demise. Her father couldn't forgive her and never spoke to her again. He passed on many years ago. After his death, the consequences of her leaving home, and of her twin brother remaining there, meant Alexander received all the benefits, while she got nothing.

It had been hard for her at first, and particularly galling, knowing that the family home in Cloverton Avenue was worth a fortune. Her father had been a wealthy man, no doubt by having taken advantage of others in purchasing and developing property to resell and he'd been good at it. Whether he had been a kind or hard-hearted man in business she never actually knew, but he had been strong willed in his dislike of her. Sadly, she deserved it all.

The way she'd lived her life until now, with regrets, must have atoned for her poor behaviour towards her parents, and now, after the long period of penance, perhaps she even deserved a little of the pots of money Alexander had?

He wouldn't miss the small amount needed to buy her a motorbike, now would he? Surely he wouldn't grudge her something small like that? He had bought her the pedal cycle, even though reluctantly, so, she told herself, *I must be capable of wheedling a motor bike out of him...*

At about this point, the tiny white angel tapped her right

shoulder, and grabbed her earlobe. *"No, don't do that. It's not your style,"* she whispered, standing right beside her ear.

Pudding Face was her name.

Thelma dubbed this stupid female angel by that name long ago. She rarely appeared over the years but, when she did, she always succeeded in getting Thelma confused over moral dilemmas.

"You like to be independent, to do it your own way, and not be relying on anyone, other than yourself..." she continued in a whisper. Thelma had to listen very carefully or else be in danger of missing the wise words. This could be due to her ageing and diminished hearing capabilities, but not hearing clearly perhaps was deliberate – Thelma often didn't like the suggestions made by this smarmy little smarty-pants...

A more regular tiny visitor on the left shoulder, who talked louder and was much easier to hear, she had called Sly Guy. He pulled at her left earlobe, and nipped painfully, which ensured her attention. Thelma and Sly Guy maintained a strong relationship. His advice had worked well. *"He's loaded, isn't he? He wouldn't miss it. Ten thousand would get a decent bike, fifteen a good one, but you'd have to add on the cost of lessons and the test, and you couldn't ignore the changes in VAT,"* Sly Guy was shouting. *"I'd go for twenty thousand, and..."*

"Just a doggone minute," interrupted Pudding Face, this time shouting so that she couldn't be ignored. Thelma thought it unusual for her to act so rudely. It was out of character. *"If you got yourself a job, you could buy your bike and pay it up, and then feel really good because then you would have done it all by yourself – legitimately,"* Pudding Face continued.

"You are not going to be influenced by this yellow-livered, spot-infested, little wimp are you?" enquired Sly Guy, in a fairly moderate manner of speaking for him.

"Don't you talk about me like that, you horn-toed red-nosed no-good lump of sh..." interjected Pudding Face, red-faced and becoming a little over-excited.

"Now, now, you guys. That's enough. Don't start becoming abusive. I'll have to think about it. This is my problem. Leave it with

me..."

Thelma said this in a calm but firm voice, but loud enough for them both to become deeply offended, and to leave.

Muriel stopped reading, looked over the top of her glasses, and gave her sister-in-law a very strange look...

14

Thelma found a job: only probation currently, and she might not last the pace, but it was a job: a means of earning: supervisor at the Old Astoria Bingo Hall. It was not exactly high profile, and not overly demanding and therefore, as a consequence, not brilliant money but at least a little step on the way towards a motor bike.

The Old Astoria Bingo Hall was open at weekends, on Saturdays, but not Sundays, so she was more than delighted that her days were Monday to Friday. A full-time job and off at the weekends – not too bad! The Manager himself covered Saturdays usually and would continue to do so for now. Sometime in the near future, he hoped, he would be having a rest-day mid-week and Thelma could be in total charge, but only when he considered that she knew all about the place, and proved to his satisfaction that she was trustworthy.

There was no complaint from Thelma about the job being mid-week; the downside for her was the lousy daily working hours – oh, and the minor grumble of having to work at all. A life of leisure can become habit forming she'd discovered.

The working day encompassed afternoons and evenings. She would be on shift, working when Sally and Muriel were not, but it did mean she could still be free in the mornings to continue housekeeping responsibilities, and help at home. Shopping in the mornings and an amazing amount of other things could be possible, if she put her mind to it, she reckoned. Keeping busy when she was on her own was essential and stopped her craving a drink. She knew she could never let up on the self-control.

The job had been hers for a week already, and she felt fairly confident in the knowledge of her duties and her ability to carry them out effectively. Her boss was the Bingo Hall Manager, and he was the man with total responsibility, but a small workforce.

She had been surprised how few fellow employees there were. The Old Astoria staff comprised: the Bingo Caller, a young fellow who fancied himself stupid, the girl who looked after the vending machines and sold ice cream round the hall, the girl who sold the books of bingo tickets and took the money on entry, and three part time cleaners. Other than herself and the Manager, who didn't leave his office too often, that was it.

Thelma decided that chatting to the customers was an important duty and would be good public relations. Their loyalty impressed her. Generally being dedicated players, fiercely loyal to 'their' club, most of them visited on a daily basis to enjoy the company and friendship of individuals they'd known for many years. Although possible, few had even considered playing this, their favourite indoor sport, on-line, from home; in many cases there was no computer at home anyway...

What did she have to do? Adjudicate in any disputes, step in to prevent heated tempers developing into all-out brawls and eject anyone who wouldn't behave in the manner to which the Bingo Hall was accustomed. These were some of the duties defined by her boss.

She also had to check toilets to ensure that no smoking, drinking or drug-taking occurred, as well as making sure the loos hadn't become bunged up. This was the unsavoury part that Thelma would gladly have deputised to someone else, if there had been someone else to do it. Did she have job satisfaction? No, not yet, but still, it was a job, she was earning some money and at least experienced no unpleasantness during her first working week.

Apparently the previous supervisor had blotted her copy-book by ejecting someone wrongly from the club. To be taking a couple of aspirins in the toilet to relieve the pressure of six hours of concentrated bingo effort, and then to be accused of being a 'druggy' by the supervisor, not surprisingly, caused a reaction. The supervisor's head-on approach led to a complaint to the manager by the indignant member. "Behave more sensibly," he instructed, but she didn't. Several more incidents followed. The eventual demise, however, came from ejecting someone for using a needle in the toilet and yes, it did happen... but the 'someone' being a diabetic...!

The motto '*act first and think after,*' was not what Thelma's boss desired. Her predecessor's history was recounted by him as a warning of the direction not to go, though it didn't take him long to recognise that Thelma was capable of recognising that herself because she was of a different calibre.

The building she worked in was built originally to serve another purpose, as with many bingo halls about the country. The Astoria had been the much loved cinema in Newingsworth, in the days when cinema paid its way and before television stole all the customers. It closed down and was boarded-up but was maintained in a reasonable condition.

After lying empty for a long time, it was purchased ten years ago and converted to become The Old Astoria Bingo Hall. In certain parts of the building a slightly fusty smell remained evident, caused by the lack of proper heating and ventilation for many years: the smell would probably never go.

This year was special for all involved in the Old Astoria Bingo Hall and one to mark – the tenth anniversary. A special little ceremony was intended by the manager to honour a client who'd attended faithfully since the club opened. She was one of the originals and had not lapsed once in her renewals of membership.

The ceremony would probably be carried out on-stage very shortly, on a mid-week afternoon. The lady would be presented with the freedom of the club for a week, and gifted with twenty complimentary lotto books of cards. The true purpose of the exercise was, of course, to obtain some additional publicity by inviting the Press to the ceremony and there-by enticing new members.

Thelma was informed that the name of the lady intended to receive this honour was Mrs Ivy Bloom and, mid-way through the afternoon, an announcement would be made by the big-headed Caller. He will request the lady to go the foyer and meet the new supervisor, "...to be informed of something to her advantage."

Obviously the ceremony would have to be on a day when Ivy Bloom was guaranteed to be in attendance. It would be stupid to attempt to make a presentation, extolling the virtues of her almost perfect attendance, after manipulating a one-off day of free media publicity, to find that she wasn't there... So, on the chosen day, just after three o'clock and at a suitable break between the games, Mrs Ivy Bloom was asked to go to meet the Supervisor.

Thelma, wearing her bright blue supervisor's hat, her bright blue supervisor's bomber jacket and her shiny chromed 'Supervisor' badge, stood as announced, at the house-front. Mrs Ivy Bloom could not fail to spot her.

A fair number of people took advantage of the gap between games and, with hands stamped to enable their return, rushed outside to the front of the building for a smoke. Unfortunately, thought Thelma, where they stood did nothing for the image of the business. They cluttered up the pavement for the good citizens of Newingsworth, and particularly the ones who wouldn't be seen dead in the place; the people who complained. Their constant grumbles to the local newspapers about 'unruly behaviour of Bingo persons blocking the pavement outside the bingo hall and the proliferation of cigarette ends in the vicinity' changed nothing...

This sort of work was a new experience for Thelma. She, herself, had never been inside a Bingo Hall in her life, and knew very little about the game, nor did she have any urge to try it. Her previous work was in private offices. Dealing with the general public was never part of that life. It was a real surprise being given the job, but she wasn't grumbling too much. It was a means to an end, wasn't it?

This afternoon she was trying to make herself as conspicuous as she could for the sake of Mrs Bloom, but Mrs Bloom did not appear. The smokers filed back inside after the fifteen-minute break, ceremoniously coughing and spluttering, and all looking forward to the next smoke-break.

Gradually the foyer cleared and Thelma was left standing on her own once again. The expected lady wasn't here today, Thelma guessed. Then a lone old woman came out of the toilet and went directly to the front desk. Thelma thought she heard her say that she was Ivy Bloom. She moved in that direction as the woman turned to look at her. Face to face, the two of them were surprised to realise that maybe each recognised the other.

Mrs Bloom became very flustered. Mrs Bloom? Surely this is little old Mrs Masterton from next door at Cloverton Avenue? What is she doing here, thought Thelma?

"Excuse me, can I be of assistance?" said Thelma, concluding this person to be a doppelganger. Mrs Masterton would find it funny when she told her – but this woman was turning away and making her way out. "Just a minute, please – Mrs Bloom, I'm the Supervisor. I have something for you," shouted Thelma. She followed the woman through the swing door and outside, several paces behind, having to step lively to try to catch up with the scurrying little shape. The bustling figure stopped and turned round, with cheeks flushed, obviously annoyed and deeply embarrassed.

"Mrs Masterton... It is you, isn't it?" Thelma blurted out.

"Shhhhhh... Not here. I'm Mrs Ivy Bloom here," she hissed, and side-stepped expertly into the doorway of the disused newsagents, two doors along from the Bingo Hall's entrance. Thelma stepped inside the doorway too.

"What's going on, Mrs M?"

"You didn't tell me you were working here, did you?" said Mrs Masterton snippily. "We were speaking only this morning and you never mentioned it. Some next door neighbour you're turning out to be."

At least Thelma had been informed in advance by Muriel about sweet little Mrs Masterton, 'Her from next door,' Muriel said. She was the eyes and ears of the neighbourhood and rarely missed any local happenings in Cloverton. Now, this afternoon, 'Her from next door,' was obviously upset at finding there was something she didn't know. Muriel said nothing about her being a bingo addict who'd rarely missed a session in ten years – which, to Thelma's way of thinking was serious addiction... Why didn't Muriel mention the bingo? She would have, wouldn't she, had she known? Then again maybe Muriel didn't know? It was amusing to think of the prim little lady doing this sort of thing... This could be a well-kept secret of Mrs Masterton's.

"I was only going to inform you that you are considered by the manager to be a VIP," said Thelma, looking over her shoulder, now infected by the need for secrecy. "You are to be honoured, on-stage, for your dedication to the cause, and have your photograph in the paper."

"What?" squealed Mrs Masterton, "You can't ...I can't. No... It mustn't – I'LL SUE!" The shock drained any hint of embarrassment from her cheeks now. Thelma reached into her pocket, ready to whip out her mobile and dial 999 for an ambulance, expecting any second that this little old lady would collapse at her feet.

"No, I don't want my photograph in the papers! I'm Mrs Ivy Bloom! I can't be the real me... No-one must ever find out at Cloverton. I'd never live it down – the shame..." and she fell forward into Thelma's arms and hugging closely, started sobbing.

Thelma felt rotten. What was she doing to this poor little person? She'd nearly exposed this tortured soul's guilty secret ...however, if Muriel was correct, this was the same woman who made sure she knew everyone else's secrets in the neighbourhood ...now that could be interesting. "I'll call you a taxi, get you safely home, Mrs M," offered Thelma.

"No, no, your uniform – you're a bingo person," she squealed. "Stay away! I'll get one myself, but not here. Just leave me alone." At that, she pushed herself free, changed into the proud secretive Mrs Masterton again, and stalked off erectly towards the far end of the street – well away from the Old Astoria Bingo Hall, and from Thelma. Thelma stood there feeling hurt, miffed – and a bit of a failure.

15

On the other side of Newingsworth High Street from the Bingo Hall, an establishment was located which began life a long time ago – the Old Astoria Cafe. Its doors were opened for the first time only three months after the original Astoria Cinema absorbed the first queues of eager filmgoers and, though people's habits changed and the big-screen film business collapsed and the cinema was closed, the Old Astoria Cafe kept ticking over.

In the first few years of its existence, a question asked of the owner by his customers was – why call it the Old Astoria Cafe when it opened only recently? Anton's father, the original owner, told them then that he wanted the cafe to have the feeling of permanence. He was looking to the future, and it would be old then. His listeners, back then, were confused... Nowadays it had been open long enough to leave no doubt. The cafe had lasted the pace – it was well established – it was old, and now it was Anton's.

It had even survived the arrival of Bisko's, the large supermarket, with its self-service, Rush-Your-Meal, counter. Many of the small businesses in the town, and over in Slatterfoot too, failed to survive the catastrophic effect of the large organisation's competition. Local customers who normally had frequented the smaller shops were, in general, wooed and won by the place with the bigger selections and bargain offers – and the large free car park.

Even though the supermarket, which should really be called a Superstore technically, had its brightly lit and garishly coloured cafeteria modernised regularly, the Old Astoria Cafe owner refused to be pressurised. He continued to serve traditional down-to-earth hot food and drinks with popular background music playing, which he would happily change at a customer's request, a bit like the old juke box he used to have but nowadays done manually and without charge. This Cafe had a special sort of welcome-we-are-never-going-to-change feel that everyone found comforting, something the superstore did not have.

The Cafe owner, Anton, was seen only rarely in the cafe now. He'd grown older and plumper and, if anyone was ever cheeky enough to discuss it, he would admit that along with his ageing, he was a little lazier. His son, Peter, looked after the place for him. Anton's boy – almost thirty-eight and still 'the boy' – didn't grudge his father's erratic attendance. Though retirement for Anton was still many years distant, hard work all his life, and ill health, was forcing a slower pace of life. It really didn't matter if he came in or not as far as staffing was concerned, everyone coped. It was just quieter when this jolly man wasn't in.

Today, the cafe was quiet. In fact, it was surprisingly empty, except for the two people sitting together at the window seats. The music was playing at the usual level which allowed conversation to be private.

"Please, call me Curly – definitely not Mr Stockman or even Graham. It would seem wrong to hear you say anything other than Curly, but what should I be calling you – Mrs Smith or Gran?"

Graham Stockman, the Boss, was directing the question at the smartly dressed, but elderly, grey-haired lady, sitting in front of him at the other side of the table. This lady had watched him grow up, had wiped his snotty nose when it hadn't mattered to him, supplied him with the same sandwiches as Derek when they'd gone adventuring, and given him the odd telling-off for letting her Derek lead him astray, or was it vice versa?

She was Derek's grandmother. In those days, one of her admirable qualities was being capable of sharing her affection between the two boys, himself and her grandson, whenever they were together with her – a fact about her that Graham remembered fondly...

"You are not a wee boy now, so I think Daisy would be in order. I don't hear that name very often, these days. Even Hector calls me

Granny."

In front of her sat the ginger-headed young man who'd succeeded in his chosen career, but it was the dirty-faced little urchin that she remembered, the one who used to cause her so much trouble, almost as much as her Derek had, though mischievous trouble rather than anything serious, most of the time.

Graham was the man in charge of 'Little Radio fm' and although she met him again very briefly before she started the radio show, she hadn't seen him since. He had stayed out of the way and let the natural chaotic events take place. His nerves couldn't have coped if he'd been closely involved, so it was all left to Carol.

He knew everything about The Granny Wisdom Show, probably because Carol, the producer, lived it – she also lived with Graham. There was a lot of discussion at their home about the show – during dinner, after dinner, before bed, at breakfast and after breakfast, but the line was drawn when it came to love-making...

It was still an unusual pleasure seeing the results of audience surveys creep up each week, due to the inadequacies of this dear little old lady. It seemed a strange idea, but Graham was glad Sweaty came up with it – because it worked.

The mugs of drinks were delivered: a large latte for Graham and something that seemed old fashioned, but that Daisy preferred, a simple plain and ordinary cup of tea with a jug of milk, to add as required. "...And I wanted to speak to you. Firstly, Daisy, are we paying you enough?"

"Curly," Daisy said, "You are paying me too much. That's all I can complain about. I don't need all the money and anyway I don't deserve it. I'm driving poor Carol to an early grave, for certain, and I still haven't a clue what I'm supposed to be doing."

The eats arrived. Curly with an iced bun – he hadn't changed in all those years, and a plain scone with low-fat spread for her. Why do they make these scones so large, she wondered to herself, because I always need another drink to wash it down? Oh... Yes ...clever...

"You are doing just fine," Curly said with a mouthful of bun, which in his younger days would have meant a telling-off from this lady for speaking with his mouth full. "...I'm afraid the anonymity bit might come apart soon though. Your MOGGIES are desperate to know what you look like. If we weren't smuggling you in and out in the laundry basket every Monday, the local press would have grabbed pictures and the mystery would be over."

An undignified entry and exit would be putting it mildly. She was jumping into a large laundry basket, to be trundled across town in the unmarked van by George the driver, for delivery to the radio station. Returning later, back inside the van, she would scramble out and be returned to Bisko's car park every Monday afternoon, stepping out of the vehicle as if nothing had happened to her all morning.

She was no youngster. It was a good job that she was fit and healthy or there was no chance that she could have continued this nonsense, even though it was only once a week. Secrecy was important, so as cover, she would buy groceries to take home to Hector, being the supposed reason for her being out that day.

Though the hamper routine was exciting at the start, it was becoming tedious now ...but the mystery of her identity and the resultant curiosity seemed to have a lot to do with her show's success. She was convinced she couldn't get away with this nonsense – the show, or the unwanted exercise – for much longer.

"Something else is happening in the background. How do you fancy the programme going out on nationally?" asked Curly.

"Whatever..." Daisy replied and made the 'W' sign which she knew was obligatory – a cool expression to use these days – but it didn't stop her feeling extremely stupid saying it. The strange look on Curly's face was disappointing, but he probably wasn't as up to date with the current slang as she was...

"The big boys down south would like to meet you," Graham continued, trying not to grin too much and hurt her feelings. "I've been talking tentatively with people who matter. We're not there yet, but if it was to be broadcast nationally, it would mean extra money, a special contract maybe ...but they'd like to meet you. It might even mean a couple of visits. You would have to go to London, with Carol. Hector mustn't be told. Sweaty knows about it and says he'll become your agent, working for you, free, if you decide to take up their offer, but he wouldn't be going with you either for the first time."

"But how would Hector manage if I'm not there to feed and look after him?"

"We could put him up in a hotel," offered Curly.

"A hotel, my Hector, no chance, anyway what reason would you give?"

Curly hadn't thought it through, had he?

"Well, what about him being with Sally and Sweaty?" Curly came back with. "He wouldn't object to staying with them for a number of days surely, if you were to sell it well. Anyway, it would be just a week. You'd be back for the following Monday's show, as usual." She nodded her assent, as a second round of hot drinks arrived on the table for each.

Curly hadn't changed much had he? He was bigger, but still with the mischievous little boy look to him. Wonder how he's managed to keep his curls – ginger, and not a sign of grey? She had the urge to run her fingers through these curls, but didn't. *He is about the same age as Derek, isn't he, and Derek's started with the odd grey hairs. Maybe Derek should go to Curly's hairdresser. I wonder if it's real...*

She was gazing idly out the cafe window when a movement across the road caught her eye. Two figures were hurrying down the Bingo Hall front steps. *Wasn't one of them Thelma? No, she wouldn't be in the Bingo Hall, anyway that woman is wearing a bright blue jacket and a bright blue hat, Thelma wouldn't be seen dead in those clothes.*

The other woman, she's... Ah, yes, looks like the wee lady who lives next door to the Davidson's. Masterton isn't it? Mrs Masterton, but she wouldn't be into bingo either. Are they having an argument, in the shop doorway? The wee one's stomped off... Great window this, you don't miss anything...

"Alright Curly, but now I'll have to think of a tale to tell Hector..."

16

There was a spring in her step tonight as she left work. A secret has been discovered, a secret which must be disclosed to someone as soon as she arrived home, and the unfortunate someone chosen would be Muriel. She would have to be told – immediately!

However, Thelma was tired, eager to get back and get her feet up after what seemed a long day for her. It was taking her a while to become accustomed to this working lark – and that manager.

Was he really trying to be a bother or was it just her? He didn't look the bullying type but... Maybe she was just imagining it?

Anyway, let him try if he wants... He might not yet realise the type of female he is dealing with – she'd had blokes like that for breakfast.

A mental correction was made to her thought about 'breakfast'; figuratively speaking it was almost correct. In truth, she'd been selective when it came to blokes staying over for breakfast in her younger days, and generally prided herself in the decisions she'd made. None of them became serious relationships though, so they hadn't been perfect choices – she'd made do.

Nowadays, she just couldn't be bothered. She settled happily for the family breakfasts here at Cloverton, generally a peaceful and relaxed meal – just Muriel, Sally and herself sitting round the table together, all reading newspapers. Of course, Sally, over the last few weeks, had become the substitute for Alexander. Sadly, he was still at Derek's because Sally was at Cloverton.

However, sitting together each morning as a family group was how it had been and taking the job changed the pattern. Getting to bed late because of her shifts meant, mid-week, that she preferred the cosiness of her bedclothes to their company. Therefore she now sat with the rest of them only at the weekend and, somehow, they were managing without her.

It was well after eleven and all quiet when she arrived back at number forty but, no matter, Muriel would be desperate to hear the news. The room was dark and silent as she tip-toed in and over to her sister-in-law's bedside. Switching on the bed-side lamp, she gently shook the sleeping mound.

"Oh, Alexander ...it is lovely you being back – beside me again like this," Muriel murmured, refusing to leave the dream... "Do that to me again, dear, it was nice..." Then her eyes opened...

"Thelma!" She was now definitely not sleeping. "What are you doing? What time is it? Have I slept in?" and suddenly, sleep was forgotten – she was very wide awake.

The extra pillow was placed in position at her back by Thelma to make her more comfortable, forcing her to sit up straight and be prepared to hear the news. Whether or not Muriel wanted to hear, she was going to be told. Thelma just had to get it off her chest...

Firstly, Muriel was forced to learn about Thelma informing an irate Bingo Hall Manager that his chosen customer had rejected his idea for the ten-year celebration – in fact, Mrs Ivy Bloom was demanding a large 'X' for anonymity as far as any possible future publicity was concerned. Then, Muriel was informed how indignant Thelma felt when her boss bounced the blame back to her. It was all her fault, he'd told her. She was being accused of having failed on her first simple mission.

All this was being supplied to her sister-in-law, chapter and verse, in a continuous stream of details by the excited Thelma.

"Do I have to do all these things myself?" he'd blustered. "Am I the only one who can get things done around here? Am I surrounded by incompetents?"

"Oh my goodness, Thelma," was all Muriel could conjure up in response, wishing Thelma would get to the end of her story quickly and let her put her head down on the pillow once more, but no...

Thelma also recounted how she calmly sat and listened to her boss, and noted his habit of waving his arms about as he stomped up and down the small office, which, she said, could be dangerous to anyone else who happened to be in the room with him but – she also made clear to her sister-in-law – if he had managed to strike her by mistake, or otherwise, he'd have received a kick in the chops from her, and that would have put his gas on a peep.

"Quite right, dear," said Muriel, to prove she was still trying to listen, telling herself, too much detail, and wanting to return to sleep but the story wasn't finished yet...

The manager ranted on, "It's taken me absolutely ages to arrange this and you come along and mess it up. You are a useless..."

"He stopped there," Thelma said seriously, "...probably because he recognised the look of superiority being displayed by me."

And there was more to come.

Thelma explained how this silly man had misread her, how he suddenly realised that there, in front of him, was someone who was actually much smarter than he was, and could easily wipe the floor with him.

Poor sleepy-headed Muriel wondered why she had been wakened up in the middle of her night to be told this, but Thelma was still talking... "Just leave me," he'd said with another wave of the arms. "I don't need you to tell me I'm wrong. I have my responsibilities. I am a man and I can take it. I'll think of something else to do and I can do it... I can... I can..."

As Thelma left his office, feeling slightly sorry for him, she realised she was going to have to support him more in the future – the poor soul was obviously struggling.

Why all this was being recounted, Muriel was failing to understand: the manager with the uncontrollable arms, who was incapable of managing: the little lady called Mrs Ivy Bloom, who didn't want to know ...what Thelma would do to him if...

Muriel tried hard to remain alert, but gradually began to drift off once more. She was nodding sleepily in response, hearing less and less, until Thelma reached – the secret.

Mrs Ivy Bloom, the bingo person was Mrs Masterton, their next door neighbour – they were one and the same person – and suddenly the fog lifted for Muriel. There was a purpose to this.

"No... Mrs Masterton...? Not ...Mrs Violet Masterton – from next door...? No..." and Muriel started giggling.

The prim and proper little Mrs Know-all-the-happenings-in-the-neighbourhood lady – she has been a bingo addict – for ten years? This was serious stuff now; no wonder she didn't want publicity... It was wise keeping it secret. This is Cloverton – people just don't do that sort of thing here. Behaviour of that nature was worse than sex and drugs and rock-and-roll...

"Mrs Masterton ...now who'd have believed it?"

Muriel didn't sleep at all after the excitement, and next day went to work at Bisko's in a very tired condition – but still smiling.

17

The 'No Smoking' laws caused dramatic changes in many public places, and the club was no exception. The result was remarkable, unbelievable, in fact.

Most of the members were up in arms complaining that the Newingsworth Old Folk's Club Committee overstepped its authority yet again – proper approval was not obtained before wasting money on new lighting – there should have been a meeting, and a full vote before that sort of thing was done ...but there was no new lighting!

As a result, this afternoon, Hector could actually see his old pal, Hamish, immediately he stepped in the door at the far end of the hall. Now that would have been unlikely before the smoking ban. It made that sort of difference, but everyone tended to hear old Hamish anyway before they saw him – there was no mistaking when he was on the premises.

"Hullaw therr, Sinbad!" was shouted from half-way up the room. "Whit urr ye wantin' tae drink? Thurr oan me."

Of course, Hamish Macintosh knew that Hector's reply was not expected to be out of his mouth before he reached his side. They knew each other very well...

"N-n-n-no, I'll g-g-g-get them. It is m-m-m-m-my t-t-t-turn," replied Hector, as Hamish plonked himself in the chair.

"Awa' man, dinna you bother. How urr ye? It's been near six weeks since ah've seen ye. Ah must say, ye're lookin' awfy guid – are ye no' weel?" and of course he laughed then at his own joke – the usual Hamish...

"Where have you b-b-b-been? Why have you n-n-n-not been in

the c-c-c-club?"

"Ah've been sellin' up the fairm, Sinbad. Hammy's no' been doin' aw that weel wi' the business. Ah'm broke, ah'm afraid tae say," and he said this with downcast eyes, and in a slightly more muted tone than normal.

Hector could never be certain when Hamish was telling the absolute truth. Based on today's demeanour, the Scotsman, pleading poverty, it could be just the nod that it was Hector's turn to buy the drinks.

These two made friends years ago when Hammy arrived with his family to take over 'Macintosh's Dairy Farm', well known in the area. Later it was to be called 'Macintosh's Chooky Hens' when it became Hammy's.

As young men, Hamish and Hector got to know each other at the amateur football and nicknames came out automatically when the two met, but the usage of these names by others was not encouraged. The exception to the rule was Daisy. She was allowed to use 'Hammy', though she never actually said 'Sinbad' to her own husband. She always called him Hector, or Grandad.

Like Derek, whose 'Sweaty' tag began in the little gang and continued at school, and onwards, Hammy's came early from his name Hamish, and started in his young days too.

It was later in life before Hector's nickname was donated, when he took up his trade in gent's clothing and he became Sinbad – Sinbad the Tailor. Sinbad was acknowledged as acceptable to be used by most of the other club members, but only in the club, not outside its doors.

The barman, Bill, who'd done the job for years, knew of the Sinbad stutter. When Hector came to the bar, of course, Bill was well aware of what was coming next but, even though he'd been given the same instruction by the old fellow time after time, an order memorised years ago, Bill had to wait expectantly to receive it. It was always a test of his patience. He couldn't react too soon and start pulling the pints, so today he waited... Hector had to spit it all out first. Eventually, it came, "The u-u-u-u-u-usual," and was paid for. The pints were carried over, and on went the conversation between

Hector and Hamish.

"And how's yer Missus, the lovely Daisy, eh?"

"Alr-r-r-r-right, I th-th-th-think..." replied Hector, and it was his turn to sound a bit low.

"Aw righ'? Is that the best ye can dae? She's jist aw righ'?" and then, much more reverentially, "She's no deid is she, Hector? Ah huvnae pit ma big boots in it, huv ah?"

"N-n-n-no, it's not as b-bad as th-that."

"Weel, whit's wrang, man?"

"I think she's g-g-g-got a b-b-b-boyfriend," and Hector now looked really crestfallen.

"Nev-ver ...no' Daisy, no' ma bonny wee Daisy..."

Hector then went on to explain how every Monday, early, she was up and out, dressed to the nines and perky as can be, having been doing the same routine for weeks now, coming back late in the day, cheeks all flushed and buzzing with excitement, as if she'd been having a good time – pretending she'd been at the supermarket – shopping all day...

"Och aye, Sinbad, that sounds serious, righ' enough. Nae wunner yer worrit..."

Now, this was not the most apt thing to say to inspire confidence in Hector. He had hoped his old friend would have told him to cheer up and not be so stupid, and that Daisy would never do that to him, but he hadn't! So, it must be true...

"But it g-g-g-g-gets even w-w-worse, H-H-H-Hammy. She keeps coming b-b-b-back with more and more shopping that we d-d-don't n-n-n-need. We've g-g-got m-m-more b-b-beans than H-H-H-H-Heinz has... and now she's t-t-t-telling me, she's g-g-got an old aunt in L-L-L-London who's n-n-not well and she m-m-might have to g-g-go to v-v-v-visit her."

"Oh dear me... That's bad ...really bad Sinbad... Should we hiv anither drink, maybe? But ...whit wid happen tae you if she's no' there?"

"I've to g-g-go to S-S-S-Sally and D-D-D-Derek's, she says."

"Huv ye tried tellin' hur, she canny go?"

"N-N-N-N-No, she wouldn't let me d-d-d-d-do that..."

So, they had another pint of 'the usual', but Hammy had his problems to air, as well. He'd sold the farm. It had become harder and harder to keep the business afloat, as he himself became older. Of course, when his wife died, and he'd been left trying to cope with tasks he never liked and couldn't do ...and then the final straw, losing Bisko's; the superstore had become his biggest customer, but they screwed him right down on the price of the eggs to the extent that it would have been stupid to try to continue.

Hammy had given in, decided it was time, time to give up fighting the cash flow. He had no family, his hard-working and very capable wife having passed away over four years ago, and his only relations far distant cousins, still living in Scotland, who weren't involved in farming. So, he'd sold the farm – to 'Tipsicorus International'. However, very little of the money went into his pocket because there was almost nothing left after clearing the debts.

Today had definitely become a mutual 'cry-in-the-beer' occasion, not a good idea when it already had been watered down (by instruction of the committee).

Hector listened with a sympathetic ear. Whereas before though, Hector had been uncertain as to whose problems were worse, his or Hammy's, now being up-to-date with Hammy's plight, on balance it was clear – his self-pity was more justified: having a two-timing wife was worse.

"...But they'll no' let me intae the fermhoose again, Sinbad," Hammy grumbled. "Ye see, afore ah left, ah furgoat tae remove the family jewels that urr hid in a boax unner the floorboards in the kitchen. Ah canny get back in tae get thum."

"G-g-g-go to the p-p-p-police, they'll h-h-help you. Oh no, you c-c-can't..."

Hammy knowingly rubbed the side of his nose with his index finger, which was admittance of the dodgy deals done in the past that he got away with, but only by the skin of his teeth as far as the law was concerned, so – no police.

"If ye're tae go tae Derek's and Sally's, that's jist doon the road fae the ferm. Ah met they twa when they moved in. She is nice is Sally. Aye ...a bonnie looker, an' a sweet and placid wee lassie, but

...come tae think o' it, you could help me, could ye no'? You're goannie be there – maybe soon?"

Hector nodded. Yes, it did look like he was going to be there – soon.

So ...by the end of this day's reunion, it would be settled; sometime in the future, Hammy and Sinbad, and maybe others, could be climbing over a high wire fence...

18

Sophie Clerkenwell-Brown's pretty ankle was feeling so much better. The diagnosis of the torn ligament had been overly pessimistic and, when she eventually arrived home and soaked herself for an inordinately lengthy time in the bubble filled bath, she felt so much better. A few days working from home allowed the pain to reduce, and it was barely noticeable now.

She could think back to the meeting, with Derek Toozlethwaite, and smile... He was a nice bloke, married and therefore, in theory, unavailable. This was always frustrating for her – unless a bloke decided to become temporarily available, which with her blokes was not an unknown happening. Of course, sometime in the future, if paths crossed for her and dear innocent Derek, she would see what developed. It was maybe lucky for him that she hadn't worn the powerful perfume. He would have been slain instantly.

How circumstances can change, and how quickly, just like last Saturday afternoon when she'd given him the lift. On the way over in the car, him describing how much he was enjoying his cosy little marriage – married for such a short time and, she'd thought, sounding blissful – then half an hour later, his little balloon popped. If sweet Derek had any more of those occasions, the enjoyment of his cosy little heaven could turn out to be very short indeed.

As for his wife!

She had been livid, went on about how little she could trust him, how he ruined her clothes, and shoes which could never be worn again, and on top of that, "...this hussy, in my house, and ...and ...she's NAKED!" It was said as if no-one before had ever removed clothes in there.

The faces of the other two females as they'd come into the room had been absolutely priceless... Sophie recognised the looks of admiration, as well as the surprise, on the two older ones. They had liked her bum. She had a nice bum, it had always been nice. 'A shape to be proud of', and, 'It looks at its best bare', were the comments from most of her past boyfriends. Yes, Derek's mother-in-law and aunt recognised quality when they saw it, but they were a bit nasty towards him: called him – Sweaty!

Admittedly, he had been perspiring freely when she stopped to offer the lift, but the boy had been running for miles. She also supposed the pressure of the situation in the cottage caused him to, sort of ...boil over as well, but it still seemed a strange way to talk, even if they had caught him, with her standing naked...

It wasn't an admiring look his wife, Sally, gave her though...

Of course, being a visitor in Derek's house, she wouldn't have just thrown off her clothes like that if she'd known they were going to come in to surprise poor old Derek – she wasn't that stupid. She didn't deliberately land him in it. In fact, it was pure chance they met, and it wouldn't have happened if she hadn't been a Good Samaritan and lifted him off a verge. Deliberately standing over him, when he was lying there, knackered, that was very naughty of her – but he seemed to have liked the view...

Ankle feeling better, spirits high, now she was back in business, and this time there would be no stops for hitch-hikers, or toppled-over, flaked-out, pretending-to-be, marathon runners. Only another few miles to go and she would be at her destination – Mrs Ivy Bloom of 38 Cloverton Avenue, Newingsworth. Maybe a phone call would have been wise to be sure to catch her at home. She'd feel silly if it turned out to be a journey for nothing. "Turn left at the next junction," the sexy male voice said from the satnav.

Being able to choose a voice on the satnav system was one of the most advanced scientific developments of the computerised age Sophie could think of. It was her own car, so her decision in the choice of voice had been slow and deliberate; the one selected was Italian, speaking strongly accented English. It didn't really matter that sometimes she had no idea what directions he was stating – it was his suggestive voice that mattered.

Approaching the destination, she liked to think the sexy Italian sitting beside her was whispering a supplementary message in her ear. "And we'll soon be at my pad, and then..." but the seat was empty.

Using her own car, this time, for the journey had been much more comfortable for her. Not knowing the controls can be annoying, but the old trick of accidentally playing with a guy's leg seldom failed, especially with the excuse of an unfamiliar car. The same caper had been played on her many times – and she'd enjoyed it, but poor Derek, he hadn't. Maybe she'd been a little too rough.

The voice gave another instruction, but it didn't tell her that very shortly her plans for today were destined to go slightly awry. She'd find that out soon enough herself...

***

Ivy Bloom (aka Mrs Masterton) was leaving home a bit earlier than usual for today's bingo session. A visit to Bisko's Supermarket on the way was needed to replenish stock in her fridge and all because anxiety, caused by the near exposure of her double life, was causing her to be nibbling at food constantly. She hadn't been sleeping well either, since the confrontation with that woman.

She was turning out to be much less likable than Muriel. Of course, this Thelma, she's only been here about a year – not really an established resident – an outsider who doesn't understand proper behaviour? *How could this person, this newcomer, living next door, have lowered herself to become a supervisor in a bingo club, especially as it is my bingo club and my domain? What is the neighbourhood coming to?*

"She'd better not blab to anyone how we met – or else..." she'd muttered to herself after the meeting the other day. What the "...or else," would be, she hadn't decided, but a hit man must be easy enough to arrange. She had the money and that's all it took. ('CSI: Miami' has a lot to answer for...)

***

"You have arrived at your destination, Pretty Baby," said the seductive voice on the satnav.

It was a nice-looking neighbourhood. She pressed the doorbell. It sounded, and could be heard clearly enough, but then there was silence. She tried again. Nope, there was no-one in.

"Damn, should have phoned."

She climbed back into the Mini-Cooper and sat thinking. What were the choices? Go away and come back again, but only after being sensible next time and phoning beforehand? She could push the package through the letterbox, and at least there would have been some indication of her visit, and then phone later to discuss it? No, it would be better face to face; she'd never met the woman or spoken to her so far: all done by snail-mail. Was she friendly with the people next door, perhaps? That could be a good way. They could at least pass on a friendly hello, on her behalf – and they might be kind enough to offer a cup of coffee. She'd been driving a long time, and was parched.

So, that is what Sophie did, tried next door...

Thelma answered the bell. Muriel and Sally were both at work. It was her usual later start, but this morning had seemed enjoyably extended. By doing less housework, she'd made it a relaxing morning. On opening the door, this young lady seemed familiar, and yet it wasn't someone she immediately recognised.

"Hello, I'm sorry to trouble you. I was actually visiting the lady next door, but it appears she's not in," Sophie smilingly said. She had a strange feeling she was talking to someone that she knew, somehow fairly intimately, but no, must be mistaken. She was dealing with so many people all the time...

"Is it about the Bingo?" asked Thelma helpfully.

"No...?" and Sophie thought what a strange question to ask. It certainly didn't look the sort of area where someone would appear selling bingo tickets at the door or whatever they did for bingo – and did she look as if she would be going round the doors...?

"No, it was about a message I was hoping you might be able to pass to your next-door neighbour for me."

"You'd better come in. I was just making a cup of coffee."

Sophie was led into the front sitting room. It was a large house, she noted, must be a well-off family. More than likely, they were lottery millionaires, lots of them about these days. Would this be the maid I'm talking to, perhaps? One of the things nouveau-riche love to do, isn't it, to employ a maid?

The moment this sophisticated young woman stepped through the front door, and walked in front of her, Thelma experienced an uncomfortable vision in her mind of buttocks – bare buttocks. This was a very attractive young lady, very attractive indeed, but Thelma had never had the urge to go in that direction before. She'd always preferred men, and men could have nice bottoms as well – she knew, and some nice experiences came to mind. She shook herself. Behave... Could this be the effects of the menopause? Why should she be thinking of buttocks, for heaven's sake?

"Coffee," said Thelma, and left the visitor to sit alone for a moment.

When she returned from the kitchen with a pot freshly brewed, it provided the most wonderful aroma to have reached Sophie's nostrils that morning, an intense nasal delight, one which almost could compete with the perfume – earlier re-applied in the car – but in a different sort of way, of course. The coffee was being served with a plateful of delicious looking sandwiches, which Sophie could have selfishly and totally consumed. What a lovely woman this was doing the service. Did this family appreciated how lucky they were, having a maid as competent as this...?

"Could I introduce myself? My name is Sophie Clerkenwell-Brown and I have come to deliver a package to Mrs Bloom, next door. Do you know her well?"

"Mrs Bloom? Oh, yes, I know a lot about her..." and some of it was hot off the press, thought Thelma, so it is about the bingo....

"Did she say she'd written a book?" asked Sophie.

"No, but she does like to keep her little secrets, does Violet..."

"Oh, I thought her name was Ivy?"

"Of course, she uses that as well – her 'nom de plume'. She doesn't like people knowing who she really is sometimes, and seems to enjoy a facade of respectability."

Perceptive old bird this, for a maid – spouts out French too, thought Sophie. "A fairly common trait for authors, especially amateurs who haven't made it," Sophie said to the maid. "A form of false modesty, I always think, having a nom de plume."

What the heck is this girl talking about – authors – false modesty? She's talking about another person. Mrs Violet Masterton couldn't write a book to save herself, surely. Why am I thinking of buttocks again?

The young lady reached into her bag and brought out a package and her visiting card. "Could I perhaps leave this?" and Sophie handed her card to 'the maid'. "If you could pass the package to her, she could perhaps phone me and arrange a suitable date to sign some documents. I'll leave her copy of the manuscript for proof-reading, if you would hand it to her with my apologies for missing her."

Sophie hesitated and questioned what she was doing. Was it wise leaving this novel in the hands of an underling? It's a pity the owner isn't here – but, for a maid, this woman seems trustworthy enough...

Thelma looked at the card she'd been handed. "Oh, you are a publisher. Derek would have loved to have met you. He's writing a book just now and could do with any help he can get, as far as I can see," said Thelma.

"Derek...?" a tiny little ringing sound began in Sophie's head, as she said the name. Her brain decided if it wasn't her mobile phone, it could be an alarm...

"Derek?" she repeated – the alarm triggered a disturbing memory – *that Derek – at the cottage? This person – she was there... This was one of the persons who... Oh bollocks!*

"Oh, very nice, and he's looking for a publisher is he?" Just stay calm Sophie – red alert or not!

"I don't think he has finished it yet, butto..." Dear me, she'd had almost said buttocks out loud just now. Thelma's innermost thoughts were coming out of her mouth – it was becoming both irritating and embarrassing to her...

Sophie suddenly felt uncomfortable. "I ...umm ...had better be going, I'm afraid. I'd love to chat but..." Sophie rose and made for the door.

Buttocks, buttocks, buttocks... "...buttocks, you haven't had any coffee or sandwiches..." *What? She'd actually said it – out loud. What was happening to her? Surely not the drink, was it? Of course not, she hadn't had any, she told herself.*

"No, thank you, very nice of you, however..." and so the younger lady left – hurriedly.

It wasn't until after Ms Sophie Clerkenwell-Brown had gone out of the door – Thelma stood on the doorstep smiling, watching the blonde-haired figure trotting down the path with her pert little bottom (M and S size 10) wobbling cheekily – that the penny dropped! Only when the door had been closed – it was then and only then!

Buttocks... They looked different covered up. No wonder she hadn't recognised them...

19

Oh, dear me. No ...surely not a wheelie bin... George said that the hamper arrangement would have to be changed, but hadn't said what it would be instead. He would have to think about it, was last week's comment but, as she climbed into the van, there it was.

The hamper was there as usual but, lying lengthwise, and waiting to swallow her was a wheelie bin. Looking at it, she wished maybe he could have thought a little bit more. How could someone her age get in and out of this thing? Luckily, she wore trousers more often than a skirt and George, the kind soul, had at least provided cushions.

As the station's driver, George was happy to have this job. Being made redundant at the last one, and him only sixty-one then, had been annoying, although not too unexpected. He would much rather have remained because he considered himself fit enough to continue. The only things wrong were his hearing, badly affected by the hammering noises over many years, and being worried that securing something else at his age would be impossible.

So, he considered himself a very lucky man to be working for 'Little Radio fm'. For two years now he'd been doing this driving job, as well as any other physical get-your-hands-dirty type of task asked of him by the company, but at sixty-three, he was no spring chicken...

George had guessed that climbing in and out of the bin might be a little awkward for Daisy. To make it easier, he thoughtfully laid the large bin down flat, so that she could crawl inside and lie on the cushions – but easier said than done, Daisy found.

How do you get into a container?

Down onto the floor of the van she got, suddenly realising how stiff she'd become, and then wriggled, feet first, into the large plastic container. *Made it, but I couldn't keep doing this for long,* she told herself, though she felt a little glow of pride for coping at least once.

Most elderly ladies of her age would not want the excitement or the pressures that recently she had been inflicting on herself, although it might be helping to keep her younger. It felt claustrophobic with the lid closed. George had fitted clips and he'd drilled plenty breathing holes. So I just might survive the journey, she laughingly thought to herself, and thanked her lucky stars she hadn't grown tall – this bin was a neat fit.

By George's reckoning, it would only be safe to travel with the bin lying flat. Upright, it would easily fall over. One thing he had not accounted for was the effect of slippage on the van's flooring. The bin shot back and forward at the slightest change of speed. As he accelerated, Daisy felt the thump as it hit against the rear door, then a change of gear and slight deceleration, and she was moving towards the front wall. In town traffic, gear changing from first, to second, to third, and back down again, was done a great deal more often than on the open highway.

When he stopped at the traffic lights in town, hearing the crashing sound, pedestrians thought he had banged into the lorry in front. Daisy was well aware of the real reason – she felt a bump to accompany every noisy bang. George might have heard it too, if only he hadn't turned off his hearing-aid...

However, George was feeling anything but complacent, with eyes peeled for any traffic police. This was the first time he had driven with someone in a wheelie bin in the back of a van, and not wearing a seat belt, a person well passed retirement age too. He wondered – does my insurance cover me in these circumstances? Chances are, if I am stopped by police, my licence goes, I lose my job, and I go to jail for life. He therefore was driving extremely carefully – but it did not seem like it to Daisy...

There was great relief when he safely reached the entrance to the building where 'Little Radio fm' studios and offices were located. He stopped the van outside. Double yellow lines, but he'd take a chance. Moving the body any other way would get too complicated. The clothes hamper was on wheels, and he'd managed over the weeks to move it easily himself when Daisy had been inside. Today, it almost moved of its own accord. What a difference a body made...

"Hi," said the young reporter as he moved forward, "Weekly washing, eh?" making an attempt at a joke to endear himself to this old guy who was ignoring him, yet again. "Do you have to do the laundry yourself as well as all your other duties?" and he moved closer. "Can I give you a hand with that?" and he did.

As George stepped forward to open the door of the building, the young lad lifted the lid of the basket.

"Oh..." There was nothing to see but clothes, clean and not very well ironed, because George had done the ironing himself. The pile was not deep enough to the reporter's eye to hold anything other than clothes. That idea had come to nothing. Should it have been the other entrance? A disappointed young man shut the hamper lid again and shot off to the back of the building. The hamper had obviously had been a decoy, but they weren't going to stop him photographing that elusive granny.

So, George was able to return quickly to the van. The bin had to be lifted from the floor and with Daisy inside lying down, this proved to be a bit more awkward than he anticipated. He succeeded but it took a bit of manoeuvring. Preventing the bin wheels turning and moving out of his control was awkward and he dropped it at the first try. After two attempts, he succeeded by bringing the base to rest against the side of the van and pushing hard. Then it was down the ramp from the van, and up the ramp into the corridor.

"Ouch! ...Ouch! ...Ouch!"

He had behaved in a cruel and heartless manner towards her, and Daisy was disappointed, as well as being sore. This was not the George she had grown to know and trust. He'd been utterly ignoring her yells and squeals, but this was a George still without his hearing-aid switched on...

He pushed the bin, and her, straight into the usual studio.

"Good morning, Daisy."

It was Carol who'd opened the lid, and looked in at a squashed-up little old lady, looking ever so slightly yellow about the gills.

"Good journey?" she enquired sympathetically.

"Nothing to complain about..." was the reply, but Carol thought there might be just a tiny hint of sarcasm...

20

Muriel arrived home before Sally on Tuesday evening. Both were cycling back and forth to work, but Sally being farther into town than Muriel tended to be delayed a little by the busier traffic, not that it really mattered. There was only about a quarter-hour between the two. (Incidentally, on the nights she was in and looking out, this was a point which Mrs Masterton had noted.) Both liked to freshen up the moment they arrived back, and that was no hardship. Having two bathrooms with showers in the house, there was no hold up for either, and it didn't have to be a race.

These evenings, when Thelma was at work, it was just like it used to be – having Sally at home and only the two of them again, well – almost like it used to be. Ah, the good old days, thought Muriel... but, to be truthful, normal most evenings back then had Sally, backed by Muriel, arguing with Alexander. Now Sally was married and shouldn't be here, and Alexander was with Derek, and shouldn't be there. Correction – nothing is like it used to be at all...

There was a plate-load of sandwiches, obviously prepared by Thelma and which hadn't been eaten, covered and lying in the fridge. They were just sitting there, saying 'eat me'. Finding them could only lead to them being sampled by Muriel, and enjoyed – and sampled again.

What was the package, lying in the front room on the coffee table, with no name or address on the front? Muriel was curious. The flap was sealed. She didn't remember it lying there last night. Whose was it? She sat looking at it, guessing what it could be, as she picked another sandwich from the plate conveniently placed beside her.

Had any post been expected? Yes, but this couldn't have been delivered by the postman though, could it? No name, no address... Could it be one of these special delivery thingies that were put through the door occasionally for, say ...a Chinese Restaurant in town, or maybe a new mail order company, or a church bazaar? Why hadn't Thelma opened it?

She would only find out if she opened it herself, Muriel decided. So she did... What is it, a typed copy of a script? No, too big for that, a book? Yes, it has a title and an author's name, 'The Big Squeak, by Ivy Bloom' – who the heck is Ivy Bloom, and what is this doing lying here? The name rang a bell. Someone she knew? No... She checked the envelope for other clues, but there were none. There was nothing else to read other than the document she was holding, no note, formal or informal. Did this perhaps belong to Thelma? Had she left it lying here by mistake? The package had been sealed but had no name or address on the front. Had Thelma been in the process of sending this somewhere – to a publisher perhaps?

That's what it is!

Thelma has been writing a book...! The sly monkey... She's been writing a book and I've stumbled on it... She'll be mad that I've looked at it – though she shouldn't have left it lying around now, should she? Maybe she left it deliberately – to break it to me gently? My goodness, I know someone who will be jealous – Derek. If he gets to know that Thelma has completed a book and he has barely started his, he will be livid, no, probably more broken-hearted, devastated – he's really a big softie... That's a bit sad though, someone else in the family beating him to it.

Our Thelma – an author... I didn't know she had it in her. The sneaky cow ...and she used a pen name: Ivy Bloom. That was the name she mentioned the other night, the same one Mrs Masterton used for the bingo. Thelma's pinched the name from her, from our next door neighbour... Ivy Bloom? Surely she could have pinched a better one.

The front door was opening. Sally was getting home now. Muriel wondered if she'd made up with Derek yet. It would be nice if she had, for her and Derek; she could go back to her own home – and

Alexander would come back here.

"Hello love, had a good day?"

"Ok."

"How's Derek then?"

"Who?"

No more questions needed, obviously...

"Were you aware, Sal, that your Aunt Thelma was writing a book? I found it lying on the table. I don't know if we're supposed to know," said Muriel, feeling guilty because she opened the sealed package.

"Aunt Thelma? Never... Oh, let's see," said Sally. She took it from her mother, opened the pages randomly and began to read the contents.

"It was dark. The floor creaked seriously with each footstep, but he had to keep moving towards the door. He didn't know what lay inside the room but he was the only one about, the only one who could do something, the only one who could save her. He slid the Magnum from his holster, gently, and stopped at the door."

"Aunt Thelma wrote this?"

"Yes" replied Muriel, feeling pride for her sister-in-law.

"This little shooter would send that guy to heaven – fast – if he misbehaves, he said to himself. The light shone under the door. Soft moans could be heard coming from inside, could be pain, but then again, it could be pleasure – it was always pleasure with his dolls. Someone started pacing back and forth, and he wasn't wearing high heels. It had to be Stefano on the other side, Stefano Davidson, the notorious drug smuggler, who recently branched out into the white slave trade, yes, that Stefano, and he had her in his vicious clutches again..."

"Is Aunt Thelma sleeping all right at nights?" asked Sally. "This is the result of a troubled mind, I'd say."

"She's good, isn't she?" said Muriel.

"And she's beaten my Derek to it, poor Derek. If he would just give up the training for that ridiculous marathon, he could concentrate more on his writing."

Now this is a good sign, thought Muriel. A little bit of sympathy?

Could it mean this temporary lodger moving out quite soon?

"But there's no chance of him doing that. He's too stupid. He prefers chasing skinny naked girls around the house."

Ah well, so much for the peace process – and the Arabs and Israelis think they have problems, mused Muriel.

Sally lifted the envelope. As she put the document inside, she sniffed the sheaf of papers, then the brown envelope. She held it out to her mother. "Do you recognise that as Thelma's perfume, Mum, I don't?" Muriel took a sniff... No... It wasn't Thelma's.

Suddenly something flashed into her head, just for a moment.

Buttocks...

21

"Derek," shouted Rob from the comfort of his office, "would you come in a minute please. I want to discuss something privately."

Derek rose from his desk, thinking to himself, Rob is deluded. With wafer-thin office walls, nothing is private in here. He hoped it wasn't going to be about him and Sally.

"A word – while Sally is out of the office," Rob began.

Having a sandwich and coffee at the place round the corner, on her own, had been the recent routine ever since the fall out, but today, for a change, she went with Spider. Therefore, Rob could have stayed where he was and talked, and Derek could have stayed where he was and listened, and it would still have been private.

"What is going on with you and Sally? The atmosphere in here is crap, and will probably remain so until you two kiss and make up. Can we all get back to normal, please?" As Derek only looked back blankly, it was obvious that subject was not going to progress very far... "Well, never mind that then. There's something else I want you to do for me. Spider bumped into this bloke in the pub last night," Rob continued.

"And this is news?" asked Derek.

"And this bloke has written a book..."

Everybody's written a ruddy book, it seems, except me, Derek murmured quietly to himself.

"Did you say something, Derek? No... He's done the self-publishing thing, apparently, and it's accessible on the internet to read, and can be purchased on-line, but it's not moving very well, and of course, he's desperate to make his fortune out of it."

"Yes...?"

"When he heard Spider say that he worked here, this bloke asked if it could be possible to use it in a serialised form in the paper, edited any way to suit us. The book would maybe at least sell better locally after some publicity. We could push the line of him being the local boy who's made the big time."

"Yes...?"

"...But I haven't the time to look at it, and I thought that you would be the perfect person to consider it, seeing you are into books. He is a policeman, so I'm sure it wouldn't do us any harm to be friends with the law, especially after all the carry-on last year with my money, and you, and Sally."

"Oh, yes..." Derek remembered it well, but he didn't sound over-enthusiastic yet, although it seemed a good enough idea. It was a premise he pushed himself and so was difficult to demur. If it was broken into weekly instalments over many episodes, and was good enough, it could keep readers coming back every week to buy The Gazette.

So, Derek accepted and was given the manuscript, with a request from his boss to forget his personal troubles, and try to generate a little more enthusiasm for his work. Leaving the confines of the 'private' office, he returned to his own desk, laid down the manuscript for later, and carried on with this week's panic, needed at the printers tomorrow.

It was a happy smiling Sally who returned arm-in-arm with Spider. They'd not been to the cafe. Today it had been pub grub and a little light refreshment obviously, but the minute she looked at Derek the scowl returned, and the office became unpleasantly normal again.

It was late in the afternoon when Derek opened the manuscript again.

Let's see how it begins... 'THE DOOR CREAKED, by Andy Woodstock'. Woodstock? Now that name seems familiar... Woodstock, hmmm... A policeman ...and local... It can't be, can it? Hmmm, possible ...the detective who arrested Sally and me, he went back to the beat. So, this is how he gets his kicks. Huh, I know where I'm putting this...

He stopped, just before the document left his hand.

Maybe the dustbin would be a bit unfair. He wasn't really such a bad bloke, a bit naive, and, he realised, *we've probably to thank him for Alexander still being a free man,* then he hesitated again. After suffering Alexander as a lodger for some time now, why should he be grateful to the policemen who failed to arrest his father-in-law?

Curiosity then made him carry on reading...

'Deep down he was a country boy, soft and gentle, with a heart of gold, but that was hidden underneath this carefully manufactured hard veneer. The veneer was an essential for what he did in the big city.

It was dawn and quiet in his office. He would have been able to hear the sound of the dust falling, if it hadn't been for the buzzing of a fly which had eluded capture all morning, but which blended with the buzz of the traffic six floors down.

He waited for the phone to ring, or a knock at the door. He needed the business. Would a visitor know where to find him? He stood and walked casually to the door, opened it, and checked the shiny black plastic plate with the name engraved in white bold capitals. It was his name, and still attached to the door with four screws. ANDY PANDOLETTI – PRIVATE INVESTIGATOR. He sat down again.

His copy of the Weekly Gazette, from his home town, was lying folded on his desk, and looking lonely too. He had subscribed, and it was posted to the office address every week. He'd already completed the Weekly Crossword, and the Sudoku, and was bang up to date with all the local hatches and dispatches. Yes, keeping abreast of the times was important in the job he did.

It was one of those kind of days, he told himself but something is about to happen – and then the phone rang. It was his mobile. He lifted it.

"Help...!" it said.

"Why didn't you ring my office number," he answered coolly, as was his style. "That's the number I do business on."

"Help...!" it cried again.

He raised his head and there she was, holding the mobile in her hand. She looked ravishing, standing in the doorway, this hot blooded female, wearing an off-the-shoulder evening gown, the backlight from the corridor giving her flaming red hair a gloriously warm glow. He could feel her body heat hitting him where he was sitting.

This doll was hot. The day could be getting more interesting...'

Not bloody likely, mate. What a load of... I'll try another bit...

Derek soldiered on.

'It was dark. The floor creaked seriously with each footstep, but he had to keep moving towards the door. He didn't know what lay inside the room but he was the only one about, the only one who could do something, the only one who could save her.

He slid the Magnum from his holster, gently, and stopped at the door. This little shooter would send that guy to heaven – fast – if he misbehaves, he said to himself.

The light shone under the door. Soft moans could be heard coming from inside...'

Derek settled for a long heartfelt sigh. As if life for him wasn't sad enough – and now he was going to have to edit this bundle. He could tell a lot of editing was called for but he decided that is enough of the office for the day. The others had already left. It was galling how Sally's cheery laughter returned again, the moment she stepped out of the door with Rob and Spider. The annoying thing about all this, he was having difficulty remembering what had caused their bad feeling in the first place...

Then he remembered – it was all about him.

22

It was a lonely journey back along Cloverton Avenue, but one which was gradually becoming more of a habit for her. She was getting well used to cycling and enjoyed it, except in the wet weather. It was dry tonight.

As she glanced around her, the impression was that the door to every household along this road was already bolted, and everyone was in bed, except her. She realised that this was a distinct possibility, taking account of the ages of the population and the habits of the resident in this snobbish stuck-up area of town, but this was where she resided too.

It was only ten o'clock, for goodness sake, and not even properly dark yet. Would outsiders consider her to be part of this ageing mob? Had she merged in with the rest? She cycled on. Pedalling home meant, at least, she wasn't standing at a deserted bus stop after work, hopefully waiting to see if the bus would actually arrive; a lonely wait, very often punctuated by a drunk wanting to be too friendly.

Her boss was getting a bit familiar, too friendly by far. Yesterday it was all bluster about the special anniversary celebration going wrong. This evening, he was saying sorry for losing his temper, explaining that it was all due to problems at home.

"My wife doesn't understand me..."

Now how many times had that been said to her? Usually followed by the suggestion, "You know that you could do well in this company, if..." *A knee in the groin will quickly cool his ardour if he tries anything like that*, she resolved. *He is not my type, at all. I don't want the job that much*, but he had something she was at least interested in; it was a motorbike.

She felt quite warm as she pedalled, and having her light anorak over the bright blue jacket was the cause. There was little choice. She couldn't be seen outside wearing the ghastly jacket, but she couldn't leave it at work, and didn't want to roll it up to carry it. Crumpled, made it look even worse. The colour had not been her choice, at all.

The light came on, automatically, as she walked up the path. Another two bikes were already sitting inside the shed, Muriel's, and Sally's. Alexander had taken his to Derek's. Sometimes the large double garage was used for bike storage, but the shed was usually handier. It was unusual for a double garage not to hold at least one vehicle, but this household had no cars. They were slightly unconventional.

There couldn't be many homes around here like the Davidson family, without a car in the garage. All other garages in the area had several cars. The indignity of pedalling a bicycle would not have even been contemplated by the Overton residents. Few adults, around here, would even be able to ride a bike!

Mrs M next door didn't have a car, of course, but neither did she have a bike. She was also an oddity. Thelma wondered if she was still mad at her. *Imagine, after all those years, no-one being aware that she played bingo, but why should she be ashamed of it? It gets her out and about. Just peeping out from behind curtains, every day, alone, can't be good for anyone, can it? She meets lovely people at the bingo, doesn't she? She met me...*

In she went, and her anorak was hung up, her bright blue bomber work-jacket was hung up too, and her silly bright blue hat was removed from her pocket and thrown expertly, spinning to land on the coat hook, just like James Bond used to do... Oops ...missed.

"And who is a clever girl then?" was the greeting from Muriel, as Thelma entered the front lounge. "You kept that a secret didn't you? Thought we wouldn't find out – but we have..."

"The light shone under the door. Soft moans could be heard coming from inside," quoted Sally in her sexiest voice.

Goodness ...I did? Me ...moan ...surely not? I didn't think anyone... Thelma was embarrassed and panicking.

"The book... When did you write it? Were you going to make us wait until it was printed, you naughty girl?" said Muriel, chucking her sister-in-law's chin, and then giving her a big hug of congratulations.

"And you beat Derek," cried out a delighted Sally, hugging her aunt, and then immediately feeling extremely disloyal to her stupid husband.

"Excuse me ...I never touched Derek. If there's any beating to be done, young lady, I'd say you were the one to do it," replied an indignant Thelma. She had no idea what they were getting so excited about. She hadn't done anything. Anyway, why were they in the lounge? Muriel was usually in her bed by now. Had they been drinking? Where's mine?

Sally held up the package, and as she did so, she noticed a very pleasant smell, again, and it was from the paper for certain.

"Oh you found it then," said Thelma.

"Yes, indeed, you Scallywag, did you think we wouldn't?" smiled Muriel.

"No, I didn't. Oh ...did you open it? It's for Mrs Masterton," Thelma mentioned in a matter of fact voice.

"WHAT?"

It was a deflated Sally and Muriel who were then told that this had nothing to do with Thelma – it wasn't her story at all. It had been delivered by a special visitor during the morning.

"Bet you can't guess who?" smiled Thelma, and, of course, they couldn't guess, and anyway, who cared? It wasn't Thelma's book after all. What a let-down. They felt pig-sick about the bursting of their bubble, so refused to play silly guessing games at this time of night.

Then as Sally held the package, she caught a whiff of the smell again. She sniffed. It was familiar. "That is a perfume..." she sniffed again, and slowly lifted her head, her eyes opened wide, with the nearest thing to a snarl that could be managed formed at her mouth.

"It was HER! It was that naked bitch – the one who sullied my dear innocent husband!"

Sally didn't know 'HER' name and didn't care – but if she had touched this... Ugh! The package was thrown down, as if red hot.

Once Sally cooled down somewhat, Thelma lifted the business card from the mantelpiece, and went on to explain the request made by her visitor. She had to refer to the card for the name, Ms Sophie Clerkenwell-Brown...

Maybe it would have been better not mentioning her name. Now the blue touch paper had been relit. The bitch had a name.

Sally stamped around the room in anger at the mention of it, and the remainder of Thelma's information was put on hold. Sally sat down, but continued to smoulder.

Eventually, and with some caution, Thelma continued... 'She' had requested that the package be handed to Mrs Masterton next door, because apparently, Mrs Violet Masterton was the author of this story. It looked as if this 'person' was about to take on the publishing of Mrs M's book.

Was it jealousy pervading the room at that moment – jealousy of the little woman next door having had a little success in her humdrum little life?

No – it was the need for revenge...

Revenge against Ms Sophie Clerkenwell-Brown... *How could she have dared to show her face again? The cheek of her ...and now, she had been in this house as well, the brass-necked little vixen.*

So, today's visitor was now identified properly by a name, she was no longer just a person; she had clearly advanced and graduated – to become a hated person...

Thankfully, the serious dislike was really only emanating from one person – Sally – but the other two could do nothing other than be her loyal supporters. Driven along by her, there was agreement that something would have to be done, but what could it be?

Hurting little old Mrs Masterton seemed unfair. She had become piggy-in-the-middle, but there must be some way for pain and discomfort to be inflicted to wipe the smugness from that little blonde's face.

Though it was becoming late, three heads began plotting – on how to achieve revenge...

Obviously, it could turn out to be a long night, so Muriel suggested she should make coffee, and that Thelma should make sandwiches. No need, said Thelma, there is a plateful in the fridge from lunch. Muriel said nothing, until the fridge was found to be bare; only then did she admit to having scoffed the lot.

Leaving Sally sitting in the lounge, with a serious expression on her face while sustenance was prepared, turned out worthwhile. In the short time between the suggestion of the coffee, and the arrival of a steaming jug of the stuff, plus sandwiches, an idea had formed in Sally's head.

It would become their book, well, maybe Thelma's book because she would be involved from the beginning. Not difficult to imagine for Muriel and Sally – they had already managed to implant this erroneous idea in their own heads earlier. For Thelma this was a little more than she thought she deserved, but it took only a few moments of persuasion to have her believe she had earned the honour.

Thelma was to become an author.

Ownership of this story would be changing – it would be made to change. Unfortunate for Mrs Masterton to have to suffer a little in the process, but at least they would be doing something, and whatever the something turned out to be, should muck up any plans that Ms Sophie Clerkenwell-Brown might have had for this little chronicle...

23

The atmosphere in the office had changed – it was worse. The request by Sally, to Rob and Spider, for her desk to be moved yet farther away from Derek's, could be taken as an indicator that the tiff was becoming much more deeply entrenched. After Rob's chat, Derek would willingly have grovelled to Sally for forgiveness, but he would be wasting his time, he could tell. This was now a long downhill struggle...

When he was in the office, Derek kept his head down and concentrated on work, if possible, but each time he heard the low murmur of voices, he couldn't avoid squinting out of the corner of his eyes. It almost certainly meant a communication from Sally to him – but only with Spider's assistance.

Rob and Spider were becoming self-conscious even when they actually talked in a normal volume to each other about subjects not associated with Derek or Sally. A deathly silence had become part of the Newingsworth Weekly Gazette office working conditions.

Concentration by Derek today was on this week's episode of *'Arthur and Charlie and their Wonderful Feet'*. Although publicity was progressing well, the backing of a large organisation was what Derek wanted. A big name always helped with the other charity sponsors, and would be the next part of his project. He needed that big name, and the biggest in Newingsworth, the one people couldn't ignore – was BISKO's.

An idea had bubbled around for a few days, and when he was out of the office he rang Muriel. She had worked at Bisko's for a long time, so, he hoped, that although she may not have much influence on main company policies, she would have good internal contacts. That was needed for starters and the top man locally would be the target.

Muriel agreed to help, however, but on her terms, and any contact either way must stay secret.

"If Sally discovers I'm consorting with the enemy, which is you, Sweaty, there will be no living with her. Be warned – if it does go skew-whiff – you will have a mother-in-law, me, as well as a father-in-law, staying with you at Toozlethwaite Manor, so ...not a word!"

Derek kept it secret...

Muriel did have influence and with the right person, the Senior Manager. Steven Tomkins had been doing the job for about a year, having come from another part of the country.

He liked Muriel. From that first sighting of her, which was when he was getting to know the range and capabilities of the store's CCTV cameras and she was changing from her outdoor cycling gear into her daily working clothes, she had been likeable.

Since getting to know her fully dressed, he found her experience of the store and the staff to be very useful, and if any ideas were put forward by her, they were given proper personal consideration by him, although this latest request was perhaps pushing it a little far.

'*Bisko's don't do charity*', had been drummed into Mr Tomkins' head since he joined the company, and that was goodness knows how many years ago. He knew of many a good manager who'd fallen by the wayside by not adhering to company rules. His loyalty to the organisation could not be questioned by anyone – Steven Tomkins was 'Mr Company Man' personified – even though, he mulled over her suggestion. Maybe this was the right time...

Is Bisko's current approach to charity really the correct one for a modern company, and justifiable to our customers? He asked himself the question – his conclusion – no.

'*Profits come first*' was another clearly defined statement in the company's internal targets, probably the most important one of the lot. Would Muriel Davidson's idea conflict with that principle, or could it be complementary, if done correctly?

Having a friend on the Board of Directors was useful. He was actually a second cousin, who'd taken a few more lucky steps than him on the ladder, and Steven decided to give him a call, and talk. It was fortunate timing because the directors were experiencing a feeling of euphoria at that precise moment. Having been informed by the MD that the profit results shown on the 'about to be disclosed' company accounts were even better than the previous year, only beaming smiles could be seen around the boardroom table. The unusually magnanimous mood prevailing within the group, just then, permitted a positive answer to feed back down the line. Anyway, he was given the go-ahead.

He would be permitted to open discussions with a view to the sponsorship by Bisko's of two runners for the London Marathon.

There was a proviso. Positive publicity had to be achieved. If it turned out to be a failure, the Newingsworth manager, Mr Steven Tomkins, would carry the total responsibility. The proviso, in writing, ended with '...and there should be no need to spell out the consequence for your relationship with the company'.

Today, Derek was working on something to offer. He was meeting Steven Tomkins in two days time. As usual, he felt under pressure, but that was a fact of life for most work involved with newspapers. Sometimes Derek felt he wasn't cut out for his chosen career of journalism.

He suffered from fluctuating confidence – and today the right words were not coming out. He did have a plan, for the outfits.

Charlie and Arthur could wear T-shirts, but not just ordinary T-shirts. His minds-eye saw T-shirts which reached to the ground, and could carry a very large advertisement for the new sponsor. Not in the least comfortable for them to be running in, he guessed, but it wasn't too much to worry about for him – having given up the hope of competing himself – for Arthur and Charlie, yes, but not for him... So, the creation of a slogan was next.

'This man wanted the runs – BISKO's helped him get them.' No, that is not quite right ...has to be short and punchy.

'BISKO's can help you with the runs.' Still not right...

'Short of breath? Get it at BISKO's.' No...

'If you need to go – go at BISKO's.' No...

'This man won't win – but BISKO's will.' Hmmm?

'Go – BISKO's – Go.' Maybe...?

Proper concentration was hard. This feeling of daggers-in-the-back constantly coming from the direction of Sally was slightly off-putting? So, he left the slogans, and switched to the serialisation of 'The Door Creaked, by Andy Woodstock'. The whole story hadn't been faced yet, but random selections were giving him an idea of the mood and the style. If he were to edit it for the Gazette, it would be best to capture the author's style.

Page 42...

'She had trusted him. He had said he could dance, "...lead her a merry dance," his actual words, but could he? The answer was no... He was just an overblown good looking suave detective with two left feet, feet which had stepped into every trap that the evil hoodlum, Frankie Doodle, had set. He could see himself reflected in the bedroom window, in a state of suspension, hanging onto the edge of the window sill, eight stories above ground, and still smiling. God, he looked good in profile.'

Had Rob looked at this before he handed it to him, Derek wondered? And he was expected to do something constructive with this... This load of...

'His muscles bulged as he inched his perfectly honed body into position. With no light spilling from the street seven storeys below, he was rendered almost invisible.

He would be dropping a mere twelve feet onto the balcony below, opening the window of that room with his penknife and then crossing the room containing the couple of youngsters, now lying exhausted after some illegal activities, open the door and exit without them even realising he had been in the room, and run up the stair, three steps at a time, to rescue her.

He went for it, landing nimbly on his toes, and the trusty pen-knife had the door open in seconds. Like a shadow he flitted into the room and out again without disturbing the two still figures lying prone on the bed after enjoying their illegal activity. He did everything exactly as he had intended, not surprisingly. He knew he was good...

She held her breath, trembling in anticipation of his strong arms encircling her, but there had been no sound from the corridor – had he failed? And then the handle of the door turned and the door was slowly opened – but the door creaked. The noise, the door creaking, broke the silence and ...it could mean curtains for them both...'

"Ohhhhhh no, great heavens..." sighed Derek, gazing to the ceiling.

He went back to the slogans...

'Race you to BISKO's – we can all be winners.' Nope, too wordy again...

'Be first and win the race to BISKO's.' ...Maybe a bit better?

He tried to visualise Arthur and Charlie, running along in the pouring rain, wet T-shirts reaching to their ankles, and clinging un-provocatively to all their parts, and them hating the conditions – and hating him – but soldiering on, because they were wearing special canary yellow t-shirts which said in big bold black lettering...

'WIN – AT BISKO's.'

He could now smile, a little more confident in his own ability...

24

Nothing much was happening this morning along the avenue, nothing that Mrs Masterton could see, and she could see everything. It was time for elevenses, coffee and biscuits, sitting in her favourite seat, by the window, all on her own. Being alone meant she could have everything her own way, which was the way she liked it now.

I wasn't always like this though, she thought. *Now, when Albert had been alive... Ah yes...*

The seat beside the window was positioned so that she missed nothing, but at a suitable angle to watch the television programme of her choice at the same time, remotely changing channels at the boring bits. Remote devices were wonderful. *There we are, stir the sugar in well, a bite of the Abernethy biscuit, and relax and...*

There was a sudden surge of energy, most unlike her. Did she put double sugar in her coffee by mistake? It could have a funny effect she'd found. *Let's brighten things up*, she decided, and closed her eyes.

She was going to live dangerously and take a random choice with her Sky remote... She stabbed at three buttons – and what came up? It was her favourite. She'd hit one of the music channels and there they were, looking good and sounding good, especially now that Robbie was back, and she started to dance around the room...

Did the doorbell sound? She turned down the volume. It didn't matter how loud she had the television when living alone. The houses were well apart, no-one could be disturbed by her noise, but she had been disturbed, by the bell... No, it's ok. They've gone away, relax again...

'Grooooovy baby...' *Goodness, there it was again – the bell...* She stopped the gyrations, which were barely perceptible anyway, switched off the telly, and went to the door.

Thelma stood on the doorstep, a package in her hand.

Mrs Masterton had liked her when she first came to live with Muriel and Alexander – but now she wasn't so sure. Now, she was bothering her, coming and interrupting her dancing, and, of course, this was the woman who was lowering the standards of Cloverton. She was now, '...the person who worked at the Bingo Hall... Riff-raff...'

The biggest smile, she could summon up, was on Thelma's face. "Good morning, Mrs Masterton. Are you well, today? I hope I haven't called at an inconvenient time," and before Mrs Masterton could come out with her true feelings and say Yes... Thelma continued, "There is something I want to discuss with you that I think would be better done inside."

There was considerable hesitation, before the invitation to enter was reluctantly given and Thelma was led along the dark hallway, into Mrs Masterton's front room – the nerve centre. For some strange reason, Thelma expected to see a telescope, and a large notepad and pencil sitting at the window, maybe even a tape recorder switched on ready; such was Mrs Masterton's reputation for being the eyes and ears of Cloverton – but there wasn't any of that.

Regular visits to her optician and appropriate adjustments to the lenses of her spectacles ensured over the years that this old woman's long-sight was as good as any modern high-tech sighting device. No hard copies of information needed either, with a perfectly good memory for the trivia of the neighbourhood. Other than the specs, no other artificial aids were required for her to maintain her vigil over the community, and she took what she considered to be her duties most seriously – except when she was at Bingo.

"Ah, you're just having a coffee break. How nice," said Thelma, "No sugar for me, please – got to watch the tummy, you know – are you the same?"

"Am I the same as what?"

"...The same as me. Oh yes, I can see you are, of course, dear...

and not too much milk."

Mrs Masterton left the room.

Thelma sat down and gazed around. She was wise enough not to go too far by sitting in the 'special' seat, where a coffee was already lying – cold. Everything in the room smacked of almost forty years ago. How styles had changed. Look at the photographs, all sorts of different frames holding photographs of either, one person, or two, and the same female and the same male pictured in all of them. One was Mrs Masterton herself, from when she must have been a teenager, although the term, teenager, probably wasn't in use in her young days. The other, Thelma presumed, would be her long-dead husband.

Thelma rose and went over to the large teak display unit. She lifted a photograph of the two of them. Hot pants were being worn. *Look at those legs... bet you didn't know the meaning of varicose veins in those days* Mrs M, Thelma thought cattily – *and the platform shoes – ruined many a neat ankle when you fell over, I'll bet. Nice hair though, long, and what lovely waves – and dark brown too. Those were the days...*

The man looked happy, smiling his best smile for the camera. Bell bottom-trousers had been his choice, a really fancy patterned wide tie, and a cool looking leather jacket which narrowed at the waist, and made him look quite skinny, *and look at his shoes... platforms, as well, and his hair... It's the same as hers.* Tall and skinny, would be how Thelma would have described him.

"Put that down!" It was a sharp rebuke from the reluctant host. "Bertie doesn't like being touched by any woman other than me."

Thelma replaced it rather quickly. She didn't want to go too far, not yet, and certainly not with Bertie.

"There's your coffee."

Thelma didn't feel that she was really and truly being made welcome. "Thank you very much. This is very kind. You have lots of photos."

"Yes. Now what do you want?"

"Ah yes. I had a visitor yesterday – a lady from a publishing house."

"Oh...?" This was a different tone now from Mrs Masterton, an interest was being shown.

"She gave me something she wanted to pass on herself to you, but you were out. Did you leave early yesterday?"

"Yes, I was..." and she stopped. What had that to do with this person?

"This book," and Thelma held out the package. It was snatched out of her hand.

"...But ...you've opened it..." was the accusation.

"What? Now why would I do that? She must have forgotten to close it. Did she leave a note for you explaining her future intentions?" The manuscript was taken from the envelope, but there was no note. "Oh, I thought she said she was leaving one... She will have phoned you since though, has she not?"

"No..." replied Mrs Masterton, a little on the back foot.

"Oh dear, that's youngsters for you, isn't it? I do hope I can remember what she told me then. My memory's not brilliant... She said of course you had written this, and that it required to be... Is it... proof read? Is that correct?"

Mrs M nodded.

"What else? Oh yes ...it unfortunately isn't up to a high enough standard for them to absorb the cost of producing it, not without a contribution from you. Vanity Publishing I think was how she put it."

"Oh," and there was now a look of dejection on the old lady's face, a look that almost made Thelma stop and state the true version – but she didn't.

"How much?" was asked grudgingly.

"It would be at least, now what was it? Nine thousand pounds... yes, that's right, nine thousand, but it would include fantastic publicity, and be on sale in all the best places, and would be a deal which would cover you for two years." There was silence. "You are disappointed... I can tell. Oh dear, it's a cruel world, isn't?" and Thelma put on a sad face in sympathy.

Again, silence, and Thelma could see the start of a lip tremble – either disappointment, or petulance, because she hadn't got what she wanted.

"I'll tell you what. I've just had an idea," said Thelma. "I've always wanted to write a book but I've never succeeded. Would you be willing to sell your book to me?"

"But I'm the author. That would be cheat..."

"No. Not really," Thelma quickly broke in, "There surely must be some way for you to get something out of it, after all your hard work? I could give you money for it, and you would have a little benefit, at least."

No, it wasn't working, was it? The silence continued, so Thelma made her way towards the door. Obviously Mrs Masterton was not rising to the bait.

Thelma walked through the now opened door. "See you later, then..." she offered cheerily, and added, when Mrs Masterton's eyebrows rose questioningly, "I was presuming, today, you would be going to the bing..."

The door slammed behind her.

Not in a good mood, then.

Thelma had the strong urge to open the letterbox to finish off her sentence, and shout loud enough for everyone to hear, "...BINGO," but she didn't...

25

Today's programme was planned to be different, although due to the haphazard way that Daisy performed her stint as Granny Wisdom, no programme ever turned out to be the same. It would be nice to say that it was all down to the skills of this little old lady – but untrue. Here was someone who was game for anything, but whose ability to control the sequence of events, the destiny of the programme, or simply the pushing of the right button at the correct moment, were all diminishing week by week, but Daisy was not the only one feeling the strain.

As Daisy's producer, Carol did not think she could last much longer, certainly not as long as Granny Wisdom and her show might possibly run. The pressure was getting to her, and the problem had been discussed by Carol with her boss.

At home, Carol's boss, boy-friend, and live-in lover, was known as Graham, not as the Boss, and certainly not as Curly. Carol always used his proper name at home. It seemed much more adult to be able to use his real name. Curly was infantile and, in consequence, a male thing. Curly, Sweaty, Twinkletoes, Jacko, Wally, Eck – all names which seemed to have figured prominently in Graham's memories of his younger days – memories which were being recalled a bit too often recently.

These nicknames, being thrown into the during-dinner conversations were being regurgitated more frequently since the re-union with Granny Smith and Sweaty, or rather, Daisy and Derek. Carol liked to think, at least, she was a grown-up and could talk and behave like one, but then again, she would occasionally envy the enjoyable boyhood Graham could recall.

Last night, however, it was not his youthful and childish memories which were discussed, it was her future and this show. At 'Little Radio fm', Carol acted as producer for several presenters, as well as Daisy, but it didn't feel the same strain with the others. Even the odd hours being worked were part of the job and just routine, but she couldn't cope much longer with Daisy, likeable though she was. Carol had been relieved initially when Graham said he understood, but then disappointed when he followed up by adding that he felt the programme hadn't quite run out of steam yet. So on it had to go...

Many weeks ago, an agreement was reached between Carol and Derek about more publicity for the marathon runners. These guys, Charlie and Arthur, had already become two of the newest sought-after personalities in Newingsworth, Slatterfoot, and surrounding districts, and more exposure was planned by having them guest on 'Little Radio fm', with more cash targeted for their future run.

This was not the first time these two blokes had done a marathon run for charity, however, although they had three under their belts from previous years, the strenuous efforts to raise money had been only modestly successful, support being from friends, workmates, and their local pub pals. This time with the backing of the Newingsworth Weekly Gazette, and the radio spot, they were hopeful of gathering considerably more than they ever had.

In accordance with the plan, today the activity for Charlie and Arthur was broadcasting, and the lucky programme, the Granny Wisdom Show. The visit by these two would be making today's programme different – two studio guests sitting opposite Daisy, but this raised a question, how could Granny Wisdom's identity be protected? It took some inspiration and ingenuity on Carol's part to solve it.

So, Mr Charlie Pollock and Mr Arthur Fletcher sat in the small anti-room, laughingly called The Green Room, of 'Little Radio fm', waiting nervously to go into the studio to talk on the radio to Granny Wisdom. Their nervousness was not on account of speaking on the radio. Dear me, no. They'd appeared quite a few times on the regional telly gardening programme and so, considered themselves to be seasoned performers.

It would be face to face with Granny Wisdom: they were to be the ones! No one else had ever even caught a glimpse of this woman. Charlie and Arthur would be the first outsiders to do this. The phantom voice of the radio world, and they would be sitting with her.

At ten-to-eleven, they were taken by Carol into the studio, sat down in position, set up with microphones and ear phones, and sound-checked for balance. They were ready.

Moments before the jingle was to be played, and while the local adverts were running, Granny Wisdom appeared. At least, they presumed this to be her – because this person was wearing a brown paper bag. The face was not visible. Admittedly, it was a brown paper bag with two eyes holes cut in it and a smiling mouth cut-out also, but it was still a brown paper bag nonetheless...

The jingle sang out, *'We may be LITT-LE – but we pack a lot of punch'*, and with the bouncy start completed in the briefest of moments, it was over to the voice in the bag.

Arthur and Charlie just sat gawping.

"Good Morning, MOGGIES, everywhere, how are we all today. Me? I'm feeling a little under the weather on account of my travelling arrangements, but no matter, we'll get cracking with a little music ...the red button, Carol? Carol, are you there? Not the red button then ...whoops ...that was close, wasn't it? This first song is being specially played for a lady who phoned in to grumble about her next door neighbour interrupting her by ringing her doorbell when she was just about to listen to her favourite group 'Take That'. Now isn't that a coincidence? They're my favourites too. Let's listen to them singing, 'Could it be magic?' ...red button, green button? Carol?"

The adrenalin was flowing, but it was Rolf Harris who was singing, 'Tie Me Kangaroo Down, Sport,' and the airwaves were filled by this for several minutes. It was a cheery way to get the show moving.

Underneath the paper bag, Daisy smiled at her two guests, to make them feel more comfortable – she wondered why they didn't smile back. Carol just gazed to the heavens for support, then the song ended and Granny Wisdom was back...

"And isn't it nice that Rolf has rejoined the band. He's always been my favourite."

Carol just had to chip in there. "Don't you mean Robbie, Granny? It was Robbie Williams who rejoined the group? The song you played was..."

"Who...?" Daisy interrupted. "No, sorry Carol, I don't know him."

Carol was wondering if perhaps she should be going to the doctor for tablets, but it was time to introduce the guests, which Daisy did.

"And now MOGGIES, a special treat, I have in the studio, two men, but only boys compared to me, that we are about to meet. They look fit and healthy as if they enjoy a life out of doors. I'm sure they have lots to tell us about themselves, and why they are here today, so what's your name then, Sonny?"

The brown bag is asking a question, Arthur and Charlie realised in a panic, but which one is it talking to?

Silence...

Carol had to apply the well defined radio principle – which had been explained very carefully to Daisy before every programme, but which she managed to forget during every programme, being that she was supposed to ensure a 'Seamless' professional show with no awkward silences on air – and jumped in with "Granny, if I can help, this is..." but before she could get the names out, she was stung by the rebuke from Daisy.

"Now Carol, do I tell you how to do your job? No. Then let me get on with mine, please."

Carol's face glowered back at Daisy, but inside she thought to herself, that if I travelled to work as Daisy did in a plastic wheelie bin, wouldn't I be feeling a little crotchety too? So, she held her tongue.

"I was speaking to these young gentlemen, Carol, if you don't mind. I'm sure they're not really shy and know their own names. They are big boys now and they should be able to speak for themselves..."

As the brown paper bag turned a little more towards him, Arthur felt compelled to blurt out "Arfur..." and then immediately dried. So much for the seasoned public performers that they thought they'd become.

"Right ...so you are – Arfur," said Granny. "You are a really talkative fellow, aren't you?" which made Arthur feel even more nervous. "Are you going to tell me what your friend's name is, or could he be persuaded to talk for himself, do you think?"

"Yus," said Arthur.

"Well, maybe a little music could be useful at this juncture. Arfur, please tell me if you know what I should be doing now, I can't see very well in here." At this point, Carol stepped in and played the music to keep things moving.

"You'll have to do better, boys. I'm getting hot in here, and you're almost putting me to sleep. So, you are Arthur and you are?" The voice, coming from the bag, was making the two visitors feel quite intimidated, but as the two cut-out eyes swung around a bit more, Charlie replied this time, and some off-air limited conversation occurred which seemed to crack the ice.

Carol took care of the fade-in and fade-out, linking sound back to the studio.

"And now, while you've been away I've met Charlie. Say hello, to the listeners, Charlie." So, Charlie obliged the paper bag. "Have you ever done this running thing before?" they were asked.

At long last, they were off. It was almost as if the starting gun had been fired. 'Running' had been the trigger. Suddenly, the two guests felt more relaxed, they were into their comfort zone, they knew about running, they had tales to tell, and they began to communicate. Carol let out a big sigh.

"Oh, yus, we've dunn free, me an' me mate Arfur ...'aven't we mate?"

"Yus, an' the best 'un 'twas Brigh'on, coz 'oo won 'at one mate, eh? Ask 'im, Granny, ask 'im..."

"...And who won that one then, Charlie?" to oblige, the paper bag asked the question.

"It warrint me," Charlie replied, a little huffily.

"Yea, 'e knows 'oo's fastest. Yea, you know don't ya mate?" but Charlie didn't respond. Was a little unpleasant history being stirred up perhaps?

"And maybe some music," suggested Carol, interrupting as the chat dried again, and the sounds of Abba floated in, seamlessly.

Abba finished, 'Take a chance,' and it was back to the interview. Daisy and Carol were both relieved to find the subject of running had loosened the tongues of the two guests, and as long as they were chatting about their marathon training and adventures, they appeared to be on solid ground.

(Listeners, who also read the Weekly Gazette, would possibly have recognised that much of the chat they were hearing, had been printed in a column, created by Derek Toozlethwaite. Many of these stories, in fact the majority, had been imagined by the very same Derek. They were being quoted, verbatim, by Arthur and Charlie, as real – but it made good broadcasting all the same.)

The chatter between the three was now relaxed, and was funny, and silly, at times. Approaching the end of the programme, Daisy changed direction of the talk, bearing in mind the purpose of them being on air was the raising of money for their charities, but the two raconteurs suddenly dried again. They'd used up most of Derek's stories, back to being themselves, and the periods of long chattering had exhausted their brains. Thinking was becoming a strain.

"Sponsors are important for you, aren't they?" Daisy commented. This time two heads nodded happily – but neither spoke.

"Do you have a major sponsor, lads?" This again, brought the nods. Daisy ploughed on.

"Obviously you'll want all the MOGGIES to sponsor you. Will we ask them?"And yet another silent nod. So Granny Wisdom asked of all her loyal fans.

"MOGGIES – will you help them raise money for charity?"

Carol reacted quickly, almost automatically, but cleverly and appropriately, and chipped in with the crowd effect shouting, "Yessssss", followed by a cheer. She'd used this sound effect several times before, but for a moment today, her timing made her feel quite professional again, and it came over the airwaves very effectively.

"Did you hear that? Now you'll have lots more little people supporting you, but do you have a major sponsor?" Daisy persisted.

"Yus," it was Charlie, with a verbal response this time. "Yus, we've gotta shuge sponsor. Our sponsor is gonna be BISK..."

Carol was quick. "Sorry, Charlie, remember you can't say the actual name." At least they had found their tongues again.

"Can we say – it's gonna be a big, big soopermarket 'ats gonna sponsor us?" It was Arthur who'd spoken out this time. "An' we're gonna be wearing shuge t-shirts an' tha'll say their name."

"Of course you can, and I'm sure we are all delighted that they are helping you," said Daisy. "I wonder if it's the same supermarket that I go to..."

"Which one, like, d' you go to, Granny?" asked Charlie.

"BISKO's," answered Granny Wisdom.

"Heaven help me" sobbed Carol and pushed another CD into action...

After the broadcast the two guests were led by Carol out of the studio, back into the Green Room, and given some more refreshments.

"Bye..." shouted Daisy as they went.

"Bye..." and two marathon runners waved a fond farewell to the brown paper bag.

Back in the Green Room they sat, bemused. Had they succeeded in gaining publicity for their marathon? Probably, yes. Had they succeeded in potentially gaining more sponsorship money? Well, that was certainly their hope, but only time would tell. Had they met Granny Wisdom? Yes ...but had they recognised her? A little bit difficult when she was wearing a brown paper bag over her head...

After the show, as usual, Granny Wisdom was to be smuggled back out of the building – the same way as coming in – and to be honest, Daisy was not looking forward to the return journey inside this plastic vertical coffin. Simply climbing back inside the wheelie bin would be difficult in itself. During the broadcast, George had placed the bin outside the door of the studio.

The girl in the office didn't know it shouldn't be used. The large quantity of scrap paper she'd collected would have to go somewhere, and she was delighted find a handy receptacle in which to dispose of it. So George, having to empty a rather full bin, sort of delayed the exiting arrangements.

Back inside the studio, how Daisy should be getting back into the bin was being debated. Carol suggested standing on a chair and jumping. This method would be quick, and at the same time could prove fatal.

After each show Carol's feelings towards Granny Wisdom were never charitable. Daisy with at least a broken leg, would have given Carol's nerves a short rest, but she might have felt a little guilty afterwards. Surprisingly, it was not the method chosen.

No, it had to be the 'putting the bin horizontally and crawling back in' method. Daisy had to do this in a most unladylike manner, and to assist getting the bin upright this time, with Daisy inside, Carol placed her foot in front of a wheel to stop it moving.

She received an enormous bruise for her trouble. Carol told herself she probably deserved it for her nasty thoughts about her favourite presenter, and hobbled off.

With Daisy inside the bin and hidden, George looked out the studio door. It was all clear. The bin was wheeled into the corridor once more, but he stupidly left the van keys behind on the desk. Parking the bin for a moment, he nipped back into the studio.

They left the Green Room, Arthur still finishing his can of orangeade, as he and Charlie tried to guess the identity of Granny Wisdom, the face in a bag. Inside the wheelie bin, Daisy could hear every word being said.

"Betcha she's bin some old dolly bird oo's got too old furra telly. I fink it was whatsername. 'Oo's 'at one ...'ad long legs ...an' like, read the news, an' like, fot she could dance? Wiff ra Morecambe an' Wise Show an' 'at... ? Angie... Angie Fing... Angie... Rippon. Yup, gorrit ...'ats 'oo, yea... it's Angie baby..."

Charlie was very positive about that, and it was a nice boost to the confidence of an old gran stuck in a wheelie bin, getting hotter and hotter. How very sweet – she was like Angela Rippon. Charlie you are a nice boy, she thought.

Then Arthur spoiled it.

"Nah, Charlie ...never 'er."

He took another swig of his orange drink.

"Yerr wrong, I tell yerr. Nowt like Angie Fingy, she 'ad legs up to 'er armpits. No ...'ead in the bag... Tha' warr..."

Arthur drained the very last drop from the orangeade can.

"...Ronnie Corbett, 'ats oo it was ...'im – an' I fott you would have known 'at, Charlie mate ...'im wiff glasses. Yupp ...li'le cuddly Ronnie, it warr."

Granny's smile was now a frown, and she was going off Arthur – fast! Then he made it worse – became almost hated – lifting the wheelie bin lid to tidily dispose of his can – onto Daisy's head...

26

By creating anecdotes about Arthur and Charlie and printing them each week in the Gazette, Derek was doing a good job in keeping the approaching marathon in the public's vision. Sometimes he wished the tales he recounted carried more truth, but they made amusing reading. His two willing subjects were quite proud of the adventures he was concocting, and the fun he was poking at them. They were having crazy adventures in a little artificial world.

Hearing some of his tales recounted to Granny Wisdom, earlier today on her programme disturbed Derek, just a tad – they told them as if they actually happened. Could it be possible, through time, that they believed them to be true? Disturbing though it was, it at least stopped him thinking for a moment about his continuing problem with Sally.

He also was fostering the mystery of Granny Wisdom; who is this mysterious person? Encouraging feed-back from readers now meant a weekly page for MOGGIES' letters in which many members of the listening and reading public chose to voice opinions. However, what was being written made them seem as mentally disturbed as the programme sounded!

Derek wasn't too sure about printing this latest long 'manifesto' lying on his desk. Alarmingly, there was a group calling itself, GWANs – Granny Wisdom's Anarchists and Nationalists.

He perceived them as having the potential of becoming highly active and the root cause of a future revolution. Their sole aim was to drive the UK into unplanned government, claiming their inspiration to be Granny Wisdom's unplanned radio programme.

'*We want Mayhem and Confusion for the People, and We want It Now,*' was their not-very-slick slogan.

To more sensitive readers, the printing of GWAN's objectives might be seen as a big mistake on his part, but the alternative was of it being seen as forward thinking journalism, for which he would be given credit. If he did proceed, tight editorial control would be essential. *Were their aims any worse than the current political situation?* He was undecided. *Would the country notice any difference?*

Wisely, his better judgement won. No, it would not be encouraged...

On Monday evening, when George sat down to his meal, his wife was pleased to note that he was much more relaxed. She couldn't be told the reason. That could not be disclosed until the show came off the air. Only then would she learn of how important he was on Mondays.

Earlier today, the new arrangement to transfer Granny Wisdom worked beautifully. He'd been busy over the weekend with the idea, but fidgety and grumpy, a man with a lot on his mind obviously, but the cause of the agitation unable to be disclosed.

"To do with work," was all he'd tell his good lady. As the radio station's driver, and the person responsible for collecting and delivering Granny Wisdom, he was determined her identity would not be revealed due to any failure of his.

His Saturday visit to the Red-Cross charity shop obtained reject clothing which he'd folded, and instead of Daisy occupying the hamper, he'd filled the usual large laundry basket with these clothes. The hamper was placed in the back of the van, beside the clean and new wheelie bin, with the cushions inside, and the hamper became the decoy...

And it worked: the photographer, foiled again. Tonight George sat back with the satisfaction of knowing that Granny Wisdom's identity remained restricted to only a few, with him being one of them. *The young guy seemed determined though, wanted to make his mark no doubt, and probably thinking himself as being the 'Newingsworth and Slatterfoot and surrounding district's Paparazzi'!*

Disappointingly, Granny Wisdom hadn't seemed quite as pleased as he thought she would have been. *The wheelie bin must have been more comfortable than the hamper, surely. Yes, this was a better way to continue*, unless he could think of something else...

The new technique had very successfully hoodwinked the photographer, but he wasn't the only one who observed this Monday's routine. Another bloke today was more successful and, unfortunately, there was little that George could have done, even if he'd known.

What occurred was without the knowledge of either Daisy or George, and before Daisy even saw the new wheelie-bin...

As Daisy said cheerio to her husband, on what should have been the start of a normal Monday for the two inhabitants of 12 Blytheton Road, she was quite unaware that events were about to form a different pattern. She was oblivious to the fact that he was becoming an increasingly suspicious Hector.

Feeling a tiny bit guilty as usual, she left Blytheton Road to meet George in the car park at Bisko's, knowing Hector left first and was safely on his paper round.

Her day was beginning in a fairly routine manner, developed over the weeks, starting with the walk from home. She liked the walk, with her shopping basket over her arm, and her umbrella always at the ready in her hand. She strode out happily, wishing that she could remember which button was supposed to generate which action, and which was the one she must never touch again? Was it red or green?

Concentrating on the road ahead and the day ahead, she didn't even think of looking behind...

Today was the day he would find out, and he'd organised this in advance – no paper round for him this morning. The other two young lads agreed to split his round between them, even though it could make them late for school, because of the good money he promised. He would trail her – a good old fashioned technique. He wasn't going to use any fancy gizmos, or whatever they were called, for hacking or bugging phones, and suchlike.

He'd learned from the masters like Philip Marlow, Sam Spade, and even Jim Rockford. They'd all used good old fashioned methods, which gave results. He read about them over the years, and watched, and learned about each one's technique, and now, he was pretty confident that he knew what had to be done – but he'd never tried it. *It was just common sense anyhow, couldn't fail this way. You had to follow at a discreet distance, maintaining the suspect in view, but remaining far enough away not to be obvious to the person being trailed.*

This would be a doddle, though an unusual activity for him on a Monday morning. He was getting used to clearing the breakfast dishes, washing and drying them, putting them away and then later, preparing a sandwich or soup, because his dear wife wouldn't return until late afternoon on Mondays. He found it hard to begin with – having been waited-on hand and foot by his wife for most of his married life – but was slowly becoming a bit more used to doing it himself. To a knowledgeable observer, it would be obvious that he had been poorly programmed for self-maintenance.

This Monday was different – he was on a quest. The part he did not look forward to was the discovery of her destination. There could be two possible outcomes as he saw it, either, she would enter Bisko's and take a long time perusing the shelves and purchase things in a leisurely manner with a coffee break included, proving it all to be perfectly innocent, and make him feel foolish, but happy – or there would be an assignation...

A glance at his watch, because something else was at the back of his mind, he had to be back by eleven – he didn't want to miss the Granny Wisdom Show.

There was a busy road to cross and it was always safer, she'd found, to use the pedestrian crossing. There was no rush. A nice pleasant walk helps the relaxation process. Push the button and wait for the green man ...ah ...well done Gran, she told herself, it was the right button for a change, and over we go. Not the sort of road you want to run across, the speed they go along here... Let's take the scenic route this morning.

Now I am on the wrong side of the road, he thought... stay this side and cross over further along. No, safer by the crossing. Push the button and wait ...and wait ...and wait... Quicker staying on this side, just keep her in sight – but walk faster to catch up. No, she's gone round the corner. I could lose her... Going to have to cross over... 'BEEEEEEP.!' – but not yet!

He waited and dodged across halfway, but was then stuck because a long line of vehicles was moving too quickly for him to make it right over. It wouldn't be wise to be knocked down in the middle of the chase by a passing car. He stood impatiently on the centre white line, feeling more and more nervous, with the racing traffic roaring terrifyingly on both sides. He was becoming rapidly apprehensive of his quarry changing direction again while out of sight. *This didn't happen in the books...*

For what seemed like ages he was stuck in the middle, until eventually all the traffic came to a halt, thanks to a pedestrian at the crossing having pressed the button and waited patiently for the 'Green Man' – as he should have done – and it gave him his chance. He was over and around the corner quickly, but where had she vanished to? There was no sign of her. He kept moving. Perhaps he was held up longer than he thought. If she is not in this road, she must be around the next corner. Out of breath, he reached the next corner, he looked along – the road was empty!

Oh no, had she reached her destination? He knew no-one living in any of these houses – but maybe his wife did.

Fortunately, he looked back in the direction of the main road, or he would have missed her, emerging from the public toilet he'd hurried passed a moment ago. One thing not taken into account about females was that, at a certain age – an age his wife was well beyond, a female will rarely pass a public toilet without using the facilities, particularly if feeling nervous...

On leaving the toilet, Daisy turned right and returned to the main road, then turned left.

He was gasping as he rushed back along. He must maintain

vision of the subject – a basic principle of his chosen task. She'd reached the car park at Bisko's, busy as usual, and now she was threading her way through the parked cars, obviously aiming for the pedestrian area, but she stopped, and he did too. She was looking in her shopping bag, and removed a piece of paper. She stood looking at it, but now turning and coming back along this path.

What is she up to? Was she wise to him trailing her? Doing the trick of doubling back to confuse the follower? If she was, it was working... He stopped; pretend to be Philip Marlow, what would he do? Of course, he would get behind her again.

Hector was too exposed, his head visible above the cars if she looked this way. A bigger vehicle to hide behind was what he needed. She was walking faster now.

Quick – the postal van – he could hide behind that, and let her pass, but she was coming towards it now... Had she seen him? She was starting to move much faster – in his direction. Discovered...

He closed his eyes and waited for the rebuke.

The letter in her hand, she'd lifted it before leaving the house, but almost forgot about it. Her 'to-do list' said, remember to post letter, but here she was in the car park, and what had she failed to do? When she looked back towards the post box, it was collection time obviously, and the Royal Mail driver was opening the front of the pillar-box. Could she reach him before the contents were emptied?

Yes ...she made it.

"Nearly didn't catch you," she gasped out. "You can't fool a husband if you forget to post the red herring," and she dropped it into the post bag, the letter addressed to herself.

It would tell that her long-lost aunt in London was unwell and could do with her niece's assistance immediately, for about a week – and would have to be opened in the presence of Hector.

The postman was given a great big grateful beaming smile.

"You are a dear," she said to him.

The comment and smile made the postman's morning. He had the kind of face that people rarely smiled at...

"You are looking good this morning, yourself, Sweetheart," the postman responded, thinking it a nice feeling for a member of the public to be friendly for a change.

"All the better for catching you," she replied in a flirty manner.

I was right! Hector blanched. He heard it all, at the other side of the van. She had been found out – but now he didn't want to know – a postman, but not only that – he was a young man...

What the...? Maybe it's not the...

Off again. Daisy turned on her heel, waved to the postman, now in his van and starting up the engine. Hector ducked behind the smaller cars and made his way in the same direction she'd gone. *Oh-oh, that's not good, she was passing the supermarket entrance, going to the far side of the car park, towards a white van.*

He stopped – shocked – there was a man, and he was obviously expecting her – so, this was not the first time for this caper. He was opening the back door of the van as she smiled and talked happily to him, and she was climbing into the back of his van.

Noooooooooooo ...and the van drove off.

27

Two days later, first thing in the morning, before he went out on his paper round, he said his good-byes to Daisy. She wasn't leaving right away, but would be gone by the time he finished. He mentioned just before leaving he hoped her old aunt would recover. "What is her n-n-n-name again? I've for-g-g-g-g-g-gotten?" he said, feeling almost certain, that this sick old person didn't even exist – and she faltered. She seemed to have forgotten the name. A problem in making up a story, you have to remember the names of the characters you've created. Though he wanted to say that to her, he couldn't, it wasn't absolutely certain that this aunt didn't exist.

Please ...let there be an aunt. He wanted her to exist. It would mean his wife was just telling little fibs, rather than outright lies. To be convinced that his eyes deceived him was his dearest wish, but he'd been shown the letter from her 'supposed aunt'.

'Dear Daisy, Please come urgently. I'm fading fast and I've no-one else to turn to in this big city of London, even though I haven't seen you for years – from your dear old failing Aunty Mary.'

The letter arrived yesterday and was less than convincing... And at least he remembered the name, why couldn't she?

"Aunty ...Mary..." Daisy had spluttered out.

A bit slow, he thought, and unfortunately confirmed the suspicions in his mind. *This business with the aunt – it was the other man, her lover!*

The arrangements for his temporary accommodation were made. Sorted out by Daisy last evening on the phone, but she hadn't spoken to either Sally or Derek because they'd been out. Alexander, who was just visiting, said it would be no problem at all for Hector to come over. When will it be, he asked? Early afternoon, Daisy responded. I'll tell them to expect him then, Alexander had replied in his usual faultless and mannerly voice.

At least Hector was pleased that she put on an act for him – pretended to be a little regretful, having to go and leave him at home. "The freezer is full," she told him, "So, you'll not starve," as if it was some sort of consolation. Now why had she filled the freezer beforehand, and then booked-him-in with the young ones?

"Sally really likes you, and you adore her, don't you?" his two-timing wife told him after the phone call. "She'll look after you – probably spoil you."

She smiled sweetly at him and he smiled sweetly back, but...

So, here he was, now turning into the farm entrance, on his trusty bike, the little suitcase with his essentials strapped onto the rack. He stopped for a rest and looked up and there was the sign as Hammy had said – really pretentious – you could order vegetables by internet, and they'd be delivered to your doorstep. At least, that is what he presumed the 'www' thing was all about. Probably cost an arm and a leg for a carrot – and Hammy wanted them to break in...? Daisy wouldn't be happy to know that, but what the heck did she care. She was off to see her lover...

"T-T-Tipsi-b-b-b-loooming-c-c-corus, we're c-c-c-c-coming to g-g-g-get you," he hollered to the surrounding countryside, and shook his fist at the sign, "... and I'm n-n-not telling D-D-D-D-Daisy. Ya-h-h-h-h-hoo...!" and the yell got rid of a little of the frustration.

An internet site for vegetables indeed – all this modern high-tech nonsense was getting too much. Everybody seemed to be at it. At least some things hadn't changed: his bike still had its reassuring squeak; *only one bike in Newingsworth could squeak, and it was his...*

Yes, think about the good things in your life, he told himself, like how he was really proud of his grandson – but tried not to show it – in case it made him big-headed.

His Derek was writing a book and using his new computer. Hector hadn't seen either yet. Bet my Derek bought a good computer, he told himself, not that he could tell a good one from a bad. Hector had never used a computer, but Derek was a wizard. Maybe he could get a shot on it – Derek would teach him. It would be something to do, seeing he would be here for a while. Anyway, everybody seemed to be able to use a computer these days, except him, oh ...and Daisy. She was absolutely useless when it came to these things. She couldn't even tune in the right station on the radio.

He was looking forward to seeing Sally again, always made him feel really welcome. A lovely girl – never said a harsh word...

Back onto the saddle again to continue along the farm road but he'd moved only a short distance when, suddenly, he was deafened by the loud roar of a motorbike coming from the direction of the farm. It rushed passed. The noise startled him, but it's what motorbikes do, make a noise. It had been a throaty roar, the sound of underused power.

Hector used to have a motorcycle; still had his driving licence, obtained all those years ago during his National Service. Some folk loved National Service, others hated it. He had loved it because that's where he'd learned to ride a motorbike. After leaving the army, he had a bantam of his own for a time.

He gave up the biking to please Daisy. She became too upset when he went out on it, too dangerous in her opinion, and she was probably correct, so, he hadn't been on a bike for years. Those were the days when she cared, when it had been just the two of them – and no fancy-man. It looked as if she wouldn't be around to stop him having a shot on a bike in the future.

The silence returned to the lane, except for the squeak as he pedalled along, his head filling with sad thoughts. He wondered what had happened to Millicent, their daughter. They hadn't heard any more of her after she ran off – leaving Derek with him and Daisy. She could be anywhere in the big wide world and he wouldn't know. It was a really sad spell then, particularly for Daisy. Mothers feel these things more, don't they?

Reaching the cottage, he leaned the bike against the cottage wall and removed the strap holding his little case, the case containing his pyjamas, three spare shirts, underwear, fresh socks, and his toothbrush. What a melancholy mood he was in. He felt lonely, with the silent countryside all around, and no one else near, his wife about to abandon him, and all his worldly possessions crushed in the little box in his hand. Things couldn't get worse...

He looked at his bike, and patted the saddle affectionately.

Bugger it! He had a puncture...

He lifted the doormat and picked up the key, unlocked the front door, and wondered why Sally and Derek even bothered locking it. They would be more careful if they lived in the centre of town, would have to be...

Derek and Sally weren't home, wouldn't be back until after six. So, he made himself a cup of tea, found some chocolate digestive biscuits, and settled down to watch the telly for a while – and promptly dozed off.

28

What a let-down! Her mind had been set on it, she could have convinced others, ethical or not, but now knocked on the head, thanks to an uncooperative next door neighbour.

So close to being an author...   It isn't going to happen now, not unless I write something myself, she realised, *and some hope of that!* Sally's desperate desire to get back at Sophie Clerkenwell-Brown, that couldn't happen either now, could it? The plan wouldn't work...

Was there anything she could have done differently? Is there anything else she could still do? The day was spoiled already and she hadn't even been to work yet.

The other two were sorely missed. Somehow being together helped her to think – it was group synergy with Sally, Muriel and herself, and much less personal effort.

Should she phone them at work? No, leave a note and ask them to wait up for her again. If nothing else, a shoulder to cry on would be the result, but maybe something could come out of the three heads getting together later.

Thelma flopped down into the chair feeling frustrated in so many ways. How things had changed since coming to 40 Cloverton Avenue. This was where she lived now, but only thanks to her brother's goodwill.

It could have been her house, but it wasn't, not one little bit of it. She lost any claim to it by the clear stipulation of her father's Will. All bequeathed to Alexander, and rightly so, although admitted only to herself, when she was thinking rationally. She behaved like a spoiled kid at a party, when she was young, but it did not excuse her.

When it had happened, she was more than a kid, old enough to foolishly up-sticks and leave home in a furious temper. She should have known better, and was totally lacking self-control. Her poor mother, she faded away, mainly because of that wilful and spiteful action.

A long spell of penance, but she'd done that, hadn't she? She'd made her own way in life up till recently, with no family links. Regretfully, any of her friendships over the years became difficult and short because of her spiteful attitude to life.

She succeeded in her work, though. She could drive herself and others fairly mercilessly. That is how it used to be. Alcohol was her solace, creating false courage on many occasions. Becoming dependent on 'another little drink' had been steadily happening, but now... No drinking, well maybe sometimes, but in moderation only. She had learned her lesson, but also knew that it could be so easy to slip again.

The biggest influence in her life was during this last year, being reconciled with Alexander and getting to know Muriel and Sally; feeling part of a family again, and living with them in this house. Now Sally was having problems. It would be nice if she could make up with Sweaty. How horrible if Sally became so entrenched that she turned out a re-incarnation of the younger Thelma.

Muriel, she liked a lot. To her eyes though, her twin brother and his wife had an odd arrangement. Love was fairly obvious, but was slightly lop-sided, with the male caring just a little bit less and getting away with murder at the same time. If her brother had been her husband, she certainly wouldn't let him off with many of the things that Muriel accepted. A simple example was the clothes, the female clothes. He seemed a normal straight-laced bank manager on the outside, but Thelma suspected there were deeper problems...

Goodness, look at the time, standing here dreaming, she'd have to be off to join her favourite Bingo Manager with the wandering hands, and a merry band of housey-housey hopefuls, but before that, there would have to be a quick sandwich, a coffee, and a note to leave for Muriel and Sally.

'Sorry to tell you, the bitch next door...'

No, terrible, couldn't put that...

'Sorry to tell you, that silly cow next door...'

No, that's worse: third time lucky...

'Please wait up for me, we must talk. That silly bitch of a cow next door refused to let me have the story. See you later, love Thelma.'

Much better!

29

Alexander was first to return to the Manor, dressed in his Lycra cycling outfit as usual – not normally viewed as the appropriate clothing for a bank manager, but definitely his preferred gear for travelling by bike.

Cycling, the favourite mode of transport for Alexander long before he met Muriel, became one of the activities that helped develop their early relationship. Nothing could have avoided it becoming a healthy habit for the rest of the small Davidson clan, as it did, but whereas cycling was a bonding process, every so often, other things put their relationships to the test, like his selfish behaviour. Time and time again he promised to be a better boy in the future.

Currently, he liked to think selfishness played no part: this staying with his son-in-law, and his choosing not to live under the same roof as his daughter. *He was doing this for Derek...*

Journeying between the cottage and the Bank in Slatterfoot, meant leaving a little earlier and returning a little later than if he'd been at home in Cloverton. Tonight, he was back before Derek, but someone else was here too. The television was blaring.

Lying in the chair snoring was Hector. This triggered a memory: *a phone call yesterday to say Hector would be arriving. Did he mention it to Derek? No. Was it too late to contact him? Yes, it was much too late. He would be already on his way. Oh well ...let the old fellow sleep.*

Anyway, there were more important things on his mind, like getting Derek to go on-line and have a look at the web site, the one advertised on the notice board at the end of the road – but he could do it himself, couldn't he, unless Derek had created a password?

He'd meant to check while at the bank, but other work had occupied him and then, when he did have a moment, it slipped his mind. This organisation, '*Tipsicorus International*' ...he was curious where their headquarters might be. They'd obviously managed without his help so far, so they must have finances with some bank other than his, possibly in Europe. He knew he wasn't the only fish in the big sea but around this area he reckoned, when people needed financial advice and assistance, he was the top minnow.

Alexander switched on Derek's computer. It seemed remarkably lacking in content for a journalist and prospective novelist. 'Must try harder' he would have written in his son-in-law's report card if he'd been his schoolmaster – and no password control on his machine either, tut, tut, tut... So, on-line he went. Surprisingly, access to the internet was reasonably quick, better than at the bank sometimes.

www.tipsicorusinternational.com/specialvegetation

Check the spelling – now input – and what do we get? Hmm...? The screen looked very strange for a bulk producing greengrocer ...was it the Amazonian jungle?

He moved the cursor to the words, 'Do you want to order some good stuff?' He typed in, 'yes'. Another screen popped up asking, "Are you sure?" and again he typed in, 'yes'.

'The best quality assured,' was on the next one on the top line, and below in red lettering, 'Check no-one is watching'. He did so and pressed 'enter' – and came to an abrupt stop!

'No access without the correct password'.

So, he was none the wiser. He closed the system down again and went into the spare room, the room with a single bed for visitors. Next door contained a double bed for the residents, and should have been Sally and Derek's. As the sitting visitor he had already claimed the single bed and would fight anyone who disputed it. Derek had the big bed.

Hector awoke, surprised to find Alexander back here tonight after Daisy telling him that he was just visiting.

"So, you'll be g-g-g-g-g-going home t-t-t-tonight then?" stated

Hector tentatively.

Alexander responded with a negative shake of the head.

"N-N-N-No... Ah... Well, who is s-s-s-s-sleeping in the ...v-v-v-v-visitor's b-bed?" continued Hector.

A diplomatic shrug of his shoulders was Alexander's reply.

"Y-y-you are. Oh, r-r-r-r-right..."

Huh... so much for Daisy booking in advance... Hector sat up straight and wakened up properly, and remembered that Hammy was coming round tonight, to talk tactics. *Would Alexander still be here?*

Anyway, no need to argue about the sleeping arrangements, someone would be home shortly who would sort it out – his Sally. She liked him and she was always arguing with her father, so if he smiled at the right time, he would get the single bed. Anyway, he'll tell her that Daisy p-p-p-pre-booked him. First booking gets priority – that has always been the rule – standard procedure when there is conflict.

Would it be Sally or Derek returning first? He sort of hoped it would be Sally. He really liked her – best thing to have happened to Derek in years.

"Grandad, what are you doing here?"

The welcome from Derek was less warm than he expected. Sally will sort it out when she gets in, he told himself, but further disappointment – Sally would not be back...

What? She's staying at Cloverton? Right... Ah well, so he would be sleeping with Derek then... Why is Derek not smiling? Grandad sensed that things would probably get worse, and he was correct...

If Derek didn't know he would be here, what would there be for tea? When he looked in the cupboards earlier he found only the chocolate digestives, no real food, and if Derek has just brought food for two...? Oh well then, it'll have to divide into three instead.

Meals had been ad hoc for Derek and Alexander, both being reluctant to cook. If it came to the bit, there was the possibility Derek could pass himself with a super cheese sandwich but only if bread, or rolls, were in the house, and if cheese was sitting waiting in the fridge – tonight – there was nothing.

Derek had been to Bisko's on the way back and grabbed two

microwaveable curries. These he carefully measured out between three, with each man jealously eyeing up the portion being allocated to each plate.

His grandad's presence had been a bit of a surprise to Derek when he returned. The next surprise came when there was a knock at the door just when he was about to take the first mouthful of food.

Opening the door, Derek discovered a man standing on the step that he'd known as 'the farmer up the road', who happened to also be his grandad's pal from way back.

"Hello, Mr Macintosh, how are you doing?" he said, and they stood looking at each other on the doorstep.

"Urr ye no' lettin' me in, Sunshine?" asked Hammy. "Yerr grandad's here, is he no'? Did he no' tell ye ah wis comin', son?"

"No, Mr Macintosh," and in Hammy came.

"Yerr supposed tae ask me, as ah come through yerr door, 'Ye'll have hud yerr tea?' because ah huvnae. Ah hope ye've goat a wee bite tae spare..."

So, Derek watched hungrily, as the three small portions of the meal were consumed by Hector, Alexander, and Mr Hamish Macintosh...

30

Muriel and Sally were worried – for Thelma. From the note she'd left, Thelma sounded upset – and small wonder – the cheek of that woman next door. It was not surprising Thelma was upset. She had set her heart on becoming an author – even though it was to be by a short cut. Then what a disappointment for Thelma when she returned home to find her theory of three heads being better than one could not stand up to close scrutiny. In fact it was proving totally wrong.

The other two could think of no way, other than blackmail, to make the plan succeed, and the strength of the blackmail threat was weak. Exposing the fact that Mrs Masterton was a secret bingo fanatic, and had been for ten years while a resident of Cloverton, wasn't quite enough. Now, if they'd had some evidence that she was actually a terrorist working secretly for Al-Qaeda – that could have worked.

Muriel and Sally gave up and drifted off to bed. Thelma took up the Motor Cycle Magazine and wondered how many years of 'bingo shifts' it would take to save enough for a bike.

To hear the front doorbell ringing at nine o'clock in the morning was neither what Thelma expected, nor wished, especially as no-one else was in the house at this time but her. She felt dreadful, hadn't slept at all well, and if climbing out of bed at nine to answer the doorbell wearing her dressing gown, meant being handed either a bottle of milk or a letter, then heaven help the delivery person.

It was Mrs Masterton.

"I'm terribly sorry to bother you, Thelma, dear. If I'd known you hadn't had a chance to put on your make-up yet, I'd have left it a little longer. I just wanted a wee word. Could I possibly come in?"

Was that the manuscript for the book she had in her hand? It looked like the same envelope – but it might not be. Thelma was now wide awake. Why was this woman who gave her the silent treatment yesterday now smiling at her? Thelma felt uncomfortable – a feeling of foreboding...

"What a lovely kitchen," said the unwelcome visitor, as she firstly looked, then sidled, into the room, wiping surfaces with her finger in a natural action as if checking for dust, and inspecting each of the many cooking and baking devices, as she did the circuit. Was this an official inspection? Did this have to happen regularly? Muriel hadn't warned her about this.

"Strange isn't it," she continued, "all these years living next door to dear Alexander and Muriel, and this the first time I've actually been in the house. How lovely..."

"Could I ask ...ehhh...?" started Thelma, not quite sure what was happening.

"...Oh yes, how lovely, but only if you are making one. Of course, you are just up, and you've not had any breakfast. So, when you are making toast..." Thelma hoped this conversation would be going somewhere pleasant – eventually. Being in the kitchen beside all these long sharp knives was such a temptation...

"Dear me," the woman continued, "I should have explained why I am here. I couldn't sleep last night for thinking of the disappointed look on your face when you left my house, and after me making you coffee..." (Thelma remembered the coffee being brought into the room, but didn't remember even having a sip of it) "...and I realised how much you must have loved my writing. So, instead of putting it away in a drawer to collect dust, just because I don't want to spend a lot of money on it, I thought it would be a nice gesture if I were to let you have it. And maybe, someday, after I've gone, you can become rich and famous, because of me."

"How much?" asked Thelma.

"Three thousand," replied the author.

"Two – maximum."

"Two thousand – five hundred."

"Done," smiled the new author, offering her hand for the deal-binding shake.

31

It is true what they say about no rest for the wicked, thought Derek. *How long is my penance to be?* He asked this question rhetorically, as he lay uncomfortably on the settee in the living room, unable to stretch out to his full length, and beginning to feel cramp in at least one leg. It was a difficult choice, either the settee, or three in a double bed, sharing with two inebriates, Hector and Hammy. They were sound asleep. He could hear them snorting and whistling.

Alexander was in the bed he'd used since he came here, the spare one, a single bed, on his own and happily sound asleep as well, if the grin on his face was anything to go by. The same grin was on display when Derek tucked him in at some ungodly hour during the night. If his father-in-law hadn't brought out the bottle of whisky, the three of them maybe wouldn't be drunk, but they'd emptied it. He shouldn't have opened the second bottle. It was inevitable then that the trio would aim to empty it too ...and they did!

Derek had shown restraint. He'd been good, for all the benefit it had been for him.... Only one drink, hence he remained sober, and then had to be the person cajoling and guiding the other three into beds – fully dressed.

Dressed already, will save them all time in the morning, he forced himself to accept in the early hours, though he didn't mean it – he really didn't give a fig.

This settee was not designed for sleeping. He tried turning, and found the first empty bottle had somehow got wedged between the cushions he was lying on, so he extracted it, stood up, lay down, and started again. He tossed and turned, but no sleep. He kept thinking about what his grandad, and his pal, were intending to do. Two old men, going to break into Hammy's old farm and repossess the box that Hammy said contained his family fortune.

Crazy... It was a ten-foot high fence...

He'd tried to talk them out of it, but wasn't overly confident of having succeeded.

Derek knew all about fences – being on the wrong side of an even higher one between him and Sally. There was still no direct communication, and poor Spider, he was doing a good job, but at some point he was going to say, no, and then what?

At work yesterday, Derek made use of him again by asking him to say how sorry he was to Sally, and also to tell her that he really loved her dearly, and wanted her back home with him, please.

He'd felt a bit of a mutt saying it to another man, but poor Spider, he felt even worse at having to listen to it, and then repeat it to Sally, but the abject apology failed, anyway. The poor guy was close to tears himself when he came back with Sally's reply. It was simply, "Get lost – and do your own dirty work." Yes, such an affectionate response.

Rob seemed scared of talking to Sally, and he gave Derek funny looks every time they spoke or if he passed his desk, as if something more serious was known by him and that it was totally Derek's fault.

Leaving the office, working mostly at the cafe, was how Derek coped with the job recently. This made it easier for the others, letting some normality return because, according to Spider, Sally was apparently perfectly sweet when he wasn't there.

Lying on the settee in the early hours of the morning, Derek was lonely. He was lonely, tired, and starving. He had been certain there were some digestive biscuits in the cupboard, chocolate covered, that he could munch and at least take away the hunger, but some sod had beaten him to them. He would be up and out before the others wakened and call in at the cafe for breakfast. That was his intention. Let them find out for themselves that the cupboard was bare.

Eventually, he fell asleep, but it was a restless sleep, and he dreamed...

He was wearing a halo, sitting on his throne, and in the big car, but the car was at a funny angle. Sophie was having a bath, in the muddy stream, modestly with all her clothes on. Sally was there too, and was in a good mood, not talking to him, of course, but in a good mood. She started washing Sophie's blonde hair – with mud. Then they had a cuddle, and someone shouted, "Surprise", and they began the wrestling match, and started ripping off each other's clothes. Derek was supposed to be referee, but he didn't like to interfere – two girls wrestling in mud? Would you stop them? He just wanted to watch. He climbed off his throne. Then, he jumped out of the car, and he was way high above the earth. So he did free fall, among fluffy clouds, and was very brave. He didn't open his parachute until he was only one hundred feet above the ground – and, even then, he just jumped the last bit, and ...he was back in the mud.

When he wakened at six o'clock, the house was silent. He wished he'd taken more of the whisky and then there would be a reason for feeling so bad. He tip-toed into the bathroom and had a shower, then with fresh underwear, and clean shirt, and a spray of deodorant, he felt like a new man. He dodged the shave, although he really needed one, not chancing the possibility of wakening the others with the buzz of his electric razor.

Anyway, who cared what he looked like – Sally didn't!

32

She was now an author. Thelma could not keep the news to herself, and in the circumstances felt justified to be phoning Sally and Muriel at their workplaces to tell them, and they were delighted to hear it, Sally especially. They would be able to get back at Ms Sophie Clerkenwell-Brown after all. The dislike Sally had for that female grew in intensity each day, though there was little justification for the hatred building steadily in her mind.

Of course, Sophie had no idea of the feelings she'd engendered by innocently assisting a collapsed runner (good old Derek), but it had been decreed by Sally that one day vengeance would be served. That is the way she felt and if Sophie had to suffer – tough! It's the way the cookie crumbled...

Derek was out on an assignment, so she didn't have to bother not talking to him. It was difficult when he was in the office, using Spider the way she did, difficult for Spider. She knew it was unfair, but it had to go on, and she didn't think Spider really minded too much.

So, now was the time. With Spider in the outer office, doing his thing, and Rob in his inner office, doing his thing, this was the chance for her to do her thing. The phone call from Aunt Thelma about securing the manuscript meant the plan for retribution could move forward. The aim now was to work out a strategy to cause the maximum inconvenience and embarrassment to Ms Clerkenwell-Brown – make life awkward for her – and at the same time earn a fortune for Aunt Thelma.

Firstly, how could Mrs Masterton's name be removed from the records officially at the publishers? Secondly, now she had sold the story, could Mrs M be persuaded to send an email to confirm it? She could be told what to send, couldn't she? Oh no, telling her wouldn't be wise, if that was done she would do the opposite. No, this requires a little soft soap...

It would need to be done carefully, so, Sally sat, and she thought, until, yes, the content could be...

Dear Ms Sophie Clerkenwell-Brown,

Before future visits are made by you, or a representative of your good-selves, to my home as happened recently, it is time for me to come clean and make a confession. I am sending you this email because it is too embarrassing to say directly face to face. I have deceived you. I am not the author of the story, 'The Big Squeal', and I am not Ivy Bloom.

Ms Thelma Davidson, my dear next door neighbour, is the true writer of this wondrous tale, and as a big favour – for someone who is an extremely shy individual and desires anonymity – I suggested that I should submit it for publishing. Having been instrumental in encouraging her to write this story in the first place, I was horrified when she said she would be putting it in a cupboard rather than giving the world the chance to enjoy it.

"Give it to me. I will submit it in my name and we will sort it all out when the time is right," I bravely told her – and the time, now, is right.

Since the visit of Ms Sophie Clerkenwell-Brown, I have convinced Ms Davidson that the world deserves her story, and I have managed to cajole this shy person into coming out of her lonely shell, and to at least be willing to talk to you, even if nothing comes of it.

I feel it would be good for her morale. My conscience will then be clear, and I may once again sleep at nights.

Your humble servant,

Mrs Violet Masterton (aka, wrongly, Ivy Bloom).

That was it – she'd done it.

Sally looked up. Rob and Spider hadn't even moved.

Last night's meeting after Thelma's return from work proved

unproductive, but tonight's started off well. Thelma and Muriel read the communication concocted by Sally, purporting to be Mrs Masterton's words and were impressed but, not surprisingly, Muriel saw Mrs Masterton as a big difficulty.

According to Thelma, Mrs Masterton's personality changed overnight, and this morning, she had been willing to sell – why? "The minute she came through the door it was, 'Please call me Violet', which just about floored me. After the nosy cow viewed the kitchen, she wanted a conducted tour of the house – updating her records, no doubt, back in her own place. 'Make me a coffee,' she said, and me still in my dressing gown, and then she said she was a 'silver surfer'. Six months now, she's been going to the Mature Citizens' Club at the library. She's learned all about computers, she tells me and then, 'I've become an expert', and her with no attempt at modesty. Oooh – I can't stand the woman!"

"So, there's the answer," said Sally, "She could send it when she goes to the library," but, would she go along with that idea, each wondered?

As they trooped off to sleep in their separate bedrooms, Muriel was pleased how this was developing, particularly for Sally. It was absorbing her evenings, and thankfully, it had stopped her playing dirges on the piano.

Next morning, Thelma called on her 'friend', Violet, expecting a difficult task, but when she asked her to send the email she received a reasonably pleasant response. Thelma was suspicious. There must be an ulterior motive...

"Of course I will," Mrs Masterton smiled, "...and I will even do spell-check, and correct it grammatically for you. I find that so easy to do..."

This was the same person who would willingly have pushed Thelma under a bus if there had been one, that evening outside the bingo hall. "But how will Sophie Thingy know it's really you?" asked Thelma. That thought hadn't occurred last night...

"I'll tell her to phone Miss Simpson, the librarian – she thinks I am wonderful and she'll vouch it's me standing beside her. Now don't you worry, dear Thelma, leave it to me," was the confident reply.

Thelma was even more suspicious ...but Sally's idea did work.

Sophie Clerkenwell-Brown was on her way.

An oddly worded email had been received with a message from someone she imagined to be a very odd person, Violet Masterton. The librarian was contacted, and happily confirmed the identity of the lady named as the one who'd sent the 'Top Secret' email, and yes, she certainly agreed, she was a very odd person indeed – but also an important member of the Silver Surfer's Club.

'Silver Surfers, oh, how exciting...' Sophie had remarked, with a grimace ...but now, she was on her way to meet the author, the real one this time.

The new address sitting on the dashboard, having been previously fed to the satnav, was still Cloverton Avenue – number 40 this time. If Masterton was 38, it was next door. Wouldn't it be funny, if it was the address she visited before – where Derek's aunt was working as the maid – no – it wouldn't be at all funny! Meeting her again could be embarrassing, particularly if there was recognition that linked her with the cottage incident. Thank goodness that didn't happen last time.

Visual familiarity of the area she was entering was comforting, and her satnav giving her the usual sexy confirmation that she was near the destination.

What would happen if I were to bump into Derek again, she wondered? She smiled to herself as she remembered him carrying her into the cottage. He would be putty in my hands. Bets are, he'd be up for it – as long as his wife and relatives didn't suddenly appear again. Sex can be ruined by that sort of thing.

Here we are then, and we are looking for number forty – but ...this is the house I have already... Oh...

"Hello again Sophie, I am Thelma, in case you hadn't remembered my name from the last time," said this very effusive woman. "Please come in."

It is the maid again, and, she remembers my name, but obviously doesn't recognise me from before at Derek's. Sophie was relieved. *The maid is surely not the one who wrote the story, but she said Thelma, didn't she?*

"This is such a thrill. It's lovely to be able to expose yourself: to admit it all, don't you think, Sophie?"

Sophie did a double-take: rumbled.

"...I mean me – as an author of course. Here I am. It was me all along," Thelma smiled. "We all have our little secrets, haven't we? Of course we have, but we can't hide them forever, dear Sophie – the truth will out, won't it?"

33

Alexander, not surprisingly, overslept, but he knew nothing rested on him being at the bank punctually. His employees were well trained and didn't need him to tell them their duties.

He was grateful that the bank was next door to the bakers – a very high quality baker. Normally he made use of this benefit only at coffee breaks – he had a standing order of 'cream cake of the day' – on his way in today though, he would order a bacon roll, and eat it in the office, privately. In fact he would order two, to make up for last night's measly portions.

As he left, the closing of the front door of the cottage was a bit noisier than intended. There were two consequences. One, was that he heard the sound to be more like a clap of thunder in his aching head, which caused him to question the legality of him pedalling his two-wheeled transporter to work. The other, was that two recumbent figures inside the cottage in the warm and cosy double bed, stirred.

Both old fellows awoke, and immediately felt discomfited by the presence of another person's nose, in close proximity. Even though they were friends of more than fifty years, waking up in a strange bed, not knowing how they got there, and finding that, while they slept, each had been cuddling his best mate, just had to lead to a swift reaction.

It was a mirror image, as two stiff elderly men rapidly swung their legs out their own side of the bed, each to grab at a head which continued to spin, and to let out a slow and pathetic "Ohhhhhh..."

Hector was quick to realise the time. He was late – for the papers, his morning papers. A large part of Newingsworth was relying on his early morning deliveries. He was letting them down. Breakfasts would be delayed, husbands couldn't leave to catch the train for work, and, if he didn't deliver, his customers would have to resort to morning telly. So, he moved quickly. Personal hygiene would have to wait. Being late was not his style.

Hammy was ignored. He didn't mind. He laid himself back down in the soft bedding and fell asleep again. For him, nothing required rushing, so, when he awoke over an hour later, he didn't mind rising. The sun was shining, the birds singing, but one thing was missing – no chickens wandering round, scraping, and scratching and pecking constantly, to talk with. They never actually talked back but they did listen to him grumble about things which bothered him on any day. Some days he told them of happy events. It might have been his imagination, but when he thought of it now, hadn't there been more eggs on the days he told them the good news?

He had hoped to have cadged a better meal than last night's effort, but as they say, beggars can't be choosers. After a late morning shower, he dressed, and in his jacket pocket found the bar of chocolate to chase off the hunger: an emergency food supply, conveniently forgotten last night. A bar of chocolate wouldn't have gone very far if he'd shared it with four, now would it?

There was plenty instant coffee, so he sat and contemplated his day. No sense in going home just now. He'd have to call a taxi, and anyway, tonight was the night. A fence to be climbed and then, Bob's your uncle.

His old farm was ringed by a high wire mesh fence, he knew that much, or at least he thought he did. He did only see the entrance, with the chain and padlock on the gate. Maybe he should have a look around, reconnoitre, as they say in France, though when Hammy said the word out loud with his accent, it didn't exactly sound French.

Going along the farm lane wouldn't be the best idea. He might meet some of the people who worked there, and be recognised later. A question triggered in his mind, which had been bugging him during his sober moments last night and for which he hadn't thought of an answer – *who did work there*?

He would have thought there would have been a minibus

delivering 'slaves' to look after the vegetables – it's what they advertised as their product – but he'd seen no workers coming and going. Surely they didn't all live on the premises. Of course, since giving up the farm, he wasn't moving in the same circle of gossips, and maybe he was just out of touch.

Last night, Sinbad said he'd nearly been knocked down by a motorcyclist, coming from the farm, so there was some activity.

The surrounding countryside was pretty well known to him, and so it should be, him having farmed here for a long time. So, leaving the cottage, it was the back path he chose, leading into the wooded area and across the fields.

It was only a mile by road, a little further by this other route, but he was in no rush and could treat it as a casual stroll. He had to be careful crossing the stream – the stepping stones could be quite slippery at times. He remembered how he used to catch rabbits in this part and they'd finish up in the pot, lovely, living off the land, thanks to the cooking expertise of his dear departed wife Sybil. Then there were the foxes – always after his poultry – succeeded sometimes. What a mess they made. He didn't relish the thought of trying to cope with all that again, anyway, he probably couldn't. Working every day and living off the land was in the past. Today, he was relying on his old mate, Hector, going to the supermarket and bringing back some tinned food – much easier.

He reached the fence.

As expected, it was a big circle but only around the buildings, the fields were all outside. Might as well follow it all the way and see the best place to climb over, he thought, but he stood for a moment, gazing at the building which had been his home for such a long time – it still looked much the same, but surprisingly with no activity to be seen. Someone should be doing something, surely, even if they were only using the farm as a depot, like transferring vegetables to delivery vehicles, but no vehicles in evidence, except a motorcycle.

The fields that his father's cows had grazed in, and his poultry had scratched and scraped at, they hadn't been cultivated either. Where were the ploughs and tractors? They'd need these surely, if they were going to make it a profitable business? Then again, he sold the farm for such a stupidly low price, maybe they didn't need to use the fields. This old place had cost them so little.

"Och well, it's their business, but Ah jist wish a' this was still mine's – ah miss mah wee chooky hens," and he carried on round the remainder of the fence. He was glad he still had the key for the back door, the door which led into the kitchen, but what if they'd changed the locks for the house, the way they changed the fencing?

Looking at his old place through slightly misted eyes, he didn't notice the three CCTV cameras, positioned at high points to give an all round view of the fence. These were new, and every footstep Hammy took was being monitored.

Though the person watching the screens was concerned at the activity, no action would be needed, provided this old guy remained on the right side of the fence – the right side being the outside.

34

"But Alexander, look on it as an investment. I'd have expected you, of all people, to jump at this chance." Muriel was amazed at his reluctance when she phoned him. It was only £2,500 and he was being niggardly with the money. Thelma had no money, and she owed Mrs Masterton.

By using her own savings, Muriel could easily have helped Thelma out, Sally could have also, but, there was a principle involved here, decided beforehand, that Muriel would persuade Alexander to donate the money to this good cause. It was his duty, the three females agreed – and anyway – he was loaded.

Maybe phoning from Bisko's cash office to the bank wasn't such a good idea. He was in the middle of a meeting with a client, they told her, but the clerk put her through right away when she said who she was and that it was urgent, which, not surprisingly, put her husband in a bad mood.

"...And your name will be at the front of the book. You will be the one to whom the book is dedicated. It will tell the world how you, Alexander, her dear twin brother, was her only truly close family, always there for her, giving her all the love and support she needed to help her write this story, the one who inspired her, the one person she could look up to, and rely on, the one who supported her in her hour of need, and all she asks of you is ...a little money."

Muriel was quite proud of that speech, impromptu too, and on reflection, only having dramatic music in the background like, 'Land of hope and glory', could have improved it...

Alexander just wanted the conversation to end. The client had left his office temporarily, because apparently it had been an important call.

"And you are trying to tell me Thelma wrote this story?"

"Who else would?" Muriel asked logically. "It wasn't me, it wasn't you, it wasn't Sally, and it certainly wasn't Sweaty. So, who else is there, but Thelma?" She hadn't directly lied to her husband, relying on his being pretty dumb at times for a bank manager, stubborn too – she knew that of old – and hence why it was decided he was to be the one to pay. It was a little personal tussle and Muriel had to win.

"And for only £2,500 a publisher will print this and sell it in the supermarkets? It certainly seems a bargain," he said to confirm he hadn't misheard.

Ah, there was a touch of submission creeping in, and a tiny bit of enthusiasm too, she sensed.

"Tell you what, it does seem too good to be true, but it might give Thelma some income of her own and she could pay for a motorcycle with her own cash – I'll do it..."

Muriel was about to add, he should think himself lucky that he was just being pestered for this small sum, because if Thelma persists with the idea of the motorcycle, it will be another twenty thousand she will be after – but some things are best not said.

"Don't tell Thelma, but I would like a copy of the story."

He considered it was his entitlement anyway if he was paying two and half grand for it. "When you get home, use my copier in the study," he instructed his wife. "I'll pop in on my way back to the cottage, and collect it."

It was obvious to Alexander, if it was something Thelma had written, and a publisher had been willing to take it on at a bargain price, then it could mean any old crap would sell these days.

He was going to show it to his son-in-law. If Thelma could do it, secretly, and with no fuss, and that is all it would cost to put it onto the shelves, then what's wrong with Sweaty's creative abilities? What the hell's holding the boy back? If it would force his son-in-law to get on with it, he might even offer to support him, he conjectured, but the emphasis was on 'might'...

Muriel put the phone down and gave a little whoop. For once, she'd beaten him at his own confidence games. She couldn't wait to tell Sally and Thelma. What a good team, and they would be happy too, now that the money for Mrs M was in the bag.

How long can we remain a team, Muriel wondered? When Sally leaves, she'll be missed, although it doesn't seem too likely yet. It wasn't right for Sally not to be living with her husband. Sweaty was a nice bloke. Muriel liked him. Why did he have the fling with the Sophie girl? It was odd. Could it be something to do with Sally, wanting a baby?

As a mother, Muriel saw the broodiness developing in her daughter – at least she was convinced she could – and as Sally's mother she knew, without having to be told, it was almost certainly because she and Derek had been trying – without success. *Yes, that is the problem – and poor Sweaty. Failure has made him behave strangely. It is so obviously the cause, yes, as usual, Sweaty's fault...*

She could see why he had been up to mischief though. *Sophie whatshername, she was really stunning. What would have happened that day if they had been discovered a moment later? Were they about to ...you know? If Sally, Muriel, and her, hadn't nipped it in the bud, who knows?*

She had a sudden vision of the scene. *There was Sophie standing naked and proudly displaying all her assets, turning and moving towards Sweaty – Sweaty standing in the middle of the floor, beside a pile of discarded clothes, baring all now, same as Sophie, and obviously becoming excited by the view before him...*

Muriel could picture it all. Sweaty with a...

She shook herself. This was not the sort of way a mother-in-law should be thinking about her daughter's husband...

35

Hector was knackered. Starting off from the cottage in the morning feeling rough, having had to quickly repair the puncture before even beginning, ploughing on with his paper deliveries, satisfying all his regulars – who, incidentally, noticed no difference in the times of deliveries – and then cycling back to Bisko's in town to do the shopping, would have floored anyone! Yet, here he was now – shopping in Bisko's.

Going around the superstore without instructions was unusual; no note in hand in Daisy's own neat handwriting, stating exactly what he was permitted to transfer from a shelf into a trolley; no re-cycled bags with him either to hold the listed items, which later would hang from the handlebars of his trusty bike for transfer home. Only one thing was with him today – the bike.

Discovering how Derek and Alexander were eating almost nothing but carry-outs and microwaveable ready-made food packs since Alexander arrived, Hector decided the other three males required a better diet: they needed real food. Now, what would Daisy have told him to buy? Concentrating like mad to remember where items should be, his march around the store began; decisions would be made by him – and him alone.

So ...what'll it be?

Potatoes, one pack: onions, one pack: carrots, one pack: minced beef, half a kilo, hmmm ...and eggs, two dozen, all right, so far. ...Milk, two plastic cartons: two loaves of brown bread: chocolate biscuits, a must-have, and two bottles of whisky – Daisy would frown at that. Anyway, would Daisy ever come back to him? He lifted two recyclable bags and placed them in the trolley, in case she didn't...

In no time at all his trolley, full of essentials, was being wheeled towards the check-out. He'd given up caring. It could be the wrong items, but he'd tried hard and exhausted himself – he was feeling the pressure.

"See – I can do it, Daisy," was murmured smugly to himself, "...without you."

"Pardon?" said the woman, standing in front of him in the queue.

Remounting the bike required extra care – he would be conveying important glass whisky bottles – off he went. Halfway along the road, he had a sudden thought – *would any of the other three of them know how to cook this stuff?* He didn't...

Access to the cottage was by a fairly fast and busy road and was a greater distance for him to travel than normal. It felt dicey, and he was relieved to arrive back safely. At times it had been a hairy journey. The heavy bags hanging on the handlebars caused his steering to feel excessively wobbly. Probably his tiredness made it seem worse but, importantly, he made it with the bottles intact.

Being welcomed at the door by Hammy was a surprise, and so too was being helped by him to carry the bags. Hector guessed correctly – Hammy was starving!

Hammy could prepare the mince, while he was having a wash.

"Huh! ...No, ah've nae chance wi' mince, Sinbad. Ye've goat somethin' ah can cook, easy-peasy, bu' whit made ye get mince?"

Yes, eggs, he could cook.

Hector was grateful and too tired for discussion, so eggs it would be – by Masterchef Hammy. For years, eggs were this man's livelihood, in fact, his life – and his party trick!

Not many people could juggle four eggs at a time, but he was getting rusty at it – stopping could turn out messy – and anyway, with only two dozen purchased, each egg was precious. The trick was left for another time.

Meanwhile, Hector grabbed a much-needed shower; the woman in the queue, at Bisko's, hadn't been standing farther away just because she thought he talked to himself...

The timing of the shower and the preparation of the meal

fortunately coincided, so, the two of them sat down to an acceptable lunch of scrambled egg on toast. As they ate, Hector heard what his friend did without him earlier in the day, the reconnoitring of his old farm.

"Thur's naebuddy aboot up therr, Sinbad – it's aw deed as a dodo, ah'm sorry tae huvv tae tell ye."

"D-d-d-did you not see the m-m-m-motorbike b-bloke?"

"Och aye, well ...ah saw the bike. Ah wis in the fields at the back, so's they widnae see me," Hammy stated confidently. "Oh an' the fence, we'll get ower that dead easy. Ah fund a long ladder at the back o' the cottage here, an' ah've cut it in twa. Tha'll be perfect for gettin' us ower."

A long ladder – cut in two – Derek's ladder? He will be pleased, thought Hector.

"We could hae anither look. You an' me," suggested Hammy.

Hector would rather have lain down on the bed, or the settee, or even on the floor, than have to go back over the trail that Hammy blazed in the morning, but he went, walking along in a daze, gamefully carrying on because Hammy needed his help.

This time, it was two old men walking around the perimeter fence being viewed on the screens inside the farmhouse, and becoming a bit more serious, decided the man viewing the screen. One of these old blokes has been here before.

As for the fence being a doddle, as Hammy suggested, seeing it for the first time Hector could only partially agree, "...Yea, for b-b-b-boys in their t-t-t-teens – s-s-s-s-stupid as well," but his comment didn't dent either Hammy's confidence or his enthusiasm.

"D'ye think maybe Alexander an' Sweaty wid like to come wae us?" asked Hammy, but seeing the look his friend gave him, he realised it had been a stupid question.

This evening, Toozlethwaite Manor was being targeted from three different directions: Derek on his bike from Newingsworth, Alexander on his bike too from Slatterfoot, and the two older ones on foot through the fields after the second farm reconnaissance, each looking forward to the next meal.

Of course, Alexander presumed someone else would be doing something about it, food being beyond his expertise. Derek hoped his grandad and Hammy between them would have cooked a scrumptious meal because they had all the time in the world to do it.

As they trudged along, Hector and Hammy hoped the other two were in the process of conjuring up something magical out of the raw food now in the refrigerator.

All four experienced disappointment.

They sat and looked mournfully at each other, each wishing the other would be the magician. Could anyone save the day? ...Then Hammy stepped into the breach.

At the drop of a hat, he produced scrambled egg on toast for which Alexander and Derek were most grateful. Hector didn't eat his share with the same enthusiasm – it didn't taste quite so good for the second time in a day, but the chef was praised no end by at least two of them, for what they described as "a magnificent feast".

Hector mentioned the bottles he'd bought, and this led to toasting the chef – in generous measures of whisky – and a break-in plan was floated. Unfortunately even with some whisky downed, the plan didn't sound so good... The chance of these two old blokes actually doing what they intended, seemed very unlikely to Alexander and Derek. They sat and listened, with slight smiles on their faces.

For the mission to be successful, an essential item was required.

"D'ye ken where Sally keeps her tights?" Hammy asked Derek.

Of course Derek knew – and he knew about all her other clothes too, he admitted to himself, with remorse.

"She wouldnie mind if we used them, wid she? We'll huv tae cut the legs aff an' put them oan – ower wurr heeds," explained Hammy, "Jist like thae real robbers dae."

They were now onto a second whisky toast to the Masterchef...

"Urr ye comin' wae us...?" Hammy asked hopefully, but not expecting anything positive to come back.

"Yes, why not?" replied Derek, thinking back twenty-five years when he'd been the one who led the Blytheton Road Gang – the big dog and the policeman ...he'd handled them, and could do it again!

"Yes, count me in too," said Alexander, lured by the mention of ladies tights, and the glasses were refilled so that all could toast the chef – yet again.

So, no sleep tonight – they'd all be involved, and zero hour would be midnight...

36

'...Nine, ten, eleven, twelve...' The four of them counted the strikes out loud. The moment had come. In the cottage the sound of the last chime faded away as the old clock – lovingly handed over as a house-warming present by Gran and Grandad when Sally and Derek moved in, the very clock which Sally treasured and Derek usually forgot to wind – gave the signal to begin...

They were off, each dressed suitably for becoming invisible in a pitch-black night. Some of the dark clothing was being worn already anyway, but where required, was supplemented by other bits and pieces, whether fitting the individual or not, and all borrowed from Derek's wardrobe, and his alone. Derek did not think it wise to allow any of Sally clothes to be used – other than the tights, of course.

The obvious route was to leave by the back garden and go across the fields as Hammy had earlier with Hector, but their start should have been seen as a bad omen – the struggle to undo the simple latch on the rear gate – because, that incident was followed by expertly going around in a large circle and discovering the gate once again, ten minutes later.

The patch of woodland was the next accidental discovery, though they eventually did manoeuvre themselves back out to reach the open fields again. Because it didn't seem quite so dark there, they moved forward more confidently.

Two ten-foot lengths of ladder were being carried – parts of the long ladder that Derek hadn't yet realised was his, and no longer twenty feet. They tried carrying each part end to end in pairs, but it was impossible to keep in step and not be tripping over bits of roots.

At one point they were falling over more than moving forward. Derek and Alexander decided, being the two youngest, they'd carry one each on their own. Better progress was made this way.

Negotiating the walls and wire fences dividing the fields was easy during the day but now, in the pitch black moonless night, it was almost impossible.

They had no torches with them – no one had thought of that, and they stumbled along behind Hammy. Even though he'd known this area like the back of his hand for years, losing his bearings totally in the wooded area was probably attributable to his not being able to see even the back of his hand – and the prior consumption of three large glasses of the hard stuff!

"Thurr's a muddy bit aboot here," Hammy warned as he stepped into it, "...so, watch oot," and of course, the rest followed. Afterwards, they would wonder why their legs and feet were so wet, but it's what happens when you fail to find the correct crossing point for a stream. They were nowhere near the stepping stones, not that it would have prevented them being soaked, and anyway, they were enjoying themselves.

It wasn't clear who started the giggling but, once begun, the four of them couldn't stop. They sat down, not knowing what they were laughing at, if anything – or why ...until Hammy said in a loud panicky voice, "Whitwizzat?"

His exclamation startled them. It wasn't anything, in fact, but it stopped the giggling at least. Hammy didn't like to tell them – it was a terrible secret for a grown man – he was afraid of the dark.

"I c-c-can see the f-f-farmhouse," said Hector. "They're s-s-s-still awake, and I c-c-can see l-l-l-l-l-light." At least it gave them a better guide. Soon, they arrived beside the fence and there they all stood, suddenly almost sober and anything but confident because of what they were about to do – was it sensible?

"Let's just go back home," whispered Derek.

"What a good idea," agreed Alexander.

"No, ye canny dae tha'. We've come this far, we've goat tae go oan wi' it..."

Hector thought the idea mooted by Derek had been better, but couldn't let his old buddy down, could he?

"Noo, remember. When we're ower the fence, you three go roon the ootside o' the hoose, in case thurrs oanybody aboot, an' ah'll mak for the kitchen, oan ma ain."

"Are you going first?"Alexander asked Derek, being both a gentleman and a coward. "You're the fittest and I'll hand up the other ladder, so we can climb down the other side."

"Aye, an' we'll follow yea, laddie – tae the death..."

Derek wished Hammy hadn't said that...

Inside the farmhouse, the watcher wakened the other two and called them over to see what was going on. No external lights were needed to permit them to observe each carefully planned part of this entry operation by an obviously highly-trained team. The viewing occupants had argued about the worth of investing extra cash for the night vision cameras when the farm had been purchased, but no dispute now, they had chosen correctly. The decision was vindicated – tonight was the proof.

Who are these guys? Two old codgers were round earlier in the day, are they back? Are they cops? Only if police retirement age has been raised to seventy? No, not cops then. Could be a rival gang? Let them climb in – deal with them inside the fence.

The screen was displaying a short ladder against the fence and one person trying to clamber up, obviously struggling and being buffeted by the strong wind, except there was no wind; another short ladder was now being lifted up, over the wire, inside the fence, and ...they almost dropped it. What are these guys – from a circus ...or real idiots?

The first one was over and making his way down the inside ladder. Another coming up – he's got stuck, can't lift his leg over the top. The old guy's come up and given him a push. Now he's over and inside. Right, get ready, let the third one come over and we'll get them all at the same time. There's one each. Go-go-go...

And they left the room.

Back outside, Hammy had dozed off while he was waiting. He was lying on the ground in the dark clothing, with a leg of Sally's tights over his head, and looked like part of the scenery.

It was lucky that in the excitement of the prospect of a punch-up, the three gentlemen inside the farmhouse had forgotten they'd seen two old men. It was the frantic hissing by Derek from inside the fence which wakened Hammy. Up the ladder and down the other side he went in a remarkably short time, and fortunately, after the screens inside had been abandoned – he wasn't even seen.

The four interlopers scattered without knowing where they were going, just stumbling along in the dark, except Hammy. He was on home ground, and could find his way about in here with his eyes closed. Being a mad Scot, closing his eyes was a trick he'd taught himself – it made the dark go away.

As Hammy scurried round to the back door, the entrance to his old kitchen, he prayed that it was still the same door lock. It was a surprise to find his prayer being answered – the last time he remembered praying was when going to bed as a tot – now he was inside the building. It took only moments to get to the loose floorboard under the old sink and lift the flap, and there was what he was looking for – the box – his Treasure Chest.

He had achieved what he'd intended. Back out of the house he went, locking the door behind him, and quickly reached the corner, to find floodlights on now. They displayed a sorry sight. One man was sitting on Derek, and Hector and Alexander were pinned against the fence by the other two. No-one was putting up any resistance. The brave invaders were obviously the worse for wear, and drink, and no match for the three burly blokes who'd grabbed them. The biggest of their captors brought out his mobile phone, and dialled a number.

Hammy could hear – *the bugger had called the police!*

37

Hammy stayed out of sight, round the corner but close enough to be able to hear every word being said, but his eyes had a will of their own tonight and he was 'huvvin' a sair fecht', as they said back up home, forcing them to stay open and focused – it was the strong drink. He really shouldn't have permitted Alexander to encourage him to have it, but then again, he told himself, *I am a Scot and, 'Ah can haud ma drink...'* but it was unlikely, whether he'd been able to hold his drink, or a total abstainer, that it would have made any difference at this moment.

Here he stood in the dark on the farm which used to be his, with his pals being held captive by these damn foreign nationals. Worse still, his pals were here with him and now captive because he'd asked them to be – this mess was entirely his responsibility.

Standing in partial shadow, it occurred to him – these floodlights, they hadn't used the master switch. It was the same ones he'd installed years ago. He recognised it was individual switches these guys had thrown, because not all the lights were on.

Hammy was grateful they did not have a dog guarding the premises, as he'd had. 'Wee McGreegor' prowled around this place for fourteen years, fiercely loyal to Hammy, so it hadn't needed a big high fence to keep strangers out then. Unwelcome visitors would have been hesitant to enter the premises when "his wee dugg wiss abooot," though it hadn't actually been 'wee'. Hammy used to inform people that he was a 'big thoroughbred mong-er-rel'.

Crouching in the partial darkness, a sudden thought went through his befuddled brain, it hadn't been a 'foreign' voice calling for the police, had it? He would surely have noticed that, but there was 'foreign' and there was 'foreign' wasn't there? His brain hesitated over that profound one – too much to cope with after too much whisky...

Tipsicorus International?

These three shouting to each other, he was hearing what they said. He understood almost every word, even though they didn't speak the Queen's English – like him. He tried to distinguish them. He'd never been very good at accents, but it sounded as if there was a Cockney, a Glaswegian, and an Irishman.

The one sitting on Derek's face was the Irishman – Derek wasn't saying much. Alexander was hard against the fence with his arm up behind his back, being held by the Glaswegian, and the Cockney had Hector in an arm-lock.

Hammy could confidently predict the moans and groans which would be coming from Hector tomorrow when he tries to get out of bed and finds he can't move any muscles because he is so sore. Hope I'm not sleeping beside him tonight, he thought uncharitably, all hell will be let loose in the morning, but, wait a minute... How will they get home?

An' thuv phoned furr the polis, he reminded himself, an' that's no sae guid.

Derek's legs kicked vainly. At least he was still breathing, but he didn't look comfortable. Hammy supposed, with twenty stones of Irishman sitting on top of his head, it would be difficult to achieve a comfortable position...

The wooden box Hammy carried under his arm wasn't heavy, but it would be awkward to hold if he was going to try to help the others. He needed his hands free but he couldn't just leave it down at his feet. Maybe he should hide it, but where? The farmhouse kitchen was still the same as he left it, but what about the rest of the farm?

Reconnoitring earlier in the day, he saw the high fence enclosed all the buildings inside its cordon, including the two barns. If he could find somewhere in one of the barns to hide the box, he could come back for it later. At least he would know where it was and return on his own.

He inched his way around the farmhouse, with the sincere hope that the three guys who were holding Derek, Alexander and Hector, were the only ones on the premises. His trousers would be severely messed up, from the inside, if he were to meet anyone else.

The gap between the farm-house and the nearest barn was not enormous, but it was out in the open, and if anyone was watching, he would be well exposed. Scot's courage, that's what he needed, and a deep breath.

"Whit a shame," he murmured softly, *"...tha' thurrs only three o' thum ...against me ...so whit chance huvv they goat...? Nane! Wha's like us...!"*

He went for it, and ...success. He stopped outside the large door and gasped for a while – running was not done very often these days.

Would the barn door roll open easily? Silently, when last here, and this time when he pushed, thankfully it still moved like a dream – but this whole episode was feeling dreamlike. He stepped into the barn...

It was a dream ...the barn looked like it was outside – but inside?

Where was all the farming equipment – in the other barn? Everything was different. All their vegetables were being grown inside, in here obviously. That's why nothing could be seen in the fields. Outside the night air was cool. In here, it was warm and humid, and they had lighting, to force the growth no doubt, and, he presumed, polythene covers around the crop to maintain a balanced temperature.

What were they growing? Why hadn't they ploughed up the fields and planted the crops out there? How would they make it pay – all done in the barn and using electricity to heat the place?

Oh well, it wasn't his problem – but what are they growing anyway? Highly curious, he opened the plastic sheet and looked under. Certainly lots of greenery to be seen, looking impressive under the lights too. It was certainly a healthy crop – but of what? He didn't recognise it. And then it came to him...

It was CANNABIS...

He had to get out of here quickly. These guys were no ordinary farmers – they were doing drugs – and that's why there was a ten-foot fence, and this was bloody dangerous...

The treasure box couldn't be left here after all. Sobering up had occurred rather rapidly, and it was a stiff drink he needed now. Closing the barn door again, he crossed the yard once more, slipped back to the corner and peeked around.

There was Derek still almost suffocating, and Hector and Alexander, still being held, but the place was becoming busier. A blue light was flashing at the padlocked gate. Two police officers were getting out of the car.

He was the only one who could do something about this – and he would have to do it quickly – but what?

38

Thelma was on duty at the front of house as usual for the start of the evening sessions, treading back and forth slowly and with no other purpose than to pass the time, creating a path on a carpet which was already fairly worn. Renovation was needed in this establishment, but she guessed that would be unlikely in the near future. Staying in business was probably more the target.

No sign of Mr Jameson so far this afternoon (Peter to his family and friends) – unusual with him being a stickler about time-keeping for others. Almost six o'clock when he came up the front steps, and obvious, to Thelma's eyes at least, to have had a few drinks before coming in. In his hand was a new plastic bag from the supermarket which did not disguise the shape of a large bottle of liquid. He smiled at her as he passed, and whispered confidentially, his breath confirming her earlier suspicion, asking her to come up to his office half an hour before closing time tonight, please.

She watched him go unsteadily up the stairs to his office. If tonight he started to get fresh with her, she decided, he would not walk comfortably for a week.

After what started as a dull and miserable day, the evening improved with a good turnout. A happy atmosphere developed in the old building, and the evening session passed without incident.

The front offices were now closed up and the girl doing that duty would be sticking around to ensure the building was emptied completely. She was to be the one tonight deputised by Thelma to lock the front doors, normally Thelma's own duty, but not possible tonight as she was wanted 'upstairs'.

Her knock at the door didn't produce a fast response, in fact, none. She knocked again, a little harder. This time there was some movement, and then, "Come in".

He had been asleep in the chair, at least that's what it appeared, and he had removed his shoes. They were sitting at the end of his desk. He'd possibly been lying with his jacket draped over himself. It was now hanging on the hook and he was in his shirtsleeves, and sitting on the desk was a bottle of 'bubbly'. It wasn't very expensive stuff, as Thelma could see, but to her surprise, it was sitting unopened.

"Sit down Thelma, please. I want to talk, in fact, I need to talk, and you strike me as a good listener. Would you mind?"

Safe enough so far – he is on one side of the desk and I'm on the other, nearer the door. Alright, I'll sit and listen for a bit. It's not time to leave yet anyway and he's the one paying me to waste time.

"Would you like a little drink?"

"No thank you, Mr Jameson."

"Please, Thelma ...Peter is my name. Please call me that."

"Right – Peter."

This was the usual start in her experience. Next stage, about his wife, followed by an invitation to go round and sit on his knee "...To see the view from here" or, maybe, it would be him jumping up and making a rush at her, but she could move quickly.

"Would you like to relax a bit? Maybe take off your jacket," he suggested. "It's a horrible colour anyway, bright blue, can't stand it, and it's not your colour at all. I don't know why you ever allowed me to make you wear it."

"I'm all right like this, Mr Jameson," was her curt reply.

Now that wasn't expected. Trying to get me to do a strip, is he? Cue music ...but you have no chance – Peter.

"I'm sorry, Thelma. You have probably got the wrong impression of me. I am a happily married man, or at least I thought I was. My wife and I had a serious argument this afternoon. She's threatened to leave me..."

Here we go. I was correct to begin with, she told herself.

"...and it's all because of my motor bike."

Suddenly the conversation had taken a more interesting turn – a motor bike? She noticed the piece of paper lying on the desk, which he'd started to prepare – an advert for the sale of a motor bike.

She always had difficulty reading upside down. It was a skill she admired in others. They would leave a colleague's, or a competitor's office, with a lot of knowledge which hadn't been intended for them, simply by using upside-down reading.

"She thinks it's too dangerous and she wants me to sell it and buy a little car instead. I've only had the bike for a couple of years, and it is part of me, but – I'm going to sell it. It is either her, or the bike, she informed me. Anyway a little car for her would be more comfortable than riding pillion."

Thelma looked at her watch. The time was getting on. She remembered that Sally and Muriel would be waiting up for her, but Mr Peter Jameson was turning out to be somewhat different to the first guesses.

"Now, would you oblige me by sharing this bottle? Since your little friend, Ivy Bloom, refused to accept any publicity, I thought we'd do it on our own, and so to celebrate the tenth anniversary, I bought something to celebrate it with. It was to be just the three of us, my wife, you, and myself, but my wife refused to come here tonight because of our argument. I wanted her to meet you."

Thelma was beginning to feel quite touched at the sentiment. *This man was different. He was a genuine family man, and he loved his wife – or he wouldn't be selling his prize possession.*

This offer of a drink was being done tonight out of respect for her. It wasn't because he fancied her at all, but now she had one little niggle – why didn't he fancy her?

So, she agreed to have a drink with him, just the one...

Two plastic tumblers were placed on his desk, the cork was popped, and bubbly poured into each glass.

Thelma was determined. No slipping back into bad habits. She would have one drink and no more. If she ventured into the dangerous area of a second one, she would want a third and a fourth.

The first one did taste nice... She allowed him to fill the glass a second time. It may not have been the most expensive champagne in the world, but it did have an immediate euphoric effect, but she was strong and determined – she wouldn't drink it.

What could she do with it though? He would be very offended if it just sat there. He'd see it. No plants to kill in this room. No wash-hand basin to pour it down. Only his shoes...

The bike was his pride and joy, he told her, and every Sunday, he and his wife went off to a pub or restaurant, a bike's drive away, and enjoyed a nice meal. What he hadn't realised was just how terrified his wife had always been, for both of them. If only he'd known. Any pleasure for her from the meal, and from their outing, was spoiled by the return journey – and that had been going on for two years – until now.

Though she could understand his wife's dilemma, Thelma told him, for her it was different. Looking at her biking magazine last night, having seen all the bikes only made her desperate to have a go. Unfortunately she couldn't drive; in fact, she had never even been on one.

A third glass was filled. Peter was consuming his as he talked animatedly, without realising that his second shoe was progressively assisting Thelma to dispose of her share.

In normal circumstances, he would have been happy to take her for a ride, he said, and let her enjoy the occasion, but he'd made up his mind – he would not be using his bike again. It was sitting at his house. Thelma would be welcome to try it for the day, if she wished, if she knew someone who had a licence and would take her.

Peter Jameson's speech was becoming more and more slurred, and the effect of the champagne, on top of whatever he drowned his sorrows with earlier, was beginning to show. Just one more little drink each – and the bottle would be empty.

Which shoe this time – left or right?

"Look – you take the ignition key and there's my address," and he searched for his business card in the drawer and handed it over, with the key.

"And help yourself to a run if you can find someone to take you. You could meet my ...dear ...wife at the ...same time."

A yawn preceded the closure of his eyes as he relaxed in his chair, and the empty plastic glass dropped to the floor.

Thelma placed his jacket over his legs, and her jacket over his top half, and left him muttering away every so often, but fast sleep.

She closed the door quietly and left – feeling a little guilty – *his shoes may not be dry before he tries wearing them again.*

39

The master switch – if he could get to the master switch before...

There was a lot of shouting going on. The blue light flashing meant they were about to be rescued, Hector and Alexander thought wrongly – they were yelling to the police. The police were on the other side of a locked gate and were shouting to be told what was going on. The three villains were shouting to each other expecting one of them to have the key for the padlock and chain on the gate, but none of them had apparently, because it was hanging on the hook inside the farmhouse.

Hammy still had the box of jewellery under his arm. Hiding it in the barn hadn't been a good idea after all, so the kitchen door was again being unlocked by him, so that he could go back through the kitchen to access the master switch in the hallway, for the external lights.

With the kitchen door open now, into the hall he went, and in different circumstances he would have stood and reminisced, and become misty-eyed, because nothing had been changed since he left. The old coat-stand, the one his father bought at the jumble sale and said would be worth a fortune some day, was still there at the end nearest the outside door. There's his old working cap hung on the hook, beside the umbrella stand and the picture of his old granny. Nothing had changed for many years, had it? The memories in this place...

Then something did change as the Glaswegian barged through the front door.

"What the f...!"

He didn't have the chance to say the naughty word, because Hammy's little treasure chest hit him squarely on the forehead, and he dropped like a stone. Hammy had never done anything like that before, but he enjoyed it and smiled to himself, then felt guilty having knocked out a fellow Scot.

He grabbed his cloth cap from the coat-stand, they're not going to notice it's gone, he decided, and put it on over the top of the nylon tights which still covered his head. As he thought about it, he realised that when he looked, his other three friends were still wearing their stockings too – a motley crew, right enough.

What about the key? The Glaswegian, lying out cold on the hall floor, had come in here for the key, where was it? Could this be it? It had the obligatory label tied to it, but the way it had always been with him and keys, the marking was carelessly done and the hieroglyphics were difficult to decipher. Was it 'Front Gate' it said? It did look like a padlock key. He'd have to take a chance.

In his heightened brain activity, Hammy looked at the body in front of him. The man on the hall floor was wearing similar clothes to him including a hat, though his was a baseball cap. He recollected as he smacked him, that the bloke had been about the same build as him, although about twenty years younger – so he swapped the caps.

He grabbed the key, crossed his fingers, and threw the master switch. The floodlights outside went dark. Some light spilled from the hall, but was behind him as he went outside.

"Y'took yer fecking toime, as usual, Mac," came from the Irishman sitting on Derek's head. "Would ya get a fecking move on. Oim gettin' cramp in moi leg sittin' here – an' whids wrong wid d'loights?"

"It wis a friggin' fuse, ya stupid..." Hammy restricted himself in his reply, making it sound as near as he could to the Glasgow accent he'd heard earlier. Saying any more than was needed would be chancing it, but, so far, so good...

Hammy hurried over to the gate, careful not to drop the box under his arm. Was it the correct key for the padlock? He fumbled a bit in his nervousness, being able to see only with the help of the police car's blue flashing light. Although it seemed like forever, the padlock clicked, and the chain was able to be removed. He opened the gate and stood back.

Should he scarper – on his own? Of course he shouldn't. He must help his mates, so, in the cover of the darkness, and as the police came in to the yard, he ran over towards the Cockney holding Hector and Alexander. Hector was being held by the collar, because he was wriggling less, and now struggling to breathe.

The Cockney was grateful for Mac coming back to help him hold this old guy while he wrestled with younger one, but he didn't wrestle for too long. Relief from his endeavours came, when Hammy smacked him over the head with the very useful jewellery box.

Grabbing Alexander and Hector, he half-dragged them towards the gate. He couldn't help Derek, because in the semi-darkness the two police persons had gone to the assistance of the Irishman with the body underneath him, and Derek was being dragged to his feet.

Pushing and pulling each other very quickly towards the open gate, Hammy, Alexander, and Hector, rushed passed the police car still flashing away, and hurriedly vanished into the darkness of the fields.

Whereas afterwards, Hammy and Hector remembered the occasion only with relief, Alexander having the mind of the experienced thespian, visualised the drama of the panicky episode in more flowery theatrical terms...

The blue strobe lighting intermittently displays the scurrying figures of the three bruised heroes, as they exit stage left, limping slightly – BLACKOUT.

40

At first, Derek didn't realise he'd been abandoned by his friends and relations, but if the truth be known, at this moment Derek didn't know anything about anything. He was just delighted to be able to breathe real air and to see vaguely the blue flashing light. It seemed for hours he'd supplied something soft (his head) for some person to sit on. He'd know who it was in future – the one with his face imprinted on their bum, obviously.

It was fortunate he'd removed his glasses at home, before pulling on the stocking, or who knows how bad his face would have been, but no spectacles meant impaired vision. That he was being held firmly by two people, he could see – because they were too close – his arms being gripped by two police officers, one of them a female and did she have a grip like iron? Her boyfriend wouldn't dare misbehave.

The man standing in front of them, the one who'd been sitting on Derek's head, was the only one of the farm's three current inhabitants who was able to stand. His mouth was going at a fast rate. Though the mouth was moving, nothing was being heard by Derek. His hearing seemed to have been affected.

Derek could see only hazily by the flashing blue light that there was another man on the ground, over near the fence, and he was moving slightly. It didn't look like Hector, or Alexander, or Hammy, thank goodness – as far as he could tell. In the lit farmhouse hallway it was possible to make out another figure. He was lying prone too. He must have walked into something in the dark, Derek assumed. Derek felt dizzy, and wobbled, but there was little chance of him falling over, thanks to the grip that the lady in blue had of him. His hearing was returning slowly.

"...and the hot coffee, getting cold... So, hurry up!"

These were the first words he heard distinctly, coming from the policewoman, which were hissed in the direction of her male companion. He seemed to be going into too much depth with his questions, while she was eager to be off. Derek's vision was blurred, but he was certainly getting that impression.

"I'll leave without you then!" were the next words she threw at her buddy, but he ignored her and continued his questioning...

Then Derek, with his arm twisted up his back and being led by her, was pushed towards the police car. They stood and waited while her mate, who with notebook in hand was still listening and recording what Derek's tormentor was saying.

However, it looked as if now he'd made his complaint, the villain was eager to be rid of the policeman, becoming irate and waving his arms about, ushering the constable towards the gate.

The policeman wasn't happy at being hassled by both his colleague and this bloke, as far as Derek could see standing in the arm-lock beside the flashing light on the car roof. Two bodies were still lying prone, getting little attention from their mate, but then again, they didn't elicit much sympathy from Derek either.

Derek tried moving a little – should he wriggle and break free and run?

"Ouch!"

The policewoman dug in her nails, her viciousness due to a combination of controlling her victim, and getting fed-up waiting on her overly-conscientious companion. She obviously hadn't taken a fancy to Derek.

"Come on Andy, the coffee will be cold," she shouted.

The moment the policeman was through, the gate clanged shut again, and the padlock and chain were quickly re-applied. This was done before any attention was given to the two who were lying on the deck. Imagine having a bloke like that for a mate, Derek thought – no thank you – and then he realised he'd been abandoned. The phrase, 'All's fair in love and war', seemed to suit.

At least I haven't been handcuffed, was his thought as he was bundled into the back of the police car and told to put on his seat belt. The policewoman was the one driving. She obviously passed her police driving test with flying colours and drove even faster than Sophie Clerkenwell-Brown. No-one spoke as they sped along, until she swung into a lay-by and stopped the engine.

Oh no... They were about to talk tough, he guessed, and he wasn't good under interrogation – Sally could vouch for that.

Earlier, the call for assistance, coming through to them in the middle of their break, proved not the best time to demand urgent action. Neither police constable was in the best of moods at having to pack up sandwiches, and return hot coffee to the flask, just at the moment they'd started, but being conscientious...

Derek didn't understand what was happening now. Was he being arrested, he asked politely? Yes, but later, was snapped back at him.

"...We've sandwiches to finish first," the girl with the grip of steel told him.

"Don't I know you?" asked the other one, using the rear view mirror to scrutinise Derek's appearance.

Andy, you can be a right pillock at times, thought his female partner. With the stocking still over his head, it is probably very likely that he looks like every other villain who has ever worn a nylon stocking and been arrested by you.

"Would you please remove the stocking, sir," requested PC Yvonne Saunders to simplify it for her colleague.

"No," responded a petulant Derek.

"You can't say 'no' to a policeman," said PC Woodstock.

"I didn't," responded Derek cheekily, and he is correct PC Pillock, thought Yvonne, I am a woman, all woman, and Andy, dear boy, you don't even realise that...

"It's a good job for you that we're now on our break, or I'd have you out of this car and knock the living daylights out of you," Andy responded gallantly.

"One sugar or two, Andy?" asked Yvonne. She was concerning herself with the important things in life by pouring out two cups of steaming coffee.

If only I'd behaved, Derek guessed, *they might have offered me a cup too – I am parched – but no chance now.* All he got was a frosty silence. Now, if he'd been a fly on the inside of this police car normally, he would have known that this was always the routine during the break for these two. Little things in life, like routine and silence, are important.

As it was, Derek just sat there, thankful for small mercies, like having removed his glasses before he put the stocking over his head. Filling in an insurance claim would have been interesting though. 'Cause of breakage – twenty-stone man sitting on face.' If only he'd had the specs with him – having limited vision was sapping his confidence...

The policeman's voice, he was sure he recognised it, but he couldn't picture the face to go with it. He hadn't seen him properly in the dark, but the voice was familiar. He thought feverishly for when he last was involved with uniformed police. The only time was with two bigger guys than this, who chased him because of Sally's handbag.

No, there was another – it was that twit, what was he called, Andy Pandy something-or-other, but he was a detective. Then Derek twigged. *Didn't the policewoman called this guy Andy? It's him... Now I remember, he became a beat policeman again after failing to deal with us. Andy Pandy...*

Oh-oh... This could get awkward. He would enjoy getting even. Derek shrank lower into the rear seat, wishing himself somewhere else, without success.

They'd eaten their sandwiches and finished their drink now, but were just sitting, not talking. *Was this the way they behaved towards each other all the time*, thought Derek? *Just like me and Sally.* It felt an uncomfortable silence to Derek, but it was probably nervousness he was feeling, he concluded, and it was then he realised he needed the toilet. He needed a pee and it suddenly felt – urgent.

Should he ask if he could leave the car? It had been all the excitement, not surprisingly. Of course he would ask – or wet his pants?

Then he noticed how quiet it was in the two seats in front of him, and it wasn't because they were giving him the silent treatment. All he could hear was steady breathing, and an odd snorting snore or two. It was the early hours of the morning, probably the night shift routine for this pair of highly energetic police persons. The two in front were having a snooze.

The lay-by the car was parked at was beside a hedge and there were high bushes beyond, bushes that Derek could quickly squeeze through. If he could quietly open the door ...like so ...and wriggle over to the edge of his seat ...like so ...and get out...

The door made a very slight 'click' as it moved back of its own volition, not quite closed. Derek stopped, waiting for a shout, or for someone to grab his shoulder and get rough with him, but nothing happened... He moved forward gingerly, and went through the hedge.

"Give him a moment," Andy whispered. He smiled to Yvonne Saunders. "OK. Off we go then," he looked smug, "... He'll lead us to the rest of the gang."

Yvonne wasn't really in the mood. She would have preferred to sit in the car and just let the idiot run off, chased by the other idiot, but she and PC Woodstock were a team, she had to remind herself. A chase in the dark, running after someone in the woods, and over muddy fields, was not her choice for this time of night, but she couldn't be bothered arguing. The thrill of the chase could be fun, but preferably at high-speed – in the car. Now, that she did enjoy.

However, through the hedging she went, following her partner. They would catch the stockinged faced villain and his gang, and they would do it together.

Now if these two had actually listened carefully as they left the car, they might have heard the slight hiss and tinkling sound, and the not-quite silent sigh, coming from someone who was being greatly relieved. Also, if it had not been dark, they might have recognised the person, who was standing zipping up his fly, still wearing a stocking on his head.

Derek had been about to return to the car when they made their move. Doing it his way seemed less embarrassing than asking, and anyway he hadn't wanted to disturb their slumbers. He knew how they must feel and sympathised because he was tired too. After all the earlier excitement, he just wanted to sit down, or better still, lie down somewhere and sleep. He was too tired to run.

Standing there, Derek wondered what they were up to. One car door having opened and been properly closed again, but gently, then the other door being opened and closed gently too, the male, in uniform, pushing through the hedge and careering off through the high undergrowth, towards the woods.

The female was right behind him, but stopped, turned, and returned to the car, opened the door and closed it again, quickly but gently once more. This time she passed, wearing her hat. She couldn't chase an escapee while improperly dressed.

Derek stood there and wondered why they'd gone and left him. *Perhaps calls of nature too. Or else, it was a more meaningful partnership than it appeared. Could they be off to the woods to...? No, they were on duty... They wouldn't, no, not while they were on duty... Or would they?*

Oh, well if they have lost interest in me, I might as well go home, he decided, I have work in the morning. So, the police car was left, empty, as Derek walked off along the road in the direction of the cottage, still wearing a stocking...

41

The knocking at the front door caused panic. Hector shot into the bathroom to hide, Alexander scrambled under the bed in the room that he claimed as his, and Hammy dived down behind the sofa. No-one was going to answer the door. It was locked. If these guys from the farm had followed them and were going to beat them up, first they'd have to break down the door.

The house lights were on. They shouldn't have made it so obvious they were back, but the three of them hadn't thought of that. They'd been desperate to get inside, and relieved to have made it across the fields still together without collapsing in a heap along the way.

The front door was being banged a moment ago, now it was the back one. Was it closed properly and locked? It couldn't have been forgotten, could it? The back door handle was being rattled. Whoever was outside was determined, but the door hadn't been forced in – yet.

Silence...

Hammy bravely raised his head above the edge of the sofa – to see the living room door starting to swing open. Someone had returned to the front door and got in. He ducked down again – rapidly.

"Who didn't put the ruddy key back where it should be?" shouted the stocking-headed figure, glad to be back to the safety of home.

"Derek? It canny be you is it, ma bonnie wee fella?" came the voice from behind the sofa, "...but ahm no' here, if it is no' you!"

Three brave souls appeared from the different hiding places, all carrying a look of guilt which comes from walking away and leaving a buddy in major danger – although actually, they'd run.

"Are you all r-r-r-r-right, D-D-D-Derek?" asked Grandad.

"How did ye get oot?" asked Hammy. "Ah thocht ye were deed!"

"I'd every confidence in you, my boy," Alexander patronisingly commented. "I knew you would talk your way out of any awkward situation."

It was a relief to remove the stocking. Derek felt it so nice to breathe again without doing it through the single leg of Sally's tights, even though the air in the cottage, with the four males living in it, did not smell very fresh. It was free – as he was.

He wondered if his nose would stay bent.

Standing centre stage and being honoured with their rapt attention, Derek told them of being taken away in the police car. Yes, of course Alexander remembered DC Andy 'Pandy' Woodstock – it had been a close call with him. Could have given them a harder time last year though – now in uniform, is he? They'd gone into the woods to do what?

Repeating in front of the two older men, how he thought they popped into the woods for a 'quickie' seemed wrong for Derek saying out loud. Maybe he should have asked the old ones to put their hands over their ears when he'd said it to Alexander the first time. Never mind, they probably wouldn't remember what a 'quickie' was anyway...

Having seen nothing of the escape of the other three from the position he was in, Derek was curious too. How did they get home? Other than bruises from banging into some walls and fences, which Hammy was convinced had jumped out in front of them, and the torn clothing from scrabbling passed the odd bit of barbed wire, it had been a doddle, Derek was told.

"...But was it all worth it?" Derek wished to know. He didn't want to find it had all been in vain, now he would have to go through the rest of life with a misshapen head.

"Of course it wiss, Sunshine," said Hammy happily. "Look ower there! It's mah boax."

There it sat, pride of place in the middle of the table: an old carved box: the Macintosh's family jewels, safely back with their true owner. Yes, it had all been worth it.

"Can I see what's in it?" asked Derek.

"Och, ah huvnae even opened it mahsel yet. Ah've only jist cleaned aff the bloodstains," said Hammy with a smile. "Ah'll tell ye, ma lad, that wiss a couple o' great moments in ma life – jist hitten thum."

"Where were you then D-D-D-Derek, when he h-h-hit them...?" questioned his grandad. "Why d-d-d-did you n-n-n-not see it?"

Derek grimaced, remembering where...

Hammy lifted the box and found the reason why it didn't burst open when he used it as a weapon. It had a lock on it. Unfortunately, he didn't have a key. A lovely looking box like this, with a carved design on the top, produced by his 'grand-faither' or maybe even his 'great-grand-faither' and it couldn't be opened without being spoiled. That was a wee bit disappointing.

"N-n-n-no," said Hector "...d-d-don't b-b-b-break it open. D-D-Derek, have you a p-p-p-paperclip or s-s-something?"

"Urr ye gonnae pick the lock then, Sinbad?" Hammy scoffed.

To their surprise, he was – and he did. As the other three watched in fascination, Hector bent the paperclip and got to work, annoying himself in taking longer than it should. The lock wasn't rusty – but he was. He should have kept practising.

"Where did you learn to do that?" asked Alexander, incredulously, as he looked at the box, now sitting ready to be opened by Hamish.

"Have you ever r-r-r-read about H-H-H-Harry 'Ace' R-R-R-Rawinsky, the jewel thief who spent most of his l-l-l-life in j-j-j-jail? He was one of my b-b-b-buddies in the army – he t-t-t-taught me. I used to be able t-t-t-to do this with m-m-m-my eyes shut."

The other three were highly impressed; definitely a handy skill.

Now, was the opening ceremony and it had to be Hammy's honour: his family heirlooms and his inheritance...

"Urr ye ready tae be dazzled?" asked Hammy, counting silently to ten, to crank up the atmosphere in the room – like on television. This was a special occasion. It was the first time the family jewels were to be seen. His father talked about them and had told him where they were hidden; he had never opened the box either. It had been his father's father, the first in the Macintosh family to own the farm, who'd been the one who hid them under the floor, with the instruction – they must only be removed in a crisis. It was the family secret.

For Hammy, the crisis had arrived.

He opened the box and...

"Michty me. would ye hae a look at that!"

They all looked...

"It's jist aw paper. Thurr's nae jewels!"

There was silence – well what could you say at a time like this? The other three could only look on, embarrassed and uncomfortable, witnessing Hammy's disappointment.

"My faither would huv laffed his heid aff at this," Hammy said bravely, "...but ah must say, ahm a toatie wee bit disappointed, mahsel," and he smiled sadly.

The Range Rover had been sold and he was glad he'd done that, and some of the money was his. At least he wasn't down to his uppers yet, but an expectation of a few thousand in the family treasure chest, hadn't seemed unreasonable...

He looked at the contents – only letters and old deeds – now null and void, of course, since the farm had been sold on. Some other bits and pieces were laid on the table – an old family bible, and a few old photographs, and a map.

The map was carefully unfolded. It seemed the most interesting thing in the box: hand drawn and roughly to scale of the farm buildings, and recognisable to Hammy as the way it was about fifty years ago. It showed the old cowsheds, removed when the new barns were built by his father. This must have been drawn by his grandfather and a very fine job he'd done too, the words done in a flamboyant style though the spelling was questionable. A smart looking compass was in the corner beside the legend together with a red cross shown about fifty feet from the farmhouse, directly due south.

Derek was looking over Hammy's shoulder and now able to see since he'd retrieved his glasses.

"The cross – it says on the map that the cross shows the position of the buried family treasure," said Derek. "There is treasure after all. Do you see?"

"Och aye, ah see it, but that canny be right. That's whaur wann o' the barns is."

"But there's no barn shown on the map," Alexander pointed out. "So, there would have been nothing to stop the stuff being buried there, would there?"

"Aye, ah ken whit ye mean – but it's righ' in the middle o' the cannabis."

"CANNABIS?!" exploded the other three.

"You never t-t-t-told us there was c-c-c-c-c-cannabis," said Hector.

"No wonder they were less than pleased to see us," added Alexander.

"Och aye, ahm pretty sure that's whit it wis," said Hammy offhandedly. "No' very much like vegetables tae me. Thu'll no dae awfy weel sellin' that stuff. Its carrots, an' onions, an' cabbages, that fowk'll be wantin'?"

"We'll have to tell the police about this," said Derek enthusiastically.

"Awa' ya dumplin'. They'll arrest ye, if ye dae. Naw, we'll have tae be mair cleverer than tha' – 'specially if we urr goin' back furr the treasure..."

42

It was Friday evening. For Sally and Muriel there was no work the following day so lounging around the house was acceptable – a bit like the old days before Sally wed – with the consumption of a few obligatory glasses of wine. The television remote, though being skilfully used by Sally, was failing to locate many programmes of interest to keep them almost awake.

So when Thelma returned from work, rather later than normal and in a state of excitement, it was to join two very drowsy females. Muriel and Sally recognised that if they had been in bed asleep, they would have been shaken awake to listen. Thelma just had to talk.

"Do we know anyone who could take me for a ride on Peter's motorbike?" she asked the other two eagerly and hopefully.

"Peter? Who is Peter?" asked Muriel.

"Why, he is my boss of course, didn't I say – and he has a motorcycle..."

"Ooh, lucky him and it is Peter now is it? I thought you couldn't stand the man."

"Don't believe everything I tell you. He's really a lovely person, but do you know anyone?" Thelma prodded again.

Muriel and Sally sat and pondered, or at least pretended to, because although it was a mediocre film they were watching, Thelma appeared at the only potentially exciting moment in the plot, but which regrettably was turning out to be an anti-climax...

"Wait a minute..." Sally said. "I know someone who used to be able to drive one, but I don't know if he has a licence – Derek's grandad, Hector. He told me, before Derek and I were married, how he'd learned to ride a motorbike in the army when he was doing his National Service. He loved using it."

"I'll phone him," exclaimed Thelma, "...immediately!"

"You can't phone him at this time of night. He'd have a heart attack. Remember his age," and Muriel brought the conversation back to earth.

"In the morning then – early," Thelma accepted.

At Toozlethwaite Manor, as Derek grandly referred to it, it had been a long night, with four bruised and exhausted males all desperately trying to get some sleep but with only partial success. The inside of the cottage was looking nothing like a manor house, and, how could it, with these four blokes sprawled about the living room, partly undressed and not smelling as fresh as maybe they should. It was now peaceful, because eventually sleep did take control, and they were snoring remarkably harmoniously...

Their alarm call was the shattering sound of Derek's house phone ringing out the good news that someone was attempting to contact them. As it was barely six a.m. on Saturday and each having had little more than two hours decent sleep no-one was eager to answer it. Derek tried to find the source of the noise, and would have been so much quicker if his brain could have reminded him where the permanent position of the phone actually was.

He found it... The receiver was lifted.

"What...?"

Manners were not likely in certain situations – this was one.

"Hello Sweaty, this is Aunt Thelma."

"Who...?"

"Aunt Thelma... Sweaty, have you been drinking? Never mind. Can I speak, please, with your grandad, it's very urgent. I know he's there with you. I wouldn't be phoning on a lovely morning like this, and stopping you going out for your training run, if it was anything else other than important."

"Grandad...? You want to speak to Grandad? Is something wrong with Gran?"

"I'm not interrupting your grandad's breakfast, am I?"

"No, you are not. Grandad...!" he shouted in the ear of the elderly gentleman who was in the chair next to the telephone. This shout, almost succeeded in wakening him. "Grandad!" The second time was considerably louder, and marginally was more successful. "Phone..." and he handed the device to him.

"H-h-h-hello," Hector managed.

"Hector. It's Thelma, Sally's Aunt Thelma. I'm told you can drive a motorbike. How would you like the chance to ride one today?"

There were only a few key words he successfully grasped – 'Thelma' and 'motorbike' and 'today'.

"Yes, b-b-b-b-but..." he almost got out.

"Oh, that would be great. If I come round for you about eight o'clock on my push-bike, we could go together to collect the motorbike, and you could drive it and take me for a run. You are wonderful, Hector. I love you. I just hope your wife appreciates you. I'll see you shortly," the voice sang out happily, and she hung up.

43

Did she have to go so fast? She was a very excitable and energetic person was Thelma and he was barely managing to keep up with her. Having had to repair another puncture before he could even start had been tough enough, and here she was, in a great rush, pedalling enthusiastically: a woman on a mission! For Hector today on his push-bike, the way he was feeling, just being a pedestrian could possibly have been hazardous for other pedestrians.

Could he drive a motorbike in this condition? More importantly, should he? He was battered, and bruised, and mentally under excessive pressure – obviously last night's excitement was more than enough.

There were also two minor factors which ought to be considered: firstly – although he was the owner of a licence for a motorbike, he had not driven one for nearly fifty years and, secondly – he had no insurance. Would he still be able to drive? At least, he was awake, and he was moving, but he knew he was chancing it. Would he live to regret this? *Would he live?*

Why was Thelma going round in circles?

The presumption that she knew where she was going was his error. Newingsworth over the years she'd been away had changed. He never had this problem with Daisy...

Life became simpler when he found out the address of her destination – just along the road from the newsagent he worked for, or rather the one he used to work for. His paper-round from this morning was no longer his, much to the newsagent's surprise. Feeling lousy and pressurised in so many ways, he'd decided to jack it in. No longer was he the oldest newspaper delivery boy in the country but a free man, being controlled this morning by the magnetic attraction of a motorbike ride – and a woman on the bicycle in front.

It was a nice shape on the saddle in front, he noticed. He realised it was a thought he shouldn't be having, but it was probably innocent compared to what his own wife could be up to, down south. He'd heard of things that happened in London.

She'd stopped. They had arrived. He noticed she possessed a nice shape off the saddle too...

The motorcycle's ignition key was in Thelma's possession already, her boss having told her to help herself, but it would be wrong to use it without proper permission, even though Peter had insisted. Anyway, he'd been tipsy last night. It was not correct behaviour, helping oneself, so, she rang the doorbell of the home of Mr and Mrs Peter Jameson and the lady of the house appeared.

"Pleased to meet you – Peter told me all about you," was the pleasant reaction from Mrs Jameson. "Of course you may use it. Have a run. Peter is upstairs, incapacitated."

It was three in the morning when he'd arrived home, wakening his wife to say he was sorry about the big argument they'd had earlier, sorry to have argued over a stupid motorbike, and very sorry that his shoes were ruined – he must have walked through an extremely deep puddle on the way home.

His wife was told of the advice given by the very wise woman at work, Thelma – his superb supervisor – that he should return to his loved one immediately, and forget about the bike.

"She told me..." his sleepy spouse was informed, "...to come home tonight and make mad passionate love to you, Sweetest."

He'd made up that part himself, but he was wasting his time, as Mrs Jameson wouldn't let him, even if he could have. In the state he was in, his wife recognised there was no chance he could even get his clothes off or be able to get into bed by himself, never mind 'make mad passionate love'. She put him to bed. He was currently sleeping it off, and was likely to be doing so for many hours.

"Go on – help yourselves," the wife said.

The bike was in the garage, together with two helmets.

Hector swung open the up-and-over door and there it was and a bit different to the one he used nearly fifty years ago. He looked closer. Bikes had changed a lot. This was a Honda Fireblade – 1000cc of modern engine power.

Hector couldn't help wondering how Thelma's boss could afford this, because he was amazed that the Astoria Bingo had even survived for all these years. This bike looked shiny and new, maybe five or six years old – must originally have cost a fortune.

Hector's own bikes had been less exciting. His learning was on a BSA M21 600cc, supplied by HM Forces and a wartime relic but still serviceable and which he used for the duration in HM forces. He grew to love that bike. When his service time ended he found one of his own, second hand, and though that bike was the same as his first, it looked so much better without the dents and the odd bullet hole.

Standing close to this shiny, exciting looking, expensive modern monster, made him feel uncomfortable, and decidedly apprehensive. He had no insurance, he would be carrying a pillion passenger, and it was someone else's bike he'd be on, but just look at this bike...

Who could resist it? It had been waiting for him. He hadn't realised how eagerly he'd been anticipating this moment. She was a beauty...

He ran his hands over the shiny red paintwork, and look at the gleaming chrome. This is power, baby – try and stop me...

Thelma had been looking forward to this moment also, but for her, now the moment had actually arrived, confidence was suddenly lacking. This machine was certain to go fast, too fast. Seeing the photographs in the magazine had inspired her; they had looked as if they would go fast – but only in her imagination.

This was for real.

Did Hector have insurance? It was very unlikely, but she didn't want to ask. Why hadn't she thought of that before? Could he even drive this bike?

"It looks fast, Hector," she said and smiled, with false bravado.

"Sure d-d-does..." he replied, already roaring halfway down the road in his mind.

Ignoring the pain of swinging his leg over, and his previous fatigue, he was sitting astride it and it felt great! She, this bike, was to be his – at least for a short run...

"S-s-s-step a-b-b-b-b-board, Sweetheart," he said to this woman, who did not now want to proceed, but who couldn't say no.

Climbing onto the pillion was awkward, and she was glad that she'd had the sense to wear jeans, but now that her feet were off the ground she was feeling more vulnerable. What a stupid notion this was. There was no way she could contemplate ever driving this thing herself. It felt dangerous – and she understood immediately why Peter Jameson and his wife had argued.

Key in the ignition, no kick start needed nowadays – he knew that much – and just press the button. (In his day, tickle the carburettor, retard the ignition slightly, piston over top dead centre, then follow through completely with a gentle but firm kick, one or two usually necessary.)

Today, he pressed the button. It roared into life!

The very slight slope allowed him to move gently forward, checking the feel of the brakes in the process. Into first gear, easy with the clutch, find the sweet spot...

Stalled! Damn! Failure!

Try again... He slowly released the clutch – mind the revs – failed again!

"Maybe we shouldn't bother after all, Hector," said the tremulous voice from the pillion, "...it's obviously not as easy as it seems."

Third time lucky – and it was.

Balance felt good. Up a gear, yes, we're on the move now, haven't lost the touch. He was glad his other bikes were foot operated gears. This felt natural already. A road junction ahead, and if he turned right, the open countryside was very close. Carefully, he turned right. Do not exceed speed limits, he told himself, must not draw any attention. This felt good, really good, and the sign ahead: 'End of speed limit'.

It had taken no time to get here – compared to his pedal bike.

The pillion passenger was not enjoying the same pleasurable experience. Thelma needed something to hold on to as he started to move off the driveway, and the loose sides of Hector's anorak were grabbed. As the speed gradually increased, the grasp changed to around his middle.

As he started moving into the corners, she could not resist it becoming a panicky tightening of the grip, finding herself involuntarily, and frighteningly, leaning over with his body towards the road surface as he started taking the corners at a more confident and faster speed.

National speed limits were being achieved easily, but control on the straight parts of this road was important, and though he wanted to push it higher, good sense prevailed. With no insurance, being stopped for speeding would do him no good whatsoever.

Feeling her body moving nicely with him when he leaned over at the corners had pleased him – a difficult thing to do, particularly for the first time. A woman holding him tightly wasn't something he'd felt for a long time, he realised, and this woman was hugging into him. He could feel her body heat reaching him. *Hmmmm... I could get to like this...* He remembered how Daisy had used to...

He slowed down enough to speak to his passenger.

"Is that far enough?" he shouted back over his shoulder.

"Definitely!" she yelled back at him.

He could tell she was really enjoying this, and took it easy on the short return journey. He was happy as he drove it confidently back inside the garage, as if he did this every day.

Thelma's legs felt wobbly, and she staggered a bit, reaching towards him. He grabbed her before she fell, and held her, until she appeared more stable. Twice in one day he'd been in the grip of this other woman. *Eat your heart out Daisy*, he thought, as Thelma smiled her thanks to him.

"I forgot to hand in the key," she said, as they pushed the pedal cycles down to the roadside. "One moment," and she went back to the house door.

"Tell Peter, thank you very much for the opportunity to try the bike," she said to the wife. "And could you give him a message please, from me?"

"I'll wake him if you like," his wife offered.

"No, no, it was just to say how very, very sorry I am, but I'll not be back at my job. I'll put it in writing. The circumstances have changed, nothing to do with him, and tell him to hold onto the wages he owes me for last week. I owe him for a new pair of shoes. I'm afraid it was my puddle made his feet wet."

Mrs Peter Jameson had no idea what Thelma, who seemed suddenly to have become a threat, was getting at – but the gentleman, lying snoring upstairs, had better be able to explain this woman's statement to her, when he awakes... *her puddle?*

44

Speaking on the telephone to her husband had always been a slow and painful business, but she'd got used to it over the years, appreciating how big a struggle it was for him, especially when he was in difficult situations. She also felt guilty with this persistent lie she was living, the double life of Daisy Smith – housewife and ever loving partner of Hector Smith, and her doppelganger, Granny Wisdom – star of the local hit radio programme.

There she was sitting in a London hotel bedroom feeling lonely, pretending she was in the next room to her ailing aunt, (what name had she called her again? ...Oh yes, Mary,) her ailing Aunt Mary, knowing that telling downright lies was wrong, but was something which had to be done. She couldn't tell Hector her secret.

It had been a hard day, and not particularly successful either. It was Carol she felt sorry for, being burdened by her all day, feeling she needed to keep Granny Wisdom entertained. It was abnormal for Daisy to drink much alcohol, but tonight a stiff drink would help a lot. She was very tempted by the bedroom's drinks bar.

The meetings they'd had to attend were short. They'd been limited by the availability of the executives. Carol was doing most of the talking and manipulating of this important production team, and though doing her best, even Daisy was unimpressed. Attempts to explain the show's style sounded pretty lame even though having been presented by Daisy successfully now for many weeks, but who knows what these people made of it? Daisy had stopped thinking.

Sightseeing in London had been the main occupation for Carol and Daisy since arrival on Wednesday, but they had been wasted days.

Wasted? That was very unfair on Carol, because she was trying so hard, attempting to keep Daisy's days full and interesting. Daisy really liked Carol and hadn't the heart to remind her of her advanced years, how each night since being here, when she went to bed she collapsed from exhaustion. However, a sound sleep every night was the result.

Madame Tussauds, Buckingham Palace, the Tower of London, the West End, Tate Modern, the London Eye, a boat trip on the Thames – you name it, they'd done it, and on top of that, two theatre shows in the evenings, as well. At this minute on the other side of the wall, Carol would be frantically planning another day.

Thank goodness tomorrow was Sunday – back to Newingsworth on Monday in time for the show and semi-normality with Hector. He must be really missing her.

The phone-call to him on Friday night at Sally and Derek's must have been the wrong number, because no-one there seemed sober, or even able to understand what she was saying. So, she left it until teatime Saturday and the call went through successfully – Derek answered.

Usually Sally was in control of the phone, but when Derek was asked he didn't seem to be sure where Sally was. She was either in the bathroom having a shower, or in the kitchen making a special meal, he said. Hector sounded a bit befuddled as well. When she asked him what surprise Sally was concocting in the kitchen for them, she was told it was a 'Ch-ch-chicken k-k-k-k-korma c-c-c-carry-out', which was most unlike Sally. She usually avoided that sort of rubbish altogether.

"Are you behaving yourself?" Daisy asked jokingly and Hector became quite shirty at that, responding with, "Wh-wh-wh-why, wh-wh-what have you h-h-h-heard?" which sounded mighty suspicious to her, so, he was obviously enjoying himself.

"I hope you are not annoying Sally?" she chided.

"H-h-h-how c-c-could I b-b-be?" he replied, thinking how could I be when I haven't even seen the girl!

Daisy started to say what a hectic day she'd had, and then

suddenly realised that she was about to tell him the truth, and quickly switched tack. It became: Aunty Mary had a really bad day, sick as a dog, and what a mess she made.

"What is she g-g-g-going to d-d-d-do if you are c-c-coming home on M-M-M-Monday?" he asked.

"Her ...eh ...home help ...y'know ...gets back ...ehm ...on M-M-M-Monday," Daisy stuttered out in reply, stumbling seriously over the lie. Although she could tell lies, she could never have claimed to be accomplished at it, and that was by far her worst attempt ever...

Now it was Monday again and here she was sitting at the studio desk back at 'Little Radio fm', with the show halfway through, the jingles and adverts being controlled by Carol. It was nice to be back, but to appear jolly and interested in the job was proving difficult today.

There was the usual mix of phone calls, crazy, silly and funny, and with the usual mix-up of music and wrong buttons, but she felt guilty about some, doing them deliberately – it was expected of her now, but ...she wouldn't be keeping going for much longer with the show. It was a recent decision by her, reached surprisingly easily, and it was her guess that Curly and Carol would not object too much about her pulling out.

Here we go again, jingles over, fade-in Granny Wisdom...

"And do we have any more phone calls, Carol?"

"Yes, there is a gentleman who says he wants to make a confession, but I'm afraid the line isn't very good. Have a try. It can't be any worse than the rest of your attempts, Granny – ha, ha, only joking," Carol sang out in the usual agreed manner.

"Hello, young man, and how can I help you?" Daisy said in a motherly voice.

"I am n-n-n-not young," said the caller.

"Oh, well what can I do for you old fellow? It's a very bad line, isn't it?"

"There's n-n-n-nothing wrong at m-m-m-my end," said the voice.

"Fine, so you have a confession, have you? You do know that it's not the same as going to the chapel to confess, don't you? It's sort of lacking in confidentiality when you come on here, you know. I might not be the only one listening..."

"I've g-g-g-got to t-t-tell someone. My wife's away just n-n-n-now."

At this point, Daisy thought she recognised the voice, but no, too much of a coincidence...

"...And since she went, I've f-f-f-found a new p-p-p-p-p-passion."

"I think I can safely say – we are all ears, aren't we, Carol? What have you been getting up to, you old rascal, without your wife there to control you?"

"My new p-p-p-passion? She's such a b-b-b-b-beautiful m-m-mover – a really f-f-f-fast one – especially when she's w-w-warmed up."

"Ooooh, what are you going to say next? Remember it's a family show."

"I c-c-c-could sit l-l-listening to her p-p-purring all day, but she's g-g-got a roar too. What I know is I l-l-l-l-l-love her, but she'd p-p-p-probably be too exp-p-p-pensive for m-m-m-me."

"Boy, is your wife going to be surprised when she gets home? She might notice if your bank balance is getting low. What else are you going to tell us about your new passion?"

"Oh – she is b-b-b-beautifully c-c-cushioned, and with her susp-p-p-p-pension, she easily c-c-c-copes with t-t-t-two..."

"Caller ...we may have to end this..."

"I'd be so p-p-proud of her. If I had her for k-k-keeps, I'd g-g-get her really c-c-c-c-c-clean. I would w-w-wash her d-d-down once a week at least."

Carol was poised with her finger on the button, knowing that when the time came to abruptly censor, or end, this conversation, Daisy would never find the right control.

"Having a r-r-ride, wearing l-l-l-l-leather is b-b-best, but when you w-w-w-want, she's easy to s-s-s-stop."

"No doubt she'll have to when your wife gets home and catches you, you dirty old devil," and that was said with all seriousness, because suddenly the penny dropped. *How could she have been so dumb? No wonder she couldn't catch him on Friday night – another woman. It was her Hector...*

"But I d-d-d-don't know where I'd k-k-keep her..."

"Sinbad – you will certainly not be keeping her," Granny Wisdom spat out. "I'll see you when I get home..."

The chat was ended abruptly, much to the caller's consternation and leaving him in a state of confusion. Only his old mates knew he was called Sinbad...

45

The show today couldn't end quickly enough for Daisy. It would have been bad enough if a friend had phoned-in with revelations about naughty behaviour, but to have her own husband, her Hector, not only phoning and confessing freely about his misdemeanours when she wasn't there – but doing it live on air! Could anything have been worse? What was wrong with the man, talking like a love struck teenager? He was over seventy years old, for goodness sake...

"An interesting bloke you had on today," said Carol afterwards. "I was surprised how patient you were with the stutter. I'd have been trying to help finish sentences for him. You seemed to have no problem. How did you manage?"

"Experience, Carol, it's all down to that – unfortunately."

The further indignity of having to leave the building by the wheelie bin could wait a little while longer. Making a phone call would come first, and she searched for Sally's number. Contacting her at her office did not feel right because she presumed for Sally and Derek that Monday would normally be a very busy day. In fact, she presumed at their sort of jobs, what they did always kept them busy – deadlines and those sorts of things.

As she held the phone, she felt jealous of the loving relationship being enjoyed by Sally and Derek. Working together as they did must be great – probably able to communicate with each other, without having to actually say certain things out loud. At their stage in marriage, reading each other's mind would still be fun. She could remember how it had been when she and Hector were married at first... The dialling tone stopped, she was connected and the voice answered.

"Sally? Hello, it's me, Granny Smith. I hope I'm not disturbing you too much."

"Of course not, Gran, are you phoning from home? Should I ring you back?"

"No," she replied hurriedly, "I'm ...uhm ...phoning from ...Auntie Mary's. I've been trying to get hold of Grandad without any success." Telling lies could quickly become habit forming, she'd found over the last few months, "...to tell him that I'm going to have to stay here with the old lady for a while longer. He is still with Derek and you, isn't he?"

"Well ...yes, I think so. Well ...I don't know Gran..."

"What's wrong, Sally?" There was a sudden bout of panic – was it a guilty conscience. Had he ended it all...? "He's all right, isn't he?"

"Probably, but I don't know because..." and the tears were starting, Daisy could tell, even over the telephone, "...because Derek and I had a big argument and I left home. I'm not staying at the cottage. I'm living with Mum and Aunt Thelma at Cloverton."

Daisy was becoming a right agony aunt, whether she wanted it or not, and she didn't want it just now – she had her own problems – but this was her Sally... Oh dear.

"So, tell me, what did he do?" Daisy realised how biased the question was, automatically blaming the male of the species, but under the circumstances...

"It was his dressing up – in strange clothes," Sally sobbed.

"Oh well, that's not so bad surely, Sally, it could have been much worse. It could have been another woman."

"It was that as well..."

What – her grandson Derek? He's turning out like his grandad, how terrible... Quick – change the subject. "Oh. So is Grandad back at our own house then?"

"I think he's still at the cottage. Look, leave it with me. I'll make sure the message gets passed to him – somehow. I'm sorry to have burdened you with my problems."

"I just wish I was nearer, to help."

"Anyway, how is Auntie Mary?"

"It could be terminal, Sally. Yes, it could be the end," and as she said it, Daisy suddenly realised – she was beginning to believe Aunty Mary actually existed.

"Oh dear, how sad," said Sally who was now back in control of her emotions, "You must be under a terrible strain."

"Oh yes, I am," moaned a self-pitying Granny Wisdom, as she said her farewell.

Provided Hector was still at Derek's, she could return to her own home, and be on her own. At this moment, although feeling hurt and unable to face her two-timing husband, Blytheton Road would not be the same without Hector. She realised sadly, over the longer term, she might have to get used to it. However – and she made a promise to herself – *if he is there when I get back, I'll probably have to kill him!*

46

Spider was late for lunch, still in the office during Gran's call to Sally, and all because of a fault with his printer. While trying to fix it, he couldn't fail to hear one end the conversation, and somehow sensed he might be required when Sally's phone call was over.

The more interesting part for Spider was learning one of the reasons for the upset of the two lovebirds – Derek had been wearing strange clothes. Spider couldn't imagine what could be so serious about that – but, he gathered, there was also something else, and it caused Sally's tears but what it was he didn't know.

Spider was deeply involved, for many weeks chasing between the two of them, passing little curt pieces of essential information. If he had been a mercenary sort of person he would have been in at Rob, demanding a substantial increase in his salary due to the additional workload and responsibilities of keeping office life ticking over.

The call had ended and Sally called out...

"Spider..."

He left the printer, and went across to her desk.

"When Mr Toozlethwaite returns, would you be kind enough to tell him, Aunty Mary is poorly and his Gran will not be returning home yet, and ask him to convey the message to his grandfather – and Spider – thank you for being such a help in a trying situation."

Now, that had been a very important 'thank you', and much appreciated – better than any financial recompense.

Errand boy again but he didn't mind – *Aunty Mary* – *Granny under great strain* – *message to be passed on to Derek.*

Derek was late returning to the office. Sally had already departed, and the boss, Rob, also. He shot off a little early to catch the bookmaker's before today's chosen race began.

More trouble with the printer for Spider and he was making another attempt to fix it when Derek came in the door. *Remember the message. Now, what was it again? Damn it! This bloody thing is still not working... Yes, the message?*

"Derek, I am glad you are back – a communication from your dear wife. Is it your aunt who's unwell or Sally's? ...Aunty Mary? Sally said she is very poorly and getting worse by the minute, and that's why your gran is staying wherever it is that she is... OK? And you have to inform your grandad, urgently. I'm glad I remembered."

"Who is Aunty Mary?" asked Derek.

"Are you asking me?"

"Well, you are the only one in the room just now who might know..." Derek noticed Spider's eyes glaze over, "...but you don't – so that's two of us."

Would Grandad understand the message? That was Derek's thought as he cycled home, but Hector wasn't yet back from the supermarket where he was buying the ready-made food for their meal. It was just the two of them again for a short spell. It certainly meant the cottage was a bit quieter for the last few days. It was like a holiday to Derek, not having Alexander and Hammy in the place.

Another gathering of the four of them would be taking place shortly.

A second attempt to enter the premises of '*Tipsicorus International*' was on the cards, and this time they were going to dig for the treasure, and planning for that could be more complicated.

Meanwhile, Hammy was sitting in his own home for a number of days, and wishing he wasn't.

He stood up, he sat down, stood up, sat down again, fidgeted, missing all the fun they'd had as a gang of four, and counted off the hours until they would be meeting and trying again.

Alexander visited Cloverton, but even limiting it to one overnight stop for the collection of clean clothing, in that short period and avoiding the mention of Derek's name, he found that neither he nor Sally had lost the knack of getting on each other's nerves.

The peaceful haven for him, over the following days, was the flat in town. His involvement with Newingsworth Farm, and the other three, wasn't over yet, so he would settle himself in the flat until the four males were to re-group.

He could be visited at the flat if required but only if he didn't bring Sally, was the message Derek received. There was no chance of that...

Why Sally and her father couldn't happily co-exist in the same house, Derek could not understand. He'd no idea who was at fault there. At least the reason for discord in his current relationship with Sally was apparent.

It was clearly all his fault and the sad part was – he couldn't see a way out of it.

His Grandad was doing a great job in cleaning the Manor.

Except for the cooking of food, he was quite a different person compared to when Derek stayed with him and Gran at Blytheton Road. There, the two males had taken full advantage of Gran's willingness to run after them. Neither had known which end of the vacuum to use, but now Grandad was a wonder. After Alexander and Hammy left, he scrubbed and polished the place, and even puffed up the cushions.

He opened windows and let in some fresh air – something unusual for the house recently. He even changed the bed-sheets and put a wash through the washing machine too. Derek still couldn't contemplate the washing machine, although he could cope, if pushed, with vacuuming carpets nowadays.

His grandad attributed his new-found skills to being left on his own on Mondays, when Gran went out 'shopping' all day.

It would be interesting to see what would happen when Alexander appeared back to stay at the cottage.

Grandad claimed the single bed the instant Alexander left. Derek knew though, that whoever lost might have to become his bedtime partner – a difficult choice.

Ah, the sound of the front door opening – the food is about to walk in the door.

"Hi, Grandad, had a good day?"

"So, so, D-D-D-Derek, I ran out of Fairy L-L-L-Liquid, so I couldn't finish all my d-d-d-dishes. And there was a q-q-q-queue at the check-outs, and then I'd to p-p-p-pump up my t-t-tyre, because some young t-t-tyke had let it d-d-d-down."

"That's nice," said Derek who stopped listening after the first two words. "Oh, while I remember, there was a message left to be passed on to you from my dear absent wife. Apparently I have an Aunty Mary..."

"Oh, h-h-have you? So, has your g-g-g-gran. Qu-qu-qu-quite a c-c-c-coincidence isn't it?"

"Gran has an Aunty Mary too? I didn't know she had an Aunty Mary."

"I d-d-d-didn't know either – until r-r-recently. Your g-g-g-g-gran went to stay with her until she got b-b-b-better she told me."

"Well maybe that's it. Aunty Mary's at death's door and Gran will be with her until after the funeral. That's what Spider said."

"Now, that's odd. I th-th-thought I saw your g-g-g-gran get out of a white v-v-van at the s-s-s-supermarket. No, I m-m-must have b-b-been wrong."

Derek doubted his grandad's eyesight.

Listening every Monday to his gran had become the norm for Derek, but today he had missed the show. He presumed it had been broadcast as normal, but if she was still in London ...at Aunty Mary's, how had she managed it? That was strange?

Hector didn't admit it to Derek, it was almost certain as far as he was concerned, but it could be all over between him and her. She'd been with the other fellow in the white van, just as he suspected all along – and then was telling people she was with Aunty Mary. *Aunty Mary is dying*, "M-m-my f-f-f-f-foot."

"Your feet bad again, did you say, Grandad?" asked Derek, but to no response, "Did you enjoy Granny Wisdom today then?"

Grandad never missed the programme. If it hadn't been

broadcast, his grandad would know.

"It was a v-v-v-very g-good show t-t-t-today and b-b-b-better than usual. It helped me get things off m-m-my chest."

Derek worried about his grandad. His mind seemed to wander at times. Maybe hunger was the cause – it was certainly Derek's problem at the moment...

47

The four portions of fish and chips were consumed with gusto and a couple of cans of beer washed them down, but after that simple meal for a Friday night, and even with filled stomachs, somehow the ideas were just not rising to the surface.

Around the kitchen table sat four of the best brains in Newingsworth. If only one of them could come up with a workable idea the atmosphere in the cottage would improve tremendously, but it looked unlikely tonight. They knew what they were hunting for, and where they had to go, but they didn't know how to do it.

It was maybe a good thing Sally had not returned. The delightful aroma of the fish drifting around the house would not have pleased her, and the smell would remain for a long time. Derek now regretted the choice of meal. If she did reappear it would be yet another thing to hold against him, and reduce the chances of her remaining.

Derek's hope had been that the foray to the farm would be all over and done with tonight, so that Alexander and Hammy could return to their own homes immediately after. If it didn't happen tonight, there could be unrest in the camp. He didn't think Alexander would be too willing to be sleeping in the same bed as Hammy. If they were all here, would a fight ensue if Grandad refused to swop from the single?

Unfortunately, the way proposals were developing, or rather the way they were not, was beginning to make the sleeping problem inevitable. A practical plan for digging up treasure, up to now was nowhere on the horizon, so they opened more beer cans to help them think.

Obviously, diversionary tactics would be required. Maybe even crash helmets could be worn, Derek suggested, remembering his suffering on the last occasion. They could expect rough handling from this gang, especially if it went wrong a second time. If they were growing cannabis in the barn, as Hammy had claimed, it was no wonder they objected so strongly to interlopers.

Why the police hadn't done something about it, they could not understand. The male and female arms of the law had been there, but treated the four of them as bad guys, and ignored the real villains. Is it possible the police didn't realise what was really happening behind the ten-foot fence? Should they be told? Yes, in the right way, and as long as it didn't bounce back to implicate them. An anonymous phone call, a tip-off, would be a possibility and the villains might then be caught, but using that idea could prevent Hammy getting at the treasure.

"Help ma Boab, ah nearly forgoat tae say tae ye – when ah got the box last time an' opened the big gate, ah forgoat tae hand back the key furr the padlock."

Now that could be useful. They had a key for the padlock on the gate, and they had a key for the farmhouse kitchen door. It was getting better, now keep thinking...

The floodlights Hammy switched off – they hadn't been on to begin with when they climbed over the fence. They couldn't have been seen, surely? How did these guys know they were there? It wasn't as if they'd made any noise – they couldn't have heard anything either.

"D-d-d-do you think they c-c-c-could have these infrar-r-r-red lights that l-l-let you see in the d-d-dark?"

Now Grandad was showing some smart thinking. They all agreed it was possible but if it was, how could they get in again if watched all the time?

The beer reached Alexander's brain. "We need a bigger problem than us to occupy their minds. Could we set the place on fire?"

"Och no ...no' ma wee fairm hoose. Ah used tae live therr remember." Hammy wasn't happy.

"No, no, around the perimeter, to draw attention away from the gate and let you get to the barn," continued Alexander. "Fire usually makes people panic, I'd say, and they always have to do something about it."

Now this was becoming interesting – a practical proposal.

"So, who goes in this time?" he continued, "The fires could be raised from the outside."

It looked like Alexander was game for living a dream – a bit of the action-man – not the sort of thing your common or garden bank manager gets up to during the normal working day, "...We could use petrol, a couple of cans of the stuff, matches, and long tapers so we don't get our eyebrows singed."

This was the first and only well-rounded action plan of the night and it received a round of applause, which Alexander took as a vote of confidence. It was the first time Derek had seen his father-in-law blush.

"Weel, ah volunteer to huvv a shovel and go inside. Urr ye comin' wi' me, Sweaty? Or urr you wantin' to be daein' some fire raisin'?"

"Grandad, are you ok on the outside with Alexander?" asked Derek eagerly.

"I wouldn't m-m-m-miss this for the w-w-w-world."

"But what happens if they don't all go to the fire and somebody sees us?" asked Derek.

"Och, ye'll be wearin' Sally's tights again, they willnae recognise ye. Dinna you worry, Sunshine – nothin' can go wrong."

48

Earlier this week, he had been slogging away with all the normal work at the office, in and out as required, but feeling the looks of hatred and distrust emanating constantly from Sally. It was poor Spider he was feeling sorry for.

It might have been imagination, but to Derek, Spider appeared to be getting thinner under the strain of being go-between. At least getting thinner hadn't happened with him. Carry-outs and fast food, more or less every night, were keeping him robust, or another way of putting it – he was becoming podgy.

The over-length T-shirts for Arthur and Charlie were organised and, now that it had been accepted by the Bisko's Store Manager, he'd arranged for the shirts to be printed with his super slogan, but he hadn't told the two runners about their outfit. He wasn't sure how they'd take it – for sure if he had been running, he wouldn't be happy.

'Little Radio fm' would be covering the marathon, with the now well-publicised local heroes, Arthur and Charlie, wearing headset mikes for interviewing fellow competitors at any time along the route. Asking them to describe how they were feeling, and to describe the surrounding townscape as they gallop along might have seemed a good idea of Carol's, but Derek had doubts on its practicality.

There were second thoughts when he remembered the day he ran behind them. Though he collapsed from exhaustion, they'd never stopped to even take a breath, chattering on about their gardening work – non-stop chattering too – yet on the Granny Wisdom Show they'd dried? Maybe, as long as no-one mentions paper bags they would be all right, but it could go either way, and anyway, it would not be his concern.

Slow progress was being made on Andy Woodstock's detective tale. Derek was forcing himself to continue, but his marker pen was taking on a life of its own as he read page after page of what he felt was utter drivel. In fact, he was now re-editing his previous edits, creating a story he preferred, while knowing inside it was not what he should be doing; this way he was destroying someone else's dreams. Why was he behaving like this? Could it be jealousy on his part? No, of course it wasn't, he reassured himself – just crap story-telling ...but Derek was biased.

Tonight, it was all happening. Alexander had his mobile in his pocket, and Derek had his. Hector had never actually owned one but didn't care, and Hammy had lost his somewhere in his new abode, and didn't care either. The older men couldn't understand this younger generation having to walk around with one of those things glued to the ear, seeing nothing of the world all around.

Hector and Hammy grew up enjoying the anonymity of where they were, what they were doing, and who they were with. They settled for the old fashioned wire vanishing into a wall, which would let you to talk to America or Australia, when and if you wanted, and only now and again. To them, it seemed like the modern generation not being able to let go of mother's apron strings. Tonight though, both older men could see the benefits of being able to communicate from outside the fence to inside, but they also displayed a worryingly cocky confidence.

There they were – four heads wearing the same shade of nylon stocking to cover and distort faces and ears, and each with the same size of nylon foot projecting provocatively from the top of each head. Derek looked at the other three and hoped he didn't look as ugly as they did. He was glad it was dark.

When the moon appeared, they were able to be seen clearly by him tonight because he took the precaution of wearing contact lenses instead of his specs. Normally, his contact lenses remained in the drawer unused, too much bother.

He wondered if Sally would be any less upset by him wearing her stockings in this manner, and sharing them with others, than she had been when he ruined her shoes. He would have to remember to replace four pairs of the same type of tights before she returned, presuming there would be a return. Nothing could be guaranteed on that score, as far as he could tell.

The same approach route as last time was being used, through the dark and obstacle-strewn fields, trees, and bushes. It seemed a long way.

Without torchlight, this time, because they'd chosen it to be that way, though they had torches with them, in case ...and they did use them once, to cross the stream successfully at the stepping stones. No reconnaissance beforehand this time either. It had been decided whoever was on look-out at the farm shouldn't be alerted by one of them appearing to be just passing the time of day nonchalantly, by wandering around the outside of the fence. It was not a public footpath.

The moon appeared every so often, which helped a bit when traipsing through the fields and undergrowth, but they were hoping the clouds would become more obliging when they arrived at the fence and do a good job of obscuring the moon.

As he walked behind, Derek could see his grandad having a struggle carrying the canister of petrol, changing hands regularly because of the awkwardness of the small handle, so he swopped with him. So now Hector had a spade, same as Hammy – Alexander had the other canister filled with the petrol.

The group trudged with awkward steps into and out of squelchy soft stuff, tripping over the boulders and tree stumps which seemed to persist in creeping onto the path they were forging. They were attempting to follow each other's footsteps closely because of the dark, with each pair of feet confronting the exact same obstacle two paces after the person in front. Each felt the tension as the destination came closer.

When Hammy thought about it earlier, he had pictured the inside of the farmhouse as he'd moved along the hallway, glancing into the rooms. He thought he had seen small televisions, sitting side by side, but these were now presumed to be monitors for the CCTV. The same room was lit again tonight and, in the bluish light, someone could be seen dimly.

The fence had been reached but they kept back from it. Their timing must be right if their diversionary tactics were to be a success. The plan for the use of the petrol had been discussed, but it was one thing to talk in the comfort of an armchair about how a task should be carried out, and actually another to do it. It was vital that they did not suffer any personal injuries. They were aware how unstable petrol could be in these circumstances, especially, if what was decided to be a 'safe' means of ignition, proved to be otherwise.

Alexander came up with the idea of using a roll of toilet paper like a fuse. One canister of the petrol would be poured out along the perimeter of the fence, close to its base; a petrol moistened roll of toilet paper would be removed from the plastic bag; they would unroll it until they reckoned they were far enough away at a safe enough distance not to be scorched by the flames, and hopefully to avoid being seen in the resulting light. Hector would light the end of the toilet paper and...

It had to be Hector who would be using the match, in case Alexander had splashed any petrol on his own shoes or clothing. He'd be wearing rubber gloves, to be discarded, but petrol could get anywhere. He hated the smell when he'd been to the local garage to fill up the cans, then paid extra to a taxi driver to allow the stink to enter his cab. Being an environmentalist had its drawbacks; sometimes it would be easier just to drive a car himself...

It would have been smarter if they'd had the gumption to do a test beforehand and prove the fire-lighting theory would work, but they hadn't. So, naturally, there was nervousness in the group, and Hector, for one, wished he'd brought extra underpants.

The timing of the first fire was to attract all the men away from inside the house, they hoped. There was no certainty of there being only three men. The motorbike which went along the lane, delivering, or collecting or whatever, the man on it – was he one of the three or, could there be actually four people involved? They had very little knowledge of what was going on in there. A presumption was also that these guys lived on the premises.

Getting from the gate to the barn across the open yard would be impossible for Derek and Hammy if the plan did not work. Derek tried not to think of that – if all went wrong, immediate surrender was his plan.

His mobile was on. He asked Alexander to check his. A glance at the time it showed, two o'clock exactly, deliberately later than last time, in the hope that sleep would have overtaken the guys who weren't doing the watching, and that the screen-watcher would be very drowsy.

So, mobiles at the ready, petrol at the ready, spades at the ready, and the highly inflammable toilet paper at the ready, it was almost time to move. Hector wished now he'd brought an extra fresh roll of toilet paper, for emergency use. He had that horrible feeling again...

This would be a team effort, but they could do without any silly group hug! Four hands were held out, to display stoicism and comradeship, with each of them failing to hide their fears, but hoping the others wouldn't notice. For a moment, four trembling hands linked – and then they were off...

49

As they came closer they discovered they could see right into the room. The dull light emitted by the three small screens showed the shadowy figure sitting in front of them. Derek decided he'd crawl closer, commando style. When they were pretend soldiers in the pretend jungle in his younger days, he'd moved about that way, but it had been a long time ago, and he hadn't found it easy even then. He regretted the macho approach the moment he dropped to the ground, but he had to go on, so it was done with a bit of showmanship and bravado that he didn't really feel.

For Hammy, he felt he had to go along with the method being demonstrated by Derek, his fellow team member. Down he went, his knees cracking as he bent, dropping onto his belly, elbows already feeling the pain. As he lay panting and about to start, he found Derek already had been there and back. They crawled away from the fence again as another brighter light came on in a different room.

Derek stood up. Hammy tried to – and failed. Derek's helping hand was not shrugged off, and with a bit of a stagger, both were upright again and moving back to be beside the other two. They could see no shadowy figure now in front of the screens. Had he moved? Was it him now in the next room?

"Whit's he daein' noo? Och, it's ok, he's gone ben tae the kitchen an' he's fillin' thur kettle," whispered Hammy. "The sink's at the windae. It's 'is tea break."

Hector and Alexander stayed well back from the fence. Their task was to be at the opposite end from the gate. No other lights were showing anywhere else in the farmhouse. One man observed and on his own, they reckoned – others presumed asleep. Derek suggested that if the only one awake was in the kitchen, maybe now would be a good time to undo the padlock and chain. When that man was in the kitchen, he wasn't seeing the screens.

"Where's the key?" Derek asked Hammy. "I'll go round and undo the padlock and chain, you three stay here and make sure he stays in the kitchen. If he goes back to the screens, you could warn me with a bird call, and I'll hide again."

Wire cutters – they should have thought of bringing them in case the key wouldn't fit. One thing they'd presumed when Hammy presented his pocketed padlock key was that the inhabitants had a spare, and would consider the other to be lost. If they hadn't, the old padlock would have already been sawn off and replaced. In that case, it would be back to climbing the fence.

Off Derek went staying well back from the fence, walking upright, and obviously moving quicker and using less energy than by belly. Straight to the gate he went, hoping, of course, their assumptions were correct that no-one else was manning the screens, and it was still the same padlock.

Reaching to the padlock was proving awkward – it was chained from the inside. He was struggling to stretch through the hand-hole, and just about to check the key, when he felt his phone vibrate. Trouble... He ran for cover as he tried to pull the mobile from his pocket. They were supposed to have used the bird call to warn him...

"Hi, this is Priscilla and I'm pleased to be calling to tell you that today is your lucky day," a smarmy American accent was informing him, "...and to congratulate you on winning a free Caribbean holiday. And all you have to do is ..."

Thank goodness, they'd set their mobiles to silent, before leaving the cottage. A free holiday communication from the States at this time in the morning, and under these circumstances, was not something he felt inclined to follow up. He stood up again and went back towards the gate, reached for the padlock, was delighted to find the key fitted, unlocked it, and was removing the chain slowly and quietly, when he heard the bird call.

"Cuckoo-cuckoo-cuckoo-cuckoo..."

Was it four o'clock on the farmhouse clock, or had they just been stupid enough to choose a cuckoo as their bird noise? He'd meant an owl... He shot back into cover and threw the chain and padlock behind the bushes. Now the phone was needed.

"Gate loosened – ready for access – send Hammy now and proceed to action stations."

Derek's message to Alexander sounded highly efficient, as if the operation was being run with military precision. Alexander and Hector hurried together to the far end. They reckoned the likelihood of any military precision, being applicable to what they were about to do, was extremely low.

While sitting around the table in the cottage last evening holding a part-consumed can of beer, the idea of throwing the petrol towards the fence, then lighting it to create an eye-catching display, had seemed an easy way to grab the attention of the inhabitants of the farm. Now, in the dark, and with the expectation of discovery any second, followed by the probability of some more rough treatment from the inhabitants, the idea seemed much less appealing. A do-it-to-yourself barbecue didn't seem smart either, but they had to proceed.

Alexander's task was the petrol, as close to the fence as could be spread, without him being seen. Hector was in charge of the toilet roll. They'd obtained the toughest quality of paper available, the sort that did the human bottom no good whatsoever and that no caring mother would touch on the supermarket shelves. A light dribbling of petrol onto the roll had been done successfully, and allowed to soak. Unwinding would have to be done carefully – this was to be their equivalent of the 'blue touch paper'. Having it coming apart, in single sheets, would not serve the correct purpose at all... In his pocket Hector carried the matches, the extra long, household ones, which they hoped would prevent setting themselves on fire.

There was hesitation by Alexander as he splashed the fuel about. Why were they doing this again? Obviously, it was to create a diversion – but petrol...

He reminded himself that if Hammy was going to regain the possessions that the new owners refused to let him have, they had to get inside the fenced compound. So, he was doing it for Hammy...

Also, but not so obviously, it would let Derek feel that he was getting his own back, if only a little, for the head-squashing of the last visit.

When they were ready they would be lighting the toilet paper, which would ignite the petrol, which would go off with a 'whoosh' and there would be panic inside, the occupants would rush outside, away from the CCTV screens, and Derek and Hammy could sneak into the barn ... Easy...

Alexander looked at Hector. Hector looked at Alexander.

The petrol had been splashed and spread about until the can was empty. The paper trail leading back to the soaked area was just discernible as a ribbon of white. The petrol covered disposable gloves now removed and ...they were ready!

A match was struck, and held tentatively by Hector, applied to the toilet paper and...WHOOOOSH...

They were very glad they were well clear. The countryside was suddenly lit by a million trillion candlepower ...and they moved back even further. That was fun!

The CCTV monitors didn't do it justice. Standing at the window gazing out, thankful for an invigorating black coffee in his hand to waken him, the sudden explosion of light had a startling effect. The coffee went up in the air, the mug went too, and the bloke yelped and ran to the door, screaming for the others to get their bloody arses out of bed, and quickly. In no time at all, three men were outside, two having had the sense to grab the only fire extinguishers, and were extinguishing the burning bushes and wood, as best they could.

Alexander phoned Derek and Hammy, all three occupants were currently suitably distracted. So, in the gate they went, closing it again behind them, but not replacing the padlock and chain – that would have been silly.

The old map and the position of the cross had been committed to memory by Hammy, having known the farmyard for a very long time. Visualising where he was aiming for, he counted paces across the yard as they went in, with Derek urging him silently to get a bloody move on, and eventually they reached the barn. Fortunately, the targeted barn had the earthen floor, the other was concrete, and the large door slid open, moving smoothly and silently.

It was unlikely the three amateur fire-fighters would have heard any sounds anyway, due to the noise they were making themselves, shouting and cursing at each other. They couldn't understand what had caused the flames...

The Irishman was pretty sure this was all to do with the badly installed electrics, done too rapidly in his opinion and at rock bottom prices when they took over the farm. He'd a bee in his bonnet about that. It wasn't the first time something proved amiss with the electrics recently. *Hadn't the lights fused the night these idiots climbed over the fence? And was anything found wrong with the fuses? No, it was definitely bad workmanship*, in his opinion.

"Oi tould ya, didn't oi?" became his favourite phrase, and was being obstinately repeated at this very moment.

Inside the barn there was light, and two interlopers with shovels. Derek and Hammy stood and gazed. It was so green, and with the fluorescent lights hanging close to the fresh vegetation, it seemed a bit like a film set for a jungle movie – but they should not be just standing there.

With a nudge and a nod to Derek, Hammy made his way around the top of the barn along a used path at the edge of the growth, and well away from the door. Where he was aiming for was nearer the far side but somewhere in the midst of all the greenery. Entering the long way would avoid the obvious footprints in the soil being seen if someone was to look in the door. Derek was close behind.

Hammy counted his steps from the end of the barn and landed about halfway along. His target was then about five metres towards the centre, in the midst of the bushy plant stalks. In he went, and again Derek followed, pushing aside the foliage, trying not to bang his head on the light fittings.

To Derek this was being destructive, and he was damaging something which was growing healthily, all very much against his nature. He had to keep telling himself he was in the midst of something illegal. Eventually this crop would be detrimental to some poor addictive mutt, who would pay dearly for the privilege of consuming it, while the bloke who sat upon his head, would become rich in the process. This salved his conscience.

At the selected position Hammy dug in his spade. Derek stood watching, leaning on his spade stuck into the soil in the professional way he'd seen Arthur and Charlie do in the park. Hammy was disappointed at the first attempt. He dug down two feet but there was nothing. The soil was moderately loose, fortunately, but he found it hard work enlarging the hole. He gave Derek the nod to start digging as well. His hitting metal initially sounded promising – it turned out to be only a horseshoe, followed by a rusty old bucket, and then an oilcan Hammy lost years ago, but sadly, no treasure...

This horseshoe was not one of the lucky ones.

"They've dumped mair soil in here than ah thocht," said Hammy. "We'll hae tae dig deeper," and so, deeper they went.

Outside the fence, two anxious figures were aware that the three men had totally extinguished the flames, had stopped arguing about the cause, and were going back inside the cottage. Outside, it seemed darker than before. The floodlights weren't used in the panic, and after the flames Alexander and Hector's eyes were taking a little time to become accustomed again to the blackness.

They were uncertain of the timing of the next part. Were the two in the barn having any success?

The next can of fuel was planned to be used to allow Derek and Hammy's escape, same sort of idea as before, but this time splashing petrol further inside the fence and in a different place. Alexander reckoned it must be nearly time – surely they'd found what they were looking for by now?

In preparation, he started throwing the contents of the can as far as he could, inside the perimeter, and saw it splash over some the scrap materials lying around. He was pretty sure Hammy wouldn't have left the yard in a mess like that.

Look where they'd parked the motor bike! Right beside the stack of wood – a stupid place.

Half the can was already used. He just kept throwing it about, making sure some would be outside the fence to make contact with Hector's touch paper again, which, much to their astonishment, did work effectively.

Hector was now doing his part too, carefully unrolling the next roll of loo paper. It had proved a creditably safe way of doing the job, and keeping well back when the loo roll was ignited had been wise. He was quite proud of himself and, surprisingly, his underpants were still ok.

This time he made sure they would be even farther away. Alexander had already removed his disposable gloves and left the empty can near the fence as he appeared again out of the darkness beside Hector. Hector had the match at the ready, but unlit.

Alexander whispered "I'm all ready to go."

Hector mistakenly heard it as, "I'm all ready, so go," and lit the match, and the paper, and... WHOOSH... again...

Wearing Sally's tights made their faces less obvious in the bright light, but no matter, they felt more vulnerable this second time, standing in the middle of the open field – so they ran...

The three inhabitants appeared outside far quicker this time, not having had the opportunity to return to a nice cosy bed, and again no floodlights, but this time the Cockney ran back inside to throw the switch. The other two grabbed buckets and fetched water, because they'd used up the fire extinguishers. The floodlights came on.

The water made little impression on the flames, if anything it helped the fuel to spread. The assorted wood and rubbish took light, and the rivulet of fire which ran over the hard ground reached the edge of the barn and started the wooden face-boards burning.

When he came out again, it was the Cockney who spotted the motor bike – the rear tyre was burning. All he could think of was to get away from it because the tank could explode, but worse still the bike was resting against the main electrical junction box. He ran to get another bucket, but could only find the plastic washing-up bowl full of unwashed dishes, so, he returned just in time to witness the bike's tank exploding – and all the lights going out...

Inside the barn, the surprise of the bang and the sudden darkness caused Hammy and Derek to fall in the substantial hole they'd created. The flames at the far end of the barn were now able to be seen inside, and they looked frightening.

They began to panic. Derek automatically whipped out his mobile and dialled 999...

"Which service do you require?" answered the very efficient sounding voice.

"Fire Service – urgently!" Derek said.

"Where are you calling from, please?" came back in a very calm manner.

"Tipsicorus International!" yelled back Derek.

"I beg your pardon?" said the voice.

"Tipsicorus International!" Derek yelled again.

"Where?"

"Tipsi..."

At this point Hammy grabbed the phone.

"Macintosh's Chooky Hens, Hen."

"Oh right, thank you. Why didn't you say that? We'll be with you in a tick," and in no time at all, the Fire Engine was roaring up the farm lane.

50

Alexander and Hector managed to stay together as they made their way back, both wishing that they hadn't panicked so readily. They were hoping at any moment to meet Derek and Hammy with the big box of family treasure, but they didn't, then when the motorbike exploded it was the closest Hector came to embarrassing himself.

The Fire Engine, arriving at the unlocked gate and was driven straight into the yard, closely followed by the police squad car which rushed to the scene of the emergency also. These arrivals came as a surprise to the three unfortunate gentlemen who were running back and forward with water (in two buckets and a wash basin), and unsure if they should be relieved, or not, the 'not' was their rapid conclusion.

Being well known to the police force, north of the border, would soon come to light if they remained with their current money-making project. The fact that they had given up a life of petty drug dealing in Glasgow, to become investors in cannabis production with the guarantee of large sales, as an entrepreneurial development might not be recognised for its true value by a nasty judge. He might not see them as they saw themselves – three hard-working farmers.

So, as the firemen and police came rushing in, the three ex-entrepreneurs left them to it, and, after hurriedly collecting a few essentials such as trousers and wallets and any obviously incriminating evidence, slipped away. Over the fields they went, accusing each other of being the effing idiot who'd left the chain and padlock off the gate. In addition, the poor Irishman kept lamenting, "Me boike, me pour ould boike..."

Hot on their heels went Derek and Hammy, still wearing the stocking masks. They'd rolled the barn door open to peep out, and been very glad to find the fire engine, with an empty police car behind it, stopped just outside.

It was not the first occasion that the blue flashing light of a police car had aided an escape from here. This time it was supplemented by the one on the fire engine. The vehicles, sitting one behind the other, made excellent cover allowing them to slip out unnoticed, the firemen having other interests and duties.

The vehicle floodlights were in the process of replacing the flames as the source of illumination.

PC Andy Woodstock and PC Yvonne Saunders went to look for the occupants of the farm, by the light of their torches of course. They were surprised that no-one could be found. In the front room of the farmhouse there was a broken coffee mug and new coffee stains on the floor, and a toppled chair in front of three unlit monitors.

Clothing was abandoned in untidy rooms, and with pride of place in one room, a motorcycle crash helmet was sitting on the window sill. They'd had their suspicions at the last visit that something odd was going on here. It certainly wasn't a family home. The fence, the padlock and chain, the three tough looking characters who'd been on the premises: the fact that there appeared to have been a gang fight, or the start of a gang war – all factors suggested to them that it would be better not to be involved...

However, here they were tonight, in the thick of it. It didn't look as if there would be any rough stuff though, if the occupants had fled. This disappointed PC Yvonne Saunders – she had some energy crying out for release.

What had been going on in the farm wasn't yet apparent to them, and then the Fire Chief came into the farmhouse to enlighten them... "You two might want to look at this. The vegetation is your problem, not ours, and anyway, I think they've buried someone..."

The barn door was now wide open with the fire engine's

floodlights directed into the space. It was a mass of green amongst dangling fluorescent lights fittings. The Fire Chief walked them round the path to the far side, and there, the man-sized hole with two shovels stuck in the ground, but no body to be seen ...yet.

"You two are going to have to dig it up," said the Fire Chief to the police officers. "It's not our department ...we don't do dead bodies..."

"Hello there, everyone, having fun? Now it looks like I've arrived just in time. So, it is dead bodies is it?" said a voice behind them. "...My favourite kind of story. I'm from the Gazette, and my sensors are telling me this could be interesting. Maybe you'd like to tell me all about it. My name's Toozlethwaite ...but you can call me Derek."

51

The Fire Chief left them and went to check on the success of the damping down procedures. Cause and effect would have to be investigated and reported, and was the part of the job which always slowed down the flow of his adrenalin. He'd been anticipating a gangland cremation, the grisly find of a body in the process of disposal by fire, but at least on this visit he'd been spared that – so far. However, he had a gut feeling...

As for the Press, to him they were a necessary evil. He had no real objection to them searching for a story. It would probably lead to the creation of bizarre headlines which didn't reflect the true facts, but provided it was not digging the dirt on him, his team, or the service, he would just let them get on with it. This person who'd appeared seemed innocuous, but you never can go on first impressions he found. This was obviously an ambulance chaser. He'd arrived quickly enough – hadn't he? It was almost as if he'd been hiding around the corner, but as Fire Chief, he couldn't afford to stand around like this – a Fire Chief had important things to do...

"And you think a body was buried then?" Derek said the police officer.

"I didn't say that," responded PC Woodstock, looking around for some back-up from Yvonne, but she'd gone off to do her own thing. He hoped she hadn't gone off in a huff again.

"It's already in the hole then?" Derek pursued.

"I didn't say that either. What did you say your name was?" and he looked closer at Derek's face.

"Toozlethwaite... but you can call me..."

"Sweaty," exclaimed a smiling PC Woodstock, "Sweaty Toozlethwaite. I remember now. And you'll remember me, don't you?"

"No," replied Derek, panicking and thinking that he'd forgotten to remove the stocking from his head. "No. My name is Derek," he insisted. It was only weeks since they had been almost face to stockinged face, in the police car. Had Andy Pandy recognised him from that incident?

"Oh yes... You prefer to be called Derek. Yes... I do remember. You and the crazy bank manager ...Davidson, wasn't it?"

Bugger it, Derek thought, he's onto us. I shouldn't have come back.

"Oh, uhmm ...is it my father-in-law you are referring to? And you think you know us, do you?" Play for time, Derek – don't lose your cool, he told himself.

"Of course I do. Do you not remember me? I was a detective then. I'm Andy, Andy Woodstock. You ran circles around me – you and that family," he smiled. "You helped me get back to what I really enjoy – being in uniform."

The man's an idiot, thought Derek, and why is he being friendly to me?

"Oh yes..." he responded.

"How could I forget the fun we had together?" Andy continued. "You even had me chasing after an aunt, an aunt who had nothing to do with the kidnap. I could have arrested her – by mistake, you know. That would have been a laugh!"

I don't think Aunt Thelma would have been too happy about it, thought Derek.

"Did you say it was the Gazette you were with?"

"Yes..." said Derek, cautiously, to his new-found friend.

"Confidentially..." and Andy looked around to make sure Yvonne hadn't crept up on him the way Derek had, "... have you heard anyone there mention...", and he checked over his shoulder again, "...my story?"

"Your ...story?"

"Yes. I gave it to a guy called Spider, in the pub. I haven't seen him again since."

"Is it called ...'The Door Creaked, by Andy Woodstock'?"

"Yes." ...The policeman's eyes started to sparkle.

"Are you that Andy?"

"Yea," the officer proclaimed proudly, but with just a touch of modesty thrown in for effect.

"Wow ...I'm the one who's editing it just now. We are going to use it, very soon." Derek refrained from adding that using it was much against his better judgement.

"Yes, it is good isn't it? I'm desperate to have it published. The best I've managed so far with the public has been on the local library intranet computer courses. They use it for their typing and editing classes," explained the author. "And you're married ...Derek. Who'd have thought it? Sally wasn't it? I bet she's a goer..."

How did he know she's gone, Derek asked himself? He was about to respond with, she hasn't left me, then he realised his mind was sitting on a different wavelength. It was none of this bloke's ruddy business whether Sally was a 'goer' or not...

"So, you think they've taken the body then?" Derek brought the over-friendliness session to an abrupt halt, "...or is it just buried very deep...?"

"Oh, well ...the fire chief has a gut feeling..." he added, and it was obvious the constable was not convinced.

"What about the cannabis?" Derek pursued.

"What cannabis?" asked the constable. "Oh – is that cannabis?"

Derek nodded.

"All of it?" asked the constable.

"Yes," Derek replied, feeling his new friend needed some help.

"But it's against the law – to grow cannabis. I've never seen it growing before," said the lawman.

Derek refrained from asking what form of it the constable was acquainted with, though it now seemed possible that the story Derek was currently editing could have been written with the aid of some hallucinogenic substance.

"I presume you'll be arranging for the destruction of this crop then," said Derek.

"It seems a shame, but yes. I might wait until the fire crew have gone and just relight the fire," mused the constable. "Do you have any matches?"

At this point Derek decided it might be wise to leave the scene. He was unsure whether PC Woodstock was joking or not. Anyway, he now had enough information from the horse's mouth and enough insider knowledge to be able to achieve a long awaited scoop, and tired though he was, Derek was eager, in few hours, to be back to work.

52

The past week had been dismal for Daisy, seven days of feeling guilty about lying to her husband, telling him she was still with a fictitious aunt in London but, she was actually staying on her own at 12 Blytheton Road – their home. She guessed that Hector was still with Derek, but she hadn't asked, being a little scared in case she found out he wasn't.

Her own daily guilt was being shared with feelings of anger, disappointment, and frustration. Hector, who'd been her husband, her love and her lover, for almost fifty years, had found someone else. How could he?

Yes, it was true, their lives gradually had become humdrum, she told herself sadly, *but don't all marriages cool a little after a long time? It doesn't stop you continuing to love a person – you just don't display the affection so often.*

In recent months she'd found her kicks away from home, getting her fun by being involved with Curly and Carol and the show – not forgetting George and a clothing hamper and a wheelie bin, of course. In the process of enjoying herself she'd excluded Hector, and losing him was no-one's fault but her own. She'd let him drift away...

There was a lack of enthusiasm for today's show. It was to be the last one. She would put on an act of jolliness, another crazy, silly attempt at not being a good broadcaster, even though now she felt professional, as a clown must feel, able to generate silliness but in a deliberately controlled way.

Still, she'd have to brighten up. It wouldn't be right making Carol feel bad about it as well.

Both Carol and Curly were very nice about her giving up the show. They hadn't expected the programme to have been the success it turned out to be, and anyway another idea was lined up to take her place. She didn't know what it was, and it was none of her business.

Daisy desperately wanted to crawl off and hide in a corner. Instead she was clambering into the wheelie bin, once again, but at least it was for the last time. Over the weeks, George had tried to make the journey for her as comfortable as a bin could be, and he had become a pal along the way. Thank goodness the photographer had given up hounding them.

Carol seemed more relaxed today, Daisy sensed. As the producer of the programme, the weight sitting on her shoulders all those weeks, of having to cope with the unexpected, was shortly to be removed. It was only two of them involved so far this morning, Carol and her. The callers would be queuing up shortly to challenge Granny Wisdom and eager to be taking the Mick probably, hoping that they'd have their moment of fame by contributing to the usual, unusual mayhem – the Granny Wisdom Show...

The jingles were finishing and the silly mix of music and sound effects which had become the introduction was playing. "Stand by..." and they were off again...

Concentrating on what was being said, and thinking ahead as to what mistakes and goofs she could create for the last time, helped her forget her preceding lousy week. She had to put on a good show. The show was the thing... Go out with a bang ...but when should she announce her farewell to the MOGGIES? She didn't want to encourage it to become the subject of the programme, eliciting calls which would be either sad at her finishing, or maybe even worse, pleased to be hearing the last of her. She would leave it until the very last moment and just keep it going brightly and stupidly ...and that's the way it went.

When the last call came in, she was actually enjoying herself again, and having a few regrets that the end was near. This caller was ready with another confession, Carol informed her off-air in advance, and her mind immediately went back to the stuttering caller the previous week...

"Hello, Granny Wisdom," said the female voice.

There was momentary silence, as Daisy's mind wandered sadly, going nowhere.

"Sorry caller," interjected Carol, "Granny Wisdom seems to have fallen asleep. Yoohoo... Granny, someone would like to talk to you."

Carol could see this little faux pas was not intentional and just hoped that fact had not been too obvious to the listeners.

"Oh sorry, dear, I was just checking my shopping list. I'm sure they've overcharged me for the six crates of Newcastle Brown. Now what was it you wanted to talk about? Something bright and cheerful I hope, to keep me awake..."

"I want to make a confession," said the caller.

"Don't tell me you are the one he ran off with. You aren't are you? Are you his new passion? Because if you are..." Daisy suddenly realised her true feelings were showing and that was not wise. She changed to her light-hearted manner, "...we want to hear more..."

"Heaven forbid," said the voice. "I'm not that sort of girl, though sometimes I wish I was, and anyway, I'm not really a girl any more. At seventy five I get my kicks in another way," the caller announced.

"Keep talking, my dear, you sound like a girl to me, but tell us why you are feeling guilty," Daisy threw in.

"No, I don't feel guilty really. I just wanted to brag to somebody about it."

"This is your chance then. There are a few thousand MOGGIES who are listening to every word I'm sure, but we're running short in time, so spit it out..."

"I've hoodwinked my next door neighbour. She thinks she's smart. She bought a story from me and paid me money for it, and I know she's going to claim that she wrote it and she is going to try to sell it."

"But that's stealing from you, is it not? If she's stealing something you've written, what are you confessing for? Why aren't you annoyed?"

The voice started to giggle. "Because I stole it from somebody else, that's why ...and she ...paid ...me..." and the voice continued to giggle, then progressed to a cackle.

"Oooooh, naughty, and you certainly don't sound too guilty. Are you going to tell us your name, or the name of the book?"

"Not on your Nelly," was the swift response, and she hung up.

"Sounds as if there should be more to that tale, doesn't it? What a strange lady. She's obviously not a MOGGIE with a conscience, is she? I'm not sure it would be nice living next door to her, but at least she is not the floosie Sinbad ran off with."

Oh dear, she was slipping into serious again.

"I must say 'Not on your Nelly' is an unusual name for a book title, but to get back to more mundane matters, and I'll try and avoid the tears, this is the last Granny Wisdom Show. Oh no, I can hear you all say. I've enjoyed chatting to you and hope you've enjoyed listening to all my blathering and silly nonsense, so, for one last time... Which button do I press, Carol, the green one? What happens if I press the red one? Oh, I've done it now."

The sound of water gurgling down the drain gradually faded into the bright and cheerful farewell music which signed off the show – and that was it. The Granny Wisdom Show was all over. No more rushing out pretending to Hector that she was going to the supermarket, but maybe no more Hector either...

As Daisy removed the headphones she heard the continuity announcement about the next week.

"Tune in to 'Little Radio fm' at eleven o'clock, next Monday, to hear the new programme, 'Dig This: the Arthur and Charlie Show,' starring Arthur Fletcher and Charlie Pollock – your very own crazy-paving gardening disc jockeys."

Life just goes on, Daisy realised.

53

Granny Wisdom's final broadcast was heard in the Gazette office. Spider said it had run its natural course, but he'd found it fun right to the end. Then Sally said to Spider it was a bit silly really, and although it could be fun at times, having confessions going on for much more than two weeks in a row could have put the local priest out of a job. Derek laughed out loud – but received a cold stare, warning him that the comment was for Spider only – not for him.

Rob pretended he couldn't hear anything in the office.

Derek was puzzled. He hadn't been aware that his gran had been intending to leave the show, but, then again, he hadn't seen her for a few weeks. She'd been away at her aunt's, hadn't she? Had she abandoned Aunt Mary, or is that why she ended the show? Could it have been to do with her aunt being poorly? He thought his gran had been enjoying doing her programme, especially with the prospect of it being transmitted nationally – but maybe the London trip had been a failure.

He would make contact with her.

As soon as she was back at Blytheton, he could get rid of Grandad, and even though Hammy and Alexander would still be with him, one less would help. The cottage had been even more like a blooming gang hut for the last few weeks.

He was missing Sally...

Hector hadn't heard the final broadcast, which was not like him at all especially as he had been an ardent fan of Granny Wisdom from the very beginning. He wore his MOGGIE badge with pride.

He hadn't heard it because, today, he was back at the Bisko's car park. This was where he first saw his wife meet the other bloke and it must have been happening every Monday. Today he proposed to stay until closing time if needs be. If she appeared to meet him today, he couldn't possibly miss her. He had to know for certain: would she return to him, or would he have to live with Derek for the remainder of his life?

This morning he slept in, just when it was important too, so, when he arrived for the stake-out, he was too late to see her leave. He waited the rest of the morning with no result, but he didn't give up.

Early afternoon and there she was, getting out of the white van, helped by her fancy man. They hugged passionately and she gave him a lingering kiss on the cheek, their hands held just a little too long, gazing into each other's eyes. Obviously this was the one, the same one he'd seen before, and what was even more annoying was his age. He was a bloody toy boy – in his sixties!

He turned on his heel, disgusted, and made for his bicycle. Tucking his trousers in his socks, he was mumbling all the naughty words he could think of, inwardly. How many years had they been married? He couldn't remember for certain, but, no matter, this was no way to be treated, even though he was at an age to be thrown on the scrap heap. He regretted having given up his paper-round – it was what kept him young. He would just go home and vegetate, or become a hermit – at Derek's place – he didn't want to starve.

Derek's old mobile rang. It was in Hector's pocket – he was the new owner.

"H-h-h-hello..."

"Grandad, hello, it's Derek. Where are you just now?"

"I'm in B-B-B-B-Bisko's c-car p-p-park. I was just g-g-going home."

"Oh, that's good. How'd you like to meet me for a coffee? You are in town anyway."

"Where w-w-w-were you th-th-thinking of m-m-m-meeting?"

"The Old Astoria Cafe?"

"O.K-K-K-K-K..."

"I've something to do first – an important phone call. See you in half an hour then. Bye."

Hector got on his bike and then realised he'd be too early if he went straight there, so he crossed over to the park. He found a seat and for the next thirty minutes succeeded in getting himself into a darker and darker mood, becoming more morose by the minute. Then he got on his bike, vowing that if Derek tried to make him smile, he'd thump him...

Arriving at the cafe, he parked his bike against the lamp-post and went in and looked around. The cafe was quite busy for the late afternoon and it took a few moments to spot Derek, but he wasn't alone. Sitting with her back to him was Daisy. Hector hesitated – then sat down. He said nothing to Daisy, and Daisy was likewise. Derek looked at one, then the other. Neither was going to take the initiative and speak first, he could see clearly, so, it would be up to him to break the ice.

"There seems to be some misunderstanding going on between the two of you, as far as I can tell," he said, but neither reacted. "I had hoped you'd be willing to help me, help me make it up with Sally, but obviously, if neither of you are talking to each other then I'm not going to get help," and as he said that he started to rise as if to leave.

"Well, there wouldn't have been a p-p-p-p-problem if she hadn't started g-g-g-going out with other m-m-m-m-men," said Grandad Smith.

"What other men? Me?" retorted Granny Smith.

"Yes, I s-s-s-saw you."

"Where was that?"

"In B-B-B-Bisko's car p-p-p-p-park."

"Oh, don't be silly. It was just George..."

"See, I t-t-t-told you so," Hector said, turning to Derek.

"Anyway, your grandfather was boasting to the whole town that he had another woman," Daisy retaliated, also directing the comment to Derek, who was quickly becoming judge and jury to his grandparents, which made him feel slightly uncomfortable. Maybe he shouldn't have become involved, but it had seemed a good idea at the time...

"When d-d-d-did I d-d-d-d-do this?" fired back Hector.

"On the radio – last Monday."

"Oh, you were l-l-l-l-listening to th-th-th-that were you?"

"I couldn't help it," replied Daisy.

Derek had missed the programme last week. His grandad hadn't said anything about it to him, as far as he could recollect. Hector had been on the radio? What had he said?

"You said you'd found a new passion, and everything you said about her sounded really erotic, you dirty old man," said his gran, filling in the gaps in Derek's knowledge.

"How d-d-d-did you know it was m-m-m-me? Anyway, I was t-t-t-t-talking about a m-m-m-motorcycle."

"What? But you said..."

"I t-t-t-took Thelma for a r-r-r-run on a m-m-motorb-b-b-bike because she asked me t-t-t-t-to," he tried to explain.

Daisy was not accepting this rubbish.

"So, it's Thelma, is it? Behind my back, it's a younger woman."

 Suddenly, Derek remembered the early morning phone call from Thelma, and how his grandad had returned nostalgic for the days when he'd ridden the motor bike in the forces, and how he'd said he wished he owned the bike he'd just been on.

"Just a moment," Derek broke in. "He's been with me and Alexander and Hammy all week. We've been..." but Derek hesitated. He couldn't very well tell her all about what they'd been up to, even if it was his gran...

"How d-d-did you know it was m-m-me?" Hector asked his wife again.

"You have a very distinguished turn of phrase," she told him diplomatically.

"Anyway, what ab-b-b-bout your t-t-t-t-toy-b-b-b-boy?" he pressed on. "Going away in a v-v-v-van indeed, every M-M-M-Monday?"

"A van? Oh, that belongs to 'Little Radio fm'. George is the driver and he was putting me into the dustbin each Monday," she explained.

"My G-G-G-God!" he exclaimed. "You're into some right k-k-k-k-kinky stuff, you are..."

"No ...it was to get me into the building without anyone knowing. Until today, I've been Granny Wisdom," said Daisy.

"J-J-J-J-Jeez," said Hector. "I'm your b-b-b-biggest f-f-f-fan."

Derek could see that things might just sort themselves out now, and as he slipped out of the cafe, neither of the two old love-birds had even noticed he had gone...

54

Of the odd goings-on at *'Tipsicorus International'* (a local farm bordering Newingsworth), nothing was recorded for the readers on the pages of the Slatterfoot Evening News (the daily news source for Newingsworth, Slatterfoot and surrounding districts). Although this may seem odd, being the daily eyes and ears of the region normally, it was entirely due to no-one telling them anything about it...

Being unusual circumstances, the Police and the Fire Service displayed reticence regarding offering any information to the Press. A single newspaper reporter, fortunate enough to appear on the scene at exactly the right moment, was the only one with the story, and that gentleman had decided to keep the story totally to himself.

Only one man had the makings of a scoop, and that man was Derek Toozlethwaite.

However, having been sort of involved in the fire escapade himself, he was being very selective with what the public would be told. The fire and police services were confused and embarrassed by the events, so he didn't want to offend them too much, for fear of retaliation; avoiding self-incrimination was another essential.

This hot story will be ready for the next weekly issue, he promised Rob. He was confident – the Gazette would be the paper to be reading this coming week...

There they'd been in Toozlethwaite Manor, after the fire early on Sunday morning, the three of them huddled together feeling totally miserable, sitting, quivering, awaiting their fate – Alexander, Hammy and Hector. They'd given up on Derek.

Derek was with him when they escaped from the barn, Hammy told the other two. They'd almost reached the cottage, and safety, when the boy seemed to go crazy. He'd snatched the stocking from his head, jumped over the stream, and scurried back along the farm road, with no explanation to Hammy at he left, other than telling him to return to the cottage.

They thought he'd felt guilty about the damage and had gone back to apologise – or confess. There they sat without him, expecting the police at any second to come knocking at the cottage door to drag them off to prison – or the villains to return for them, and drag them off to a hole in the ground somewhere.

To the palpable relief of the other three, Derek was the only one who did come knocking, and when he entered, each took a turn of giving him a big welcoming bear-hug, which he found extremely embarrassing – not manly behaviour, now was it?

He'd whipped off the stocking to become the intrepid reporter (he told his appreciative audience of three), and with a brass-neck, returned to the farm to quiz the Police and Fire Service. It raised a smile when Derek told them, when the fire engine left, he'd cadged a lift back along the lane on it.

Before leaving, he'd felt a little awkward being introduced by Andy Woodstock as a 'buddy' to the female police officer. She was less friendly than Andy Pandy though, almost suspicious Derek suspected, so he was pleased to leave them behind, but he'd popped up at the backs of the emergency services, looking for a story – and success, success – he had a beauty!

Though they were gratefully relieved to have him back beside them, it was now four sweaty, unshaved and tired male bodies, stinking of petrol fumes and smoke, all together in an over-crowded and smelly cottage. However, they agreed that sharing the cottage like this was preferable to spending the next few years in jail.

It was over, but he was not able even to consider sleep. The other three were the same – hyper. So, in the early hours of the morning, Derek was gazing out of the window, watching a bright new day dawn – when he saw the flames. The farm was on fire once more – so he called the Fire Service again.

The Fire Chief had checked and been satisfied that all embers were totally extinguished when he left, so having to return to the same incident about an hour later was suspicious. This was a man already with doubts about Derek conveniently appearing so quickly at the first fire, so his suspicions went in Derek's direction – the obvious conclusion any sensible fire chief would come to – the bloke who reported it must have started it...

Of course, Derek had not set the barn alight and he had witnesses with him in the cottage when he'd seen the smoke, although, with two of the witnesses having put a match to the earlier blazes, maybe involving them would be unwise...

Derek had his own suspicions. There were two possibilities. Either: the three drug farmers, and he used the term 'farmers' loosely, had returned and attempted to burn the evidence; or his new friend, PC Andy Woodstock had done what he'd threatened to do, once Derek left. Could he have destroyed the crop using the borrowed matches?

Derek didn't think the three villains would be daft enough to return, but he felt very confident that PC Woodstock was daft...

Yes, it had been an eventful weekend.

It was Tuesday, at the office. Sally phoned claiming to have a cold, and would be late in, Rob was told. Surprisingly, this news helped Derek relax a little. He had lots to do and felt slightly easier working at his desk without having Sally silently criticising his every move.

His top story for this week's edition of the Gazette would be about the drug farm, it would be given priority, but he also wanted to progress the editing of Andy Woodstock's tale, with serialisation starting in a few weeks time. Scanning his eyes over Aunt Thelma's book was the other task.

The copy of Thelma's tale was in front of him on the desk. He'd not had a chance to look at it yet. It would have to be done shortly because Alexander had phoned about his sister and a development. Visiting her today would be a publisher with a contract for signing. The promise that it would be looked at urgently, satisfied Alexander, but the pressure was on Derek.

He was being asked by his father-in-law to judge if Thelma's book would sell and – seeing the cash used had been Alexander's – was there a likelihood of a return? Derek wasn't sure he would be the best judge.

He hadn't said how much he was paying for it to be published, but Derek knew vanity publishing usually cost a lot. He hoped that when he wrote his book, publishers would be falling over themselves, begging him to give them permission to print it – for free.

Imagine being able to afford to pay for publishing? No chance for him and anyway he hadn't written his book yet. Even Alexander was a bit miffed about the delay. Everyone else could do it; what was wrong with him?

Sally arrived as promised, late, but she was smiling as she sat down at her desk. That should have pleased Derek but it didn't, and his shoulders tensed once more – but there was work to be done.

First settle on a headline for the drugs article. The outline for the story was already sketched out, begun at home on Sunday and continued during Monday, although he hadn't been concentrating properly in the office with the radio being on. He'd been listening to that stupid old woman supposedly confessing to Gran about stealing a story, then hoodwinking her neighbour. Yea... pull the other one.

Of course, his gran ending the show had been a shock, but at least all was sorted between her and Grandad. People fall out for the silliest things, but sometimes the cause is worse than silly.

He wished he could turn the clock back. *Dressing up in her clothes ...that had been stupid.* If Sally had arrived home a little later, he would have had none of her clothes on – though being sozzled, he would probably have been standing naked instead. *Would that have been more acceptable?*

No, maybe not – and the standing 'naked' thought brought back the memory of the Sophie Clerkenwell-Brown episode – even more trouble, he remembered ruefully. He'd been stone cold sober then. So, drink was not the common problem – he was!

Now he'd thought of her, it wasn't easy to remove the picture in his head of Sophie, the pert bottom, her little buttocks ...and how her perfume had affected him... What would it have been like if...?

Suddenly he realised he was standing in the middle of the office gazing into space with his naughty thoughts – and being observed strangely by Spider, Rob and Sally.

His awkward smile didn't stop them looking questioningly at him, so he went over to his desk and shuffled the papers around a bit, squinting out of the corner of his eye until they stopped looking.

Now, Toozlethwaite, get on with it...

A MENACE IN OUR MIDST

It was fortunate that the green foliage in the barn did not reach the stage of maturity which could have created the recognised effect of the finished article, or for days the whole of Newingsworth, Slatterfoot and surrounding districts would have been high on the inhalation of cannabis fumes. A gang of drug producers were secretly growing their crop of cannabis, under the noses of our ever watchful local police force, but without their knowledge. 'Tipsicorus International' was the trade name hidden behind, as they cultivated an illegal product, while their sign, which we all probably saw on the way into the town, was openly advertising vegetables. This secret location was discovered only due to a fire caused by an electrical fault in the extensive but cheap make-shift modifications they made to the farm. If they had achieved their purpose – that of producing an illegal drug – it would have brought nothing but shame and disgust to the good citizens of Newingsworth and Slatterfoot and surrounding districts so we say, thank goodness these villains did not succeed. Your intrepid reporter for the Gazette, the good-looking and daring young Derek Toozlethwaite, who lived to tell the tale, was the one and the only one, on the heels of the brave police and fire personnel who tackled the fierce blaze which ensued, to record the unfolding drama...

Ok, it's underway, and now for a look at Mr Andy Pandy Woodstock's story – red pen at the ready.

Sally was at her desk, just sitting thinking and feeling a bit guilty and unsure what to do – if anything. Granny Smith phoned her last night from her own home in Blytheton Road. The words had just poured out of her – obviously delighted to be able to talk to someone, and desperately having to get a lot of things off her chest.

Aunty Mary wasn't ill now, which was nice to hear. It had been a surprise to Sally, especially after the gloomy prognosis of the other phone call. Dying had not been possible after all – because she was a figment of Granny Smith's imagination. Hector was back in the fold but she wasn't forgiving him – because there apparently was nothing to forgive. At this point Sally's head began to spin and she struggled to keep up.

"Ever gone to work in a wheelie bin?" Sally was asked and answered no.

"...Well don't!"

Granny Smith was really Granny Wisdom, or rather had been, but now wasn't, and she had been working, travelling back and forward each Monday – 'it was hell' – and relieved it was all over.

The good news was, and this part Sally actually managed to understand, that Derek had behaved like a devoted grandson and smoothed out the little misunderstandings which developed between her and her Hector. Daisy sounded so pleased about Derek – he was such a clever and understanding grandson – an angel.

"You are really lucky to be married to such a wonderful person," said Granny Smith. "You must be really happy together – you are so suited."

Yea, right... Sally had thought during Gran's phone-call – but now today, as she sat looking at him standing in the middle of the office looking helpless, so obviously worried about their relationship, thinking only of her...

55

She was on her way, due in about half an hour and bringing the contract, just as promised at the last visit, which seemed ages ago but wasn't. Thelma wanted everything about the book, the printing, its appearance on the bookshelves, the interviews, her name on the large posters somewhere, anywhere, to happen quickly.   Although deep down, she knew it wouldn't move fast, it didn't stop her getting excited about the whole business, and wishing. Being an author was so exciting...

Signing a deal and receiving money, was the way it happened, she hoped. She could pay back Alexander – though maybe not right away. If he thinks he's paying for the story to be printed, then he won't expect any money until it sells, and even then it would be probably after that. By the time the first cheque arrives, he'll have forgotten all about it.

Anyway he is loaded, he could afford the modest outlay, but thank goodness he didn't realise he was making his next-door neighbour happy. Heck, what was a twin brother for, if you have to worry about paying back a paltry sum of £2500 to him?

Sophie Clerkenwell-Brown was due about lunchtime. The salad was prepared, and a dessert, but Thelma guessed the dessert would be refused by the visitor. It wasn't possible to retain the figure that girl possessed by eating real food. Thelma also hoped that her visitor's expensive perfume wouldn't flavour the salad too much.

Ding-dong... She was bang on time.

Thelma hoped her next door neighbour would be sitting gnashing her teeth with jealousy, and that Sophie's car would be parked at the front of the house for Mrs Masterton to see clearly. She'd be wishing she hadn't sold the story so cheaply. Although Thelma reckoned she'd driven a hard bargain, it had been galling, all the same, to have to hand the cash over to that woman – once Alexander eventually forked it out.

Thelma opened the door. There she was looking as neat and as polished as the last time, and wearing the perfume. Yes, not only would the salad be tainted, the smell would be guaranteed to remain in the house for at least a fortnight.

"Hello again, Sophie," Thelma gushed, "How lovely to see you again."

"Hi," said Sophie, feeling a touch wary about entering the premises. She'd had a disturbing sensation about this whole thing while driving up and felt uncomfortable – trouble was anticipated!

As she stood on the doorstep the feeling remained, and if anything, it was worse. Would the owners of this place be here today, or would it be just this maid again: the author, who unfortunately happened to be a relative of Derek's?

Could it be that she was terrified she would be recognised as the 'no clothes' girl? She knew she hadn't been fully undressed, but somehow, in her own mind now, the near nakedness had become total. What if Derek's wife appeared, what was her name, Sally, wasn't it? If she appeared, there'd be a quick departure; it would be out immediately – by door or window.

"Do come in," said Thelma using her welcoming-the-publisher voice, and beginning to feel famous already.

Sophie smiled, stepping inside, wishing now she hadn't used her special perfume. It did a great job with the fellows, but if anything it just made females jealous of her looks and man-appeal.

They went into the front room and sat down. Sophie was pleased to find no-one else waiting in there, although seeing Derek again would have been interesting. He would be fun, eventually, but only if she could break down his reserve. *The poor lamb, hadn't been married long he'd told her, but obviously was under the thumb already.*

"Now, I have some good news, and some bad news for you," said

Sophie, bracing herself and bringing out paperwork.

"Oh..." said Thelma, not sure whether it should be a happy "Oh," or not.

"The good news is that we want to begin the process right away. The bad: all we can offer, as an advance payment, is ten thousand..."

"Oh," said Thelma again, trying not to appear over-enthusiastic, but inside, with a heart thumping away like mad.

"All the details of how and when further payments will be made are in the document I have here."

It seemed mundane under the circumstances, but Thelma offered some lunch anyway, and Sophie said she'd appreciate that because she had not stopped on the way.

Going into the kitchen to collect the food was Thelma's opportunity to do a little victory dance, but she almost dropped the salad bowl on turning around. Sophie, having mistakenly thought that they would be eating in the kitchen, was standing right behind her as she performed.

Sophie was smiling because everything was turning out to be more pleasant than she'd thought it would.

"I think I'd dance too, in your shoes," she said to Thelma – though I wouldn't have such a big bottom to wobble, was also her smug thought.

The food was taken into the front room, and idle chat ensued.

"Yes, I'd love some," Sophie replied, when asked if she would like some trifle. "We'll be looking for some personal details about you and your family to help determine the most suitable publicity for your story," explained Sophie. "For example, the question which inevitably will be asked of you – is this your first novel?"

"Oh yes," replied Thelma.

"Did you work on it for long?" she asked.

"No..." replied Thelma, guardedly.

Sophie could tell that radio and television appearances by this lady would be highly unlikely.

"How about your family – have they been supportive?"

"Oh yes. They think it's wonderful, and Alexander – he'll get his winnings," she said proudly.

"His winnings – was it a bet?"

"Oh yes, he bet that I would be successful – to give me confidence." Not bad, Thelma said to herself, that's the first untruth today she'd told.

"Of course I'm not the first in the family to be writing a novel. Derek's in the process too, but he struggles to get the time and the inspiration. By comparison, I had it easy, I have to admit." No lie this time either.

"Derek? Who is that then – one of the family?"

"Oh, you remember Derek ...surely. Little Miss Bare Buttocks."

Any make-up having been applied earlier by Ms Sophie Clerkenwell-Brown was surely scorched, as the glow spread from her cheeks, rapidly progressing to the rest of her face and neck, and kept going until she was burning with embarrassment – all over.

Ring-ring, ring-ring, ring-ring.

It was the phone in the hall which Thelma went to answer. Sophie was glad of the respite and attempted to regain her composure, but unfortunately, it was very likely the bell had only signalled the end of round one.

The uncomfortable feeling had returned...

56

A good job well done, Derek told himself. The drug story should be complete with descriptions of the three villains now included. They were still on the run. Anyway he'd used artistic licence for them as he had for the rest of the story.

What they looked like had been limited to only having had a rear view – or should that be a view of the rear – of the one who'd sat on his face. Detail was supplied by Hector, Hammy and Alexander, even though they had only really seen them in semi-darkness. There was no doubt about their accents so he made good mileage from that. Information selected from government leaflets, emphasising the stupidity of drug usage and addiction, and a photograph of the smouldering barn would also be included in the centre page spread.

It was ready for the printer.

Now, he could spend some time on the other two stories – it would be Thelma's first.

THE BIG SQUEAK, by Ivy Bloom.

Deep down he was a country boy, soft and gentle, with a heart of gold, but that was hidden underneath this carefully manufactured hard veneer. The veneer was an essential for what he did in the big city. It was dawn and quiet in his office. He would have been able to hear the sound of the dust falling, if it hadn't been for the buzzing of a fly which had eluded capture all morning, but which blended with the buzz of traffic six floors down. He waited for the phone to ring, or a knock at the door. He needed the business. Would a visitor know where to find him? He stood and walked casually to the door, opened it, and checked the shiny black plastic plate with the name engraved in white bold capitals. It was his name, still attached to the door with four screws. ANTONIO PANCHETTI – PRIVATE INVESTIGATOR. He sat down again. His copy of the Weekly Gazette, from his home town, was lying folded on his desk, and looking lonely too.

Some of this seemed familiar. Had he read something like this before? It seemed recently too. No, must be mistaken. He'd have recognised the character's name.

He must plough on ...though the feeling was persisting...

Sally was looking over at him. Was she smiling? No, she'd looked away again. She'd been laughing at him, hadn't she? Or had it been a sneer? Concentrate, Derek, you have a lot of reading to do...

He had subscribed, and it was posted to the office address every week. He'd already completed the Weekly Crossword, and the Sudoku, and was bang up to date with all the local hatches and dispatches. Keeping abreast of the times was important in the job he did. It is one of those kind of days, he told himself but something is about to happen – and then the phone rang. It was his mobile. He lifted it. "Help..." it said. "Why didn't you ring my office number?" he answered coolly, as was his style. "That's the number I do business on.

Derek stopped again.

His instincts, when reading someone else's work were becoming blunted almost to the point of not caring, and sadly this was not a new feeling. Was his own lack of success causing him to grudge helping others? It was how he shamefully saw himself, these days. It was happening again with this book.

He was belittling it because it was Thelma's – deliberately trying to find fault again. Clear your mind of your own feeble frustrations and concentrate, Derek, he told himself. Try another chapter.

The dress just fell away. It was obviously designed with a quick release mechanism and he was the one with the key. He could see she wanted him. Her eyelashes were going into overdrive, but he would play hard to get for a change. He casually bent down and picked the blue silk evening gown from the dusty floor and walked over towards the wardrobe, letting the material of the dress gently brush all the way along the outstretched stockinged leg. His hand was on the wardrobe door. He snatched it open and grabbed hold of the necktie of the hoodlum standing inside and pulled. The body was cold. He was dead – as dead as the proverbial dodo. He looked at the dame lying there. The look on her face said she was not happy. He knew instinctively – she ...was the killer.

Good grief. This was nearly as bad as the one he was currently working on, the one he was trying to edit, the one covered by red pen.

Wait a moment – that's it... This one in front of him was the same style as Andy Woodstock's – pseudo Mickey Spillane. He opened the other manuscript on his desk, with the red marks.

What about the titles? 'The Big Squeak, by Ivy Bloom'. 'The Door Creaked, by Andy Woodstock'.

The hero is mentioned in the first chapter by both, isn't he? Andy called his, 'Andy Pandoletti' – wanted to put himself into his story, thought Derek, while Thelma, or Ivy, as she'd called herself, had gone for, 'Antonio Panchetti'.

Hmm, were his suspicions correct? *Try the first chapter again.*

He'd gone through a lot of other material since reading Andy's first chapter a while ago, and did not have the benefit of a photographic memory. He searched and found it...

Deep down he was a country boy soft and gentle, with a heart of gold, but that was hidden underneath this carefully manufactured hard veneer. The veneer was an essential for what he did in the big city. It was dawn and quiet in his office. He would have been able to hear the sound of the dust falling, if it hadn't been for the buzzing of a fly which had eluded capture all morning, but which blended with the buzz of traffic six floors down. He waited for the phone to ring, or a knock...

And Thelma's –

Deep down, he was a country boy, soft and gentle, with a heart of gold. But that was hidden underneath this carefully manufactured hard veneer. The veneer...'

Oh no, what has she done? Who was first? There was a date on the front of both. Thelma's wasn't the original one. *What was she up to?* He'd have to ring her right away. She could land herself in big trouble if she'd copied someone else's story...

Should he say to Sally? No. She wouldn't know anything about this, and telling her would drag her into it. If she had known she would have stopped her aunt, prevented her from being so stupid. Sally was as honest as they come and wouldn't stoop to that sort of thing.

He lifted his mobile and scrolled down to the Cloverton home number, and pressed. It was ringing.

Lift the phone, Thelma, please.

He hoped she hadn't signed any pieces of paper yet. Look at the time. Sophie would have been arriving about an hour ago.

"Hello," said Thelma, a little perturbed that her comment to dear little Sophie had maybe been taken the wrong way. It was alright trying to be funny, but the other person has to see the joke too. This could have an effect on her chances of clinching the deal.

"Thelma, this is Derek. I've been reading your story."

"Oh, that's nice Derek. We've just been talking about the story too, and you, as a matter of fact. We were having a laugh about Sophie being caught in just her knickers, weren't we, Sophie dear?"

Thelma smiled sweetly to Sophie. The look that Sophie returned indicated something different.

"Fine, now I'm going to ask you some very simple questions. Please answer them truthfully. It is important."

"Of course, Derek, but you sound upset..."

"Have you signed any pieces of paper?"

"No, but we were just about to do so." Thelma, having said it, was now experiencing some doubt on it happening.

"Good. Now this is very important. Did you steal the story?"

"No, of course I didn't," she replied indignantly, "I paid good money for it ...Alexander's, in fact."

That's when Derek remembered yesterday's Granny Wisdom Show. *The old lady who was confessing – no, who had been crowing – about putting one over on her neighbour, it couldn't have been Thelma she was referring to, surely? Not Mrs Masterton... Was she the author – or rather the thief?*

"Thelma, you have heard of plagiarism haven't you? Did you

write this book?" pushed Derek.

Sophie was not hearing all of this conversation, but moved close enough to Thelma to understand the gist of it – and was not surprised. Something had been destined to go wrong today – the bad feeling was rumbling away.

"No ...but..." Thelma started out.

"Do you know who wrote it?"

"I thought it was her next door... Was it not?"

"No, I don't think so, and if you sign any documents, you could be the one who could be sued by the real author, if he were to find out."

"Oh dear... Thank you, Derek. I feel very foolish now," said a contrite Thelma.

"That's all right. You can always write your own in the future."

"Yes, you are correct, sometime in the future I will proudly add my name to the list of best sellers, and my best friend, Sophie, will help me do it," said Thelma confidently.

Sophie was shaking her head sadly in the background, searching for her jacket and satchel, as Thelma ended the call. Sophie just wanted out.

"Don't go just yet," insisted Thelma. "You haven't had coffee... I'll give you it in a moment – but I have something to do first," and she made for the outside door...

Back in the office, Sally overheard Derek's end of the conversation and she had a tear in her eye. She was the one who encouraged her aunt to do this. *This is the second very good deed Derek has done. Yesterday, he brought his gran and grandad back together, and now today, he has saved Thelma. If Derek hadn't been so brilliant and of such a strong character, Gran and a Grandad could have been suing for a divorce – and my poor aunt could have finished up paying out a fortune in a court somewhere, or gone to jail – and it would have been my fault.*

Oh dear, Sally Toozlethwaite, you have been a very naughty girl. She felt bad. How could she have had the cheek to treat this fine upstanding man who'd worn her clothes so daringly and proudly, in such a cruel and unfair manner, when she was the one who should be castigated? She stood up and walked across the office.

"Derek," she said in a tearful voice, "I've been nasty and unfair to you; can you possibly forgive me? May I come home again ...please? How could I make it up to you? A special meal perhaps? Or is there something else?"

A smile slowly appeared on Derek's face, and in a bit of a daze his head nodded, yes, but something else could wait. He would settle for real food, cooked by Sally again. Yes, he'd happily settle for that!

As a hug clinched it for the two of them, Spider and Rob broke into spontaneous applause: for them too, relief at last.

57

Thelma threw open the door, walked down her path, and back up the path next door. She now stood at the doorstep of Mrs Masterton, the little old lady who'd sent the manuscript to Sophie in the first place. Sophie halted, still in the hallway at the front door, curious to see what the original author looked like.

Thelma put her finger on the bell and held it there. A voice came from the other side of the door.

"Who is it? Would you stop ringing the bell and go away."

Thelma didn't. Eventually the door was opened a little, and Mrs Masterton looked out.

"Oh, it's you. I might have known. What do you want?" she grumbled.

"Just a little word with you please," said Thelma in a reasonable level-headed manner. "Your story..."

"Yes..."

"It wasn't yours..."

"Oh..."

"You sold it to me under false pretences."

"Oh ...so what?"

"So what...? I want my money back."

"What money?" and at that Mrs Masterton made to push the door closed, but Thelma was too quick. "Get your big foot out of the way, you silly woman," said the little old lady.

"Don't you 'silly woman' me, you conniving old sausage," Thelma retorted.

"Ladies ...this is no way to behave," shouted Sophie, climbing over the wall, and in doing so, ruining a perfectly good pair of shoes in the clay soil borders.

"Some people don't know how to behave," said Mrs Masterton, "...taking advantage of an old woman like me, and making me sign documents, telling lies about me, and stealing my story from me!"

"You lying cow!" exclaimed Thelma. "You stole it from someone else and tried to take advantage of my innocence, and stupidity, and now you have my money, well ...maybe not exactly mine, but..."

Leaning forward, Mrs Masterton gave Thelma a push and off-balance, she fell backwards into Sophie who stopped her from falling, but in the process was knocked backwards herself, landing on her beautiful buttocks. Unfortunately, while Thelma was still unbalanced, another little shove by Mrs Masterton and backwards she went again – on top of Sophie...

Sophie Clerkenwell-Brown found just then that neither the twice a week visits to her local gymnasium, nor the highly active sex-life enjoyed by her, had prepared her abs for the landing of this twelve stone woman. Sophie just lay there, gasping, as Thelma struggled to her feet, getting madder at her neighbour by the moment, but Mrs Masterton wisely had quickly put the heavy front door between her and Thelma, by slamming it closed.

This was getting totally out of hand the mini-skirted publishing executive decided, still gasping and fumbled in her pocket to find her mobile.

"I'm calling the police," she shouted at Thelma, and did so, while lying there in the flattened shrub trying to summon up the will to move, resolving to claim danger money for any future visits to clients...

The door was being thumped furiously by Thelma now, and lots of naughty words were pouring out. Sophie wanted to contribute herself, because being in the words business she'd picked up a good few unusual ones which would have been apt, but she hadn't yet regained her normal lung function. Noises in reply could be heard coming from the other side of the door too, which were of a similar nature.

In no time at all, a police vehicle pulled up at the front of the house. Sophie was full of admiration at the speed of response – so unlike London – but fast only because today had been a quiet day, even for Newingsworth.

PC Yvonne Saunders ran efficiently up the path and made for the action at the door, which now had descended to Thelma yelling a chant over and over through the letterbox. This was successfully making Mrs Masterton even more furious with her being totally unable to make Thelma stop.

"Bingo addict, bingo addict. Mrs M's a bingo addict. Bingo addict..."

PC Yvonne was accompanied by her male counterpart, who wandered up the pathway a little more casually hoping that the fracas might have ended by the time he got there, and found his attention taken up by the mini-skirted legs sticking out of the shrub. Being chivalrous, he decided to help the obviously injured party, Sophie, back onto her feet.

That was when PC Andy Woodstock received the first and fatal whiff of the perfume. As usual, Sophie was well aware of the effect. It showed – his glassy-eyed stare was fixed on her – and her alone.

"Excuse me, Constable Woodstock, could I have your assistance here please!" called out Yvonne, while trying to calm down the agitated Thelma to find out what this was all about. Her shout did break the spell and Constable Woodstock went over to the door to take a shot at conversing with Mrs Masterton – through the letterbox, of course.

"Please open the door, madam. We'll have this sorted out in no time if you will just come out and talk to us," he said soothingly. "The alternative is we use the battering ram and break down the door."

Yvonne was surprised at the macho tone in Andy's voice, and the tough guy image which had suddenly appeared. This was not the colleague she'd become used to, and occasionally fancied... *Was he trying to impress her, at long last*, she wondered? Then she realised he was more likely to be angling after the mini-skirted bimbo he'd just dragged out of the bushes.

The door opened slowly. Mrs Masterton's head cautiously appeared from behind it, her eyes shooting daggers in the direction of Thelma; there was a reciprocal arrangement. The black notebook appeared as if by magic in the constable's hand, and the pencil was poised to record the outpourings from the two protagonists, but there was only a stony silence, and a staring war going on.

It was Sophie who offered some information and Andy was delighted to be reminded of her presence.

"It's to do with a manuscript," she said. "Somebody wrote it, and someone else stole it, or maybe someone paid good money for it, but found out it was stolen, and then decided to speak to the person who said they'd written it, and..."

PC Andy Woodstock stopped writing – partly mesmerised by the movement of the lips of the blonde beauty standing before him, and partly because he hadn't a clue what she was talking about.

"Is this the one?" asked PC Yvonne Saunders, picking up the bound manuscript from the path, which was now looking slightly tatty. "The Big Squeak, by Ivy Bloom," she read out with feeling. "Deep down, he was a country boy, soft and gentle, with a heart of gold."

She stopped reading, and looked at Thelma and then at Mrs Masterton "...and you are fighting over a load of crap like this?"

She handed the document to her colleague.

"Evidence?" Yvonne suggested.

He took it and she brought out her notebook, in an attempt to progress the procedure along a little or they'd be here all day.

"Right, so, who started all this?" asked PC Saunders.

"She did!" This, of course, came back from both.

For another five minutes the argument jumped back and forward, with little progress achieved. PC Woodstock lost interest in the babbling, leaving the thinking part to PC Saunders. He'd begun to read the offending manuscript, to pass the time...

"Hey!" he yelled suddenly. "This is mine! How did the pair of you get hold of this?"

"I got it from her," said Thelma, nodding at Mrs Masterton,

"...and wasted my money obviously."

Mrs Masterton wasn't keen to talk, but all eyes were now on her, and they were waiting, so she decided that confession could be good for the soul. She didn't think crowing about it would be wise, like she did on the radio programme, so it was said in a sad-put-upon-little-old-lady voice, looking to the ground in a manner which could only elicit sympathy, she hoped.

"It was the computer classes – at the library. We had to paste and cut and edit and save and do all the things you have to do, and this was what we used. Everybody did. I just printed mine out every week and brought it home. I don't have a computer..." and she looked up sadly, for the sympathy that everyone had these days for anyone who's fallen behind in the technology race – and the sympathetic looks were there – except from Thelma.

"I thought it was such a good story, that when I found it hadn't been published properly, it didn't seem right. So, I sent it away to Ms Sophie Clerkenwell-Brown, and she said she would publish it ...and then I was going to try and contact the author so that he would get the credit."

Mrs Masterton looked up again. She was winning, wasn't she? She could even see the tears in the eyes of the blonde bimbo, so she turned her attention to the policeman.

"Are you the real author then? Are you the Andy Woodstock? You are my hero," and Mrs Masterton fluttered her eyes at him, and he almost blushed.

She was triumphant. She'd beaten the silly woman from next door, well and truly, and she still had her money – but then she went one step too far and lost the plot, by adding, "...And if she hadn't made me sell the story to her..."

Thelma dived at her this time with her fist extended, and Mrs Masterton received the start of a black eye. Yvonne had to get physical again, separating them.

Meanwhile, PC Andy Woodstock had ushered Sophie down the path. Having the interview carried out in the privacy of the squad car seemed preferable to standing out in the open, and close up he could enjoy her perfume.

"So, you are the real author," Sophie gazed into the big policeman's eyes. "I'll give you my card. We will have to meet again – for business, of course – but incidentally, my home number is on there too."

There was a future here, she could tell, and she had a fascination for uniforms...

58

Alexander was fast off the mark. The fire had hardly cooled down before he made contact with the dodgy solicitor, the one who dealt with the purchase when Hammy was forced to sell. By pushing for a fast decision Alexander successfully put on extra pressure and the sale was going ahead. He would be getting the farm and the land for a snip.

What would happen next about Alexander's latest deal hadn't been stated yet, but Derek guessed there might be a chance it could involve Hammy – at least that was the hope. The farmhouse hadn't been damaged, other than by smoke. It would be nice to see Hammy get another chance back in his old home, but they'd have to wait and see on that one.

With the farm now unoccupied, and after obtaining the permission of the new owner, and friend, Hammy felt compelled to go back for another look for the family treasure. Alexander didn't really want to miss out in anything but couldn't afford the time off, much to his regret – he had enjoyed their escapades, so it was just Derek and Hector accompanying Hammy, each armed with a spade.

It was so much simpler in daylight for the three of them, and not having to peer through a leg of Sally's tights made clear thinking a little easier. Of course, not having to worry about being attacked by vicious drug-thugs helped too.

Outside the deserted farmhouse the three mighty brains looked more carefully at Grandad Macintosh's map and debated whether the position of the cross on the map could possibly be accurate. Of course, finding the treasure was the only way it would be proved.

Was the treasure really a figment of the old man's imagination, or was Grandad Macintosh maybe just not very good at drawing and measuring? Another possibility had to be faced; Hammy had got it wrong!

"Are you s-s-s-sure your l-l-l-legs are the same l-l-l-length as your g-g-g-grandad's?" asked Hector.

They had to give Hector due credit for that particular question as it had not been asked before, although neither Hammy nor Derek could see what difference it might make! However, they paced it out again ...the exact same distance from the house, and at right angles to the little window for the farmhouse scullery, and where did they land? The same distance away from the house as before, but this time on the outside of the barn wall's charred remains.

"Och aye then, we micht as weel gie it anither wee go..."

And they found it: what they were looking for – the treasure: Silver Three-penny Pieces: hundreds of them – in a large, Ministry of Food Dried Milk Tin, from the good old days of rationing, no doubt! It must have taken the old fellow years to gather that amount, each coin valuable in his day, and, unfortunately, long before decimalisation. Now the whole tin full of coins was almost worthless, other than to a coin collector perhaps. In fact, the tin itself was probably more valuable.

Hammy would one day get round to counting the little silver coins, he promised himself, though the temptation at the time was to dig another hole and lose them again! At least the treasure had been found, the family honour satisfied, and Hammy's dear ancestors, Grandad Macintosh and Macintosh Senior, could now be permitted to rest in peace.

One thing was certain, for many years to come it would almost certainly become a valuable tale for Hammy to recount in the Newingsworth Old Folks Club.

59

Live for the moment was Derek's decision, and, for a change, no worries for Derek. Well ...other than the not-very-well-thought-out offer Sally chose to make yesterday – to Hammy!

The suspicions were correct, about what Alexander would be doing with his new purchase, and it pleased everyone that he was behaving like a gentleman and inviting Hammy to return to the farmhouse. He was to become the sitting tenant, with Alexander as his landlord, but it wasn't stopping at that. The house was to be modified extensively and destined to become a hotel, and Hammy was to look after the building modifications; he was to make it happen.

"Why not stay with us," Sally had offered, "...when you are ready to start work? No sense in having to travel from the far side of town when you could be here with us, five minutes down the road from the work, especially with you being on your own. It wouldn't be for long, would it?"

Derek was apprehensive. He liked Hammy but...

He hadn't moved in yet, and of course, it might never happen, but it niggled Derek ever so slightly that his newly returned wife had not asked for his opinion. Arguing with Sally about it just now, even though it had not been discussed with him, would not be a wise move. She was not long back with him, and he didn't want to rock the boat again: not so soon...

Sitting relaxing in the sunshine, making the best of the moment, with a glass of chilled white wine on the table beside him, was the extent of his activities today. It being Saturday and with only himself and Sally in the cottage, it was the next best thing to heaven for Derek. All was forgiven. The occasional misdeeds, which he could claim were misconstrued and hadn't justified the punishment, were past history.

Together again they were, and simply feeling good.

There would be a family gathering tonight, for a celebration. He'd promised to make some of the meal – part of the new house rules – share and share alike in all duties. He was tackling the curry for the first time, but he wouldn't be telling the visitors that, of course, not unless they became ill. Sally would be doing the rice. He couldn't cope with curry and rice, not at the first attempt.

There would be eight of them in total, Gran and Grandad Smith, Alexander and Muriel, and Thelma, of course. Hammy had been invited along too; after what the males did together, Hammy was almost like one of the family now.

As he sat there in the sun, he caught another whiff of the smell drifting over from the charred remains of the barn along the road, and thought again of Sally's offer to Hammy, but, forget that for now, there were other things to think about...

A big event was nearing fruition.

Tomorrow is the marathon. It had been sensible, his giving up silly thoughts of participating. This was a much wiser option, lying here comfortably with a glass of wine, totally immobile. Today, even thinking of the effort involved was too taxing...

Arthur and Charlie were ready, and thankfully laughed their heads off when they saw the extra long t-shirts he'd organised. Anyway, the weather forecast didn't include rain, and it was for charity, so it wasn't critical to run a fast race. Bringing-in cash for the hard strapped charity organisations was the important thing.

Their taking over Gran's Monday morning show on 'Little Radio fm' engendered a lot of publicity, and with the radio programme and Derek's tales in the Gazette running in parallel, their fund-raising was turning out to be the success he had hoped.

To be invited back on their show as the agony aunt had been great for Daisy – and for Carol, who was still the producer. They got on like a house on fire again. Coming together only emphasised how much they'd missed each other. The ex-Granny Wisdom was regularly reminded by Arthur and Charlie of having been 'the paper-bag-lady' but they weren't cruel enough to make her actually put it on when she visited them. The 'bag' took pride of place, in the corner of the studio, just staring at them all during their broadcast, every Monday...

This was now more enjoyable for Daisy, particularly because she and Hector went along to the studio together. There weren't any silly secrets spoiling their life.

Derek still found it strange when his gran and grandad arrived on their motor scooter, both togged-out in the crash helmets, and Granny Smith hanging on grimly on the pillion seat. She'd decided it would be a good idea to care about Hector's passion, but they agreed that going for the full blown motorcycle was a little over the top, so instead it was the scooter – a Vespa 125cc GTS Super Sport, in bright red.

The money Gran made from the radio programme was considered well-spent on his scooter's purchase. Hector had been tickled pink when she suggested it. They were out and about on it, everywhere, and more importantly, together ...and every time when they were on the scooter, Hector enjoyed Daisy's arms wrapped around him, even if it was because she did it out of fear...

For Derek, going to work felt so much more pleasant too. Not having the bad feeling in the office between the two of them had made life easier all round, and especially for Spider and Rob. To Derek's eyes, Spider seemed to be putting on a little weight, something to do with now not having to act as go-between. He must have been using a lot of nervous energy, particularly when Sally had been in a grumpy mood. He'd been the poor soul absorbing it and acting as her temporary punch-bag.

An email arrived at the office, the other day, to Derek from his new friend Andy, who'd become even friendlier since being called to the little misunderstanding between Thelma and 'that woman next door'. The two fighting ladies had been lucky, a caution from the judge for a first offence, mainly due to Andy speaking up for them and emphasising they were really the friendliest of neighbours – normally.

He was moving south, the email said, and could they meet for a drink before he left? Going to live with someone in London, it stated also, and he was transferring down south to the Metropolitan Force. 'My girl's name is Sophie, and she apparently thinks she's maybe met you at some time in her life, but can't remember where.'

Incidentally, it also told Derek not to bother doing the serialisation of the story. 'It is all working out better than expected, because I found a friendly publisher.' Derek sat back in his office seat and wondered how that had been manipulated with it being such lousy writing; could this be equivalent to sleeping with the producer, like film stars did? If it was – he was a lucky sod.

It was quite a coincidence too – her name being Sophie. Derek knew a girl called Sophie; she'd also been in publishing...

As he sipped the chilled wine, he pondered on the other house rules now agreed, in addition to the shared cooking.

1) Derek was to stop the training runs, immediately. Sally was refusing to let him participate because that had been one of the causes of the blow-up. Derek had said "Alright then," in a reluctant manner, not wanting to admit that he'd given them up, weeks ago.

2) There were to be no more naked or semi-naked, size ten, blonde, publishing executives permitted to enter the cottage. If Derek ever reached the unlikely stage of completing his story and was to meet a publisher, it would have to be male, fully clothed, on neutral ground with Sally in attendance.

3) Dressing-up in inappropriate clothing was banned. No more incidents of him venturing into Sally's clothes would be tolerated. Also, any 'special' meetings with her father would require a justifiable reason requiring sanctioning beforehand by her.

As he sat there, in the morning sunshine, he lifted his glass. He was happy, as happy as he had been in a long, long time – and long may it continue. He took a sip of the cool liquid, lay back, and closed his eyes...

"Swea-ty..." Sally called from inside.

"Yes, darling" he called back lazily.

"Sweaty, I had five pairs of expensive spare tights in this drawer. The type I don't wear every day..."

"I apologised, sweetheart, remember, we used them for covering our faces when the four of us did the raids – eight legs. I told you that. Had you forgotten?"

"No, Sweaty dearest, you said you'd used four pairs and you would replace them. What happened to the fifth pair?"

"Uhhhhmmmm..."

"DEREK! What are you wearing under your jeans...?"

Oh dear, here we go again.

How easily little things can ruin a weekend...

Please... Call Me Derek

ISBN 978-1-908135-10-0

Derek travels from child to confused adult, from reporter for the local paper to any job available, doing everything he thinks he should, but doing it his way. Pursuing life and employment leads Derek to fling himself into the sort of sticky situations difficult to explain to his friends or his family. With determination, gritting his teeth, doing everything for the best, how could anything go wrong?

The first in the Derek series, 'Please... Call me Derek' is available in paperback from all major book shops, online through the publisher's book shop www.uppbooks.com and through Amazon.

It is also available on Kindle

ISBN 978-1-908135-21-6

If you would like to find out more about Derek and his adventures, please follow Mac Black on www.macblack.info

Derek's Revenge

is next !